"[It's] a humdinger . . . Perfect for suspense fans."
—*Kirkus Reviews*

"Lucinda delivers every time. Unputdownable."
—Tarryn Fisher, *New York Times* bestselling author

"Lucinda Berry's latest, *Under Her Care*, is her best thriller yet! A dark, riveting read that will keep you up late, racing to the chilling end."
—Kaira Rouda, *USA Today* bestselling author of *The Next Wife* and *Somebody's Home*

"Lucinda Berry's *Under Her Care* is stunning, diabolical, and gripping, with one of the best and most gasp-worthy twists I have read in a very long time. Fast paced, fabulous, and enthralling, the pages practically turn themselves. Absolutely captivating."
—Lisa Regan, *USA Today* and *Wall Street Journal* bestselling author

"Creepy and chilling, *Under Her Care* is a tense page-turner that leaves you questioning everything you ever knew about motherhood and the family bond."
—Tara Laskowski, award-winning author of *The Mother Next Door*

## The Secrets of Us

"Those looking for an emotional roller-coaster ride will be rewarded."
—*Publishers Weekly*

"Combine Lucinda Berry's deep understanding of the complexities of the human mind with her immense talent for storytelling and you have *The Secrets of Us*, an intense psychological thriller that kept my heart racing until the shocking, jaw-dropping conclusion. Bravo!"
—T. R. Ragan, *New York Times* bestselling author

"*The Secrets of Us* is an unputdownable page-turner with two compelling female protagonists that will keep readers on their toes. Fantastic!"
—Cate Holahan, *USA Today* bestselling author of *One Little Secret*

"Lucinda Berry's *The Secrets of Us* is a tense psychological thriller that explores the dark corners of the mind and turns a mind can take when it harbors secret guilt. The interplay between sisters Krystal and Nichole and their hidden past is gradually revealed, and in the end, the plot twists keep coming. Right and wrong can be ambivalent, and this story explores all shades of gray, from their dysfunctional family to an old childhood friend to a husband who may or may not be too good to be true. Berry's background as a clinical psychologist shines in this novel with a character so disturbed they spend time in seclusion lockdown at a psychiatric ward. Don't miss this one!"
—Debbie Herbert, *USA Today* and Amazon Charts bestselling author

"*The Secrets of Us* is an utterly gripping, raw, and heartbreaking story of two sisters. Berry's flawlessly placed clues and psychological expertise grab you from the first word, not letting go until the last. Compelling, intricate, and shocking, this inventive thriller cleverly weaves from past to present with stunning precision. I was absolutely enthralled."
—Samantha M. Bailey, *USA Today* and #1 national bestselling author of *Woman on the Edge*

"The past and present collide with explosive consequences in this addictive, twisty thriller from an author at the top of her game. *The Secrets of Us* grips from the first page and doesn't let go until the final shocking twist."
—Lisa Gray, bestselling author of *Dark Highway*

## The Best of Friends

"A mother's worst nightmare on the page. For those who dare."
—*Kirkus Reviews*

"*The Best of Friends* gripped me from the stunning opening to the emotional, explosive ending. In this moving novel, Berry creates a beautifully crafted study of secrets and grief among a tight-knit group of friends and of how far a mother will go to discover the truth and protect her children."

—Heather Gudenkauf, *New York Times* bestselling author of *The Weight of Silence* and *This Is How I Lied*

"In *The Best of Friends*, Berry starts with a heart-stopping bang—the dreaded middle-of-the-night phone call—and then delivers a dark and gritty tale that unfolds twist by devastating twist. Intense, terrifying, and at times utterly heartbreaking. Absolutely unputdownable."

—Kimberly Belle, international bestselling author of *Dear Wife* and *Stranger in the Lake*

## The Perfect Child

"I am a compulsive reader of literary novels . . . but there was one book that kept me reading, the sort of novel I can't put down . . . *The Perfect Child*, by Lucinda Berry. It speaks to the fear of every parent: What if your child was a psychopath? This novel takes it a step further. A couple, desperate for a child, has the chance to adopt a beautiful little girl who, they are told, has been abused. They're told it might take a while for her to learn to behave and trust people. She can be sweet and loving, and in public she is adorable. But in private—well, I won't give away what happens. But needless to say, it's chilling."

—Gina Kolata, *New York Times*

"A mesmerizing, unbearably tense thriller that will have you looking over your shoulder and sleeping with one eye open. This creepy, serpentine tale explores the darkest corners of parenthood and the profoundly unsettling lengths one will go to, to keep a family together—no matter the consequences. Electrifying and atmospheric, this dark gem of a novel is one I couldn't put down."

—Heather Gudenkauf, *New York Times* bestselling author

"A deep, dark, and dangerously addictive read. All-absorbing to the very end!"

—Minka Kent, *Washington Post* bestselling author

# IF YOU

# TELL

*A Novel*

# A LIE

# OTHER TITLES BY LUCINDA BERRY

*Keep Your Friends Close*

*Off the Deep End*

*Under Her Care*

*The Secrets of Us*

*The Best of Friends*

*When She Returned*

*A Welcome Reunion*

*The Perfect Child*

# IF YOU TELL A LIE

*A Novel*

# A LIE

## LUCINDA BERRY

THOMAS & MERCER

Text copyright © 2024 by Heather Berry

Published by Thomas & Mercer, Seattle

www.apub.com

Amazon, the Amazon logo, and Thomas & Mercer are trademarks of Amazon.com, Inc., or its affiliates.

ISBN-13: 9781662512629 (paperback)
ISBN-13: 9781662512612 (digital)

Cover design by Kimberly Glyder
Cover image: © AleksandarNakic, © Aleksandra Konoplia / Getty

Printed in the United States of America

*To all the queer nineties kids who grew up in the rural Midwest. Those of us who made it out and those of us who didn't. Love always and forever.*

—*LB*

# PROLOGUE

Seven seconds.

That's how long it took him to slip his fingers down my pants and change my life forever.

Seven seconds.

That's all it took to change your life forever too.

My mom always warned me to keep my legs closed and watch out for the predators. But she told me they were out there. She never told me they were at home.

Seven seconds.

That's how long it took me to forget and exactly how long it took for me to remember when they told me what you'd done.

Seven seconds.

That's all it took to kill you.

# CHAPTER ONE
## *NOW*

## THERA

*It was just supposed to be a joke. Nobody was supposed to get hurt. Definitely nobody was supposed to die. We were just kids. Stupid teenagers. Everyone makes mistakes when they're young.*

That's what I kept telling myself as I frantically pawed through the back of my closet, searching for my suitcase. It's the same thing I told myself the night it happened, and every single time the memories pushed their way to the surface over the last twenty-six years. That's how I forced them down. It hadn't been easy, but I did it.

*We were just kids.*

*We didn't mean to do anything wrong.*

*We were just kids.*

Over and over again. A steady mantra until I tricked myself into believing it was true. You could do anything if you put your mind to it. At least I could. That's what happens after your mom dies of breast cancer when you're seven years old. Your brain figures out all kinds of ways to cope. It doesn't have any other choice.

I couldn't believe I was going to see the girls again—Cabin Naomi strong—after all this time had passed. It was like a weird fever dream. To have suppressed any memory of them for so long and then, suddenly—bam! Just in your face again. I still hadn't caught my breath. My emotions were all over the place. I had barely left the house in six years. Not since Dad's stroke. I shouldn't have been going now, but I didn't have any other choice.

Blakely started the group text and sent it out to everyone. How'd she get our contact information if none of us were supposed to be in touch? That was part of the plan. *Absolutely no contact no matter what. We never talk about this.* Blakely must've said it ten times before we left the bathroom that night. Have the others been in touch? I just figured everyone else followed the plan, same as me. It'd never occurred to me it might be otherwise. What if I was the only one that cut them all off and never looked back? Had they all gotten together without me? Were they setting me up? But I hadn't done anything wrong. Not anything worse than what they'd done.

Blakely had way more reason to keep quiet than me. Than anyone, really. Unless they'd gotten together and were trying to make me take the fall for what happened. But why would they do that? And why now? After all this time? My head spun and my stomach hurt. I couldn't think straight. I pushed the fears aside. These were my oldest and dearest friends. I was being silly. Totally illogical and paranoid. But it was hard not to be, given the situation.

"We never tell anyone what we did. Not tonight. Not tomorrow. Not ever. Do you understand me? We forget everything and pretend like we never knew each other when we leave here. This"—she pointed to all of us—"never happened." We were huddled in the bathroom together. Squished in one tiny stall. All the way in the back. Every camper's parent had been called to come pick up their child, and the ones that were close had already started arriving. "And this"—she pointed outside, in the direction of the main lodge, where all the emergency vehicles and police had gathered—"wasn't our fault."

I listened to her. So did the others. Because you listened to Blakely. You didn't question her. She'd always been the natural leader of our group, and that night wasn't any different. We walked out of the bathroom in silence, and nobody spoke while we hurriedly shoved our things into suitcases. The only sounds in the cabin besides our own breathing were the crickets chirping outside the window, punctuated by Grace's quiet sobs in the background. She hadn't quit crying since we'd heard the news. But we didn't stop what we were doing to comfort her like we normally would. We didn't even look at each other. We just kept our heads down and packed. I walked out of Cabin Naomi, the screen door slamming shut behind me, without even saying goodbye. I'd known at the beginning of the summer that it would be the last time we'd all be together. We'd be off to college the following year and moving on to the next phase of our lives. But it wasn't supposed to end like that. It was supposed to be the best summer of our lives.

None of it had felt real. That's what I remembered the most about those final moments with my friends. The last few hours at Camp Pendleton were just like when my mom died. *This doesn't feel real. It isn't happening.* That's all I could think about then, too, as I lay next to her on her hospital bed in our living room, listening to her wheeze as she took her last breaths, struggling with each one. Even as she hovered with one foot in this world and her other foot in the afterlife, I felt nothing. Completely detached, because it truly didn't feel possible that it was my life. My mom was supposed to live. She wasn't supposed to die. What about all our prayers? *This isn't happening.*

All my therapists asked what I was feeling in that moment with her, and I never told them the truth. Because that's not what you're supposed to be thinking about when the greatest woman in the world dies. The day you lose your heart. Part of your soul. You're supposed to have something profound to say about that. Except I didn't.

Just like the day my mom died, my dad swooped in to save me from camp in the same way. He was always my center of gravity when the world flipped upside down. My hero. He ran to me as soon as he spotted me coming down the hill, grabbing me and scooping me up the moment he got near. His familiar muscular arms wrapped around me, and he held me close to him for the longest time, his heart racing against mine. He finally pulled back and cupped my face in his hands.

"Are you okay, bug?" His big brown eyes peered into mine. Filled with nothing but concern and love. He was doing his best not to cry. Fiercely working his jaw as he tucked my hair behind my ears.

I nodded. Too scared to speak. Did I still have blood on my face? I still felt like I did even though we'd washed it off in the sink.

"Let's get you out of here," he said, grabbing my bag with one arm and throwing his other arm around me. He paused for a second and looked up at the sky. "God, help us through this moment." He took a deep breath, then turned his gaze back to me. "Now, you just close your eyes and keep 'em shut, bug. Don't look at anything when we walk through all the commotion down there, you hear me? There's a ton of people. Lots of things going on, and you don't need to see any of that. You understand?"

I nodded. I understood it was a crime scene. A brutal massacre on campus, and he didn't need to tell me to close my eyes. I'd already squeezed them shut and buried my face in his chest, wishing he could protect me from the images. But it was too late. I'd already seen too much. The police scanners crackled. The air smelled metallic. Almost like it smelled after it rained. Except it wasn't rain—it was blood. I didn't look at anyone or anything else while we walked through the masses of law enforcement, people multiplying by the second and crawling around the property like ants. I kept my head buried in Dad's chest all the way to the car.

The memories made me shudder. I didn't want to remember the car ride or what the first few days back home had been like. I was so sick and scared. Mostly from anxiety. The images. What we'd done. The part we played. I kept waiting for the phone to ring or a police officer to knock at my front door and take me down to the station, but nobody ever called. Nobody ever came. I watched the story from afar, and eventually, I stopped worrying about it. I didn't have any other choice if I wanted to go on with my life. You couldn't stay stuck in trauma forever.

That's what my mom made me promise when she died: "Don't you dare use this as a reason to throw your life away, Thera. You hear me?"

So, that's what I'd done with that last summer of camp. Same as I'd done with my mom. Moved forward. But now everything had come to a screeching halt.

I'd never looked up any of my cabinmates once you could do things like that on social media. It'd been hard in the beginning, but they'd been dead to me for years now. Decades, really. What would it be like to see Blakely after all this time? To this day, she was the best friend I ever had. Would she still snort when she laughed? Did she ever have the mole on her cheek removed, like she swore she'd do when she was an adult? Was she still the same person? Was I? Were any of us?

So many questions. But I didn't let myself think about the most important one—the one that mattered the most. Were we finally going to tell someone what we'd done? Make things right after all this time?

# CHAPTER TWO
## *NOW*

### GRACE

I was the last one to say yes when Blakely asked if we could have an emergency meeting at her house in Atlanta this weekend. The others had immediately jumped at the opportunity, but I'd held back. What if it wasn't her on the phone? How did I really know who anyone was on the group text? Everyone said who they were so we could save the number with their name in our contacts, but it's not like we asked for an ID. I didn't trust this. I didn't trust any of this.

The entire conversation had been all of four minutes:

**Who sent this???**

That's how she started it. No *Hello. How are you? This is Blakely. Sorry we haven't talked in twenty-six years. How have you been getting along since we destroyed an entire family?* No, there was none of that. Just her question followed by a picture of a white note card. The same one I held in my hand now. The corners already worn from fingering it so much:

## I KNOW WHAT YOU DID THAT SUMMER AND I'M GOING TO MAKE YOU PAY.

The message was just like the movie the line came from and sent an alarm racing through my entire body.

The summer of 1998.

The year after *I Know What You Did Last Summer* came out. It was the slasher movie of the year, and we were just as obsessed with it as everyone else. We stole the VHS tape from one of the counselors' cabins, and we must've watched it a hundred times in the basement of the rec room. Memorizing every line. Each scene. Playing them out in our cabin late at night. It was the perfect horror flick for us.

But unlike the movie, it wasn't last summer they were referring to on the card. It was *that* summer. Even seeing the words gave me chills. That summer wasn't a year ago, like in the movie. It was over twenty-six years ago. Another lifetime.

One I'd put away. Tucked it inside a box labeled "Grace's memories" all those years ago. The same way I hid my parents' wedding photos. They couldn't stand any evidence that showed they didn't always hate each other, but I knew the truth. Those pictures told a different story. A story where they were happy. In love. It was the same way with that summer.

Who sent this?

People didn't even send Christmas cards anymore. It was sealed in a white envelope just like it'd been in the movie. The perfect copycat. It wasn't just that whoever sent the note had mentioned that specific summer. It was the implication they were going to make us pay for what we'd done. That was the scariest part and the only reason I'd agreed to anything. Nobody knew what really happened that summer except us. Our very small circle—me, Thera, Blakely, and Meg. Cabin Naomi. Nine consecutive summers together.

Why would they send this? And why now? After all this time had passed?

I hadn't been paying attention yesterday when my assistant brought the mail into my studio. Fans were constantly sending me flowers and cards and gifts, but this one hadn't come with any of that. Only a single white envelope with my name stamped on the front.

I'd kept it with me ever since, constantly pulling it out and rereading it like there was some secret message hidden in the sentence that I wasn't seeing. Turning the paper around like it'd read differently upside down. I tried to calm down and go back to work, but I couldn't. All I kept doing was looking at my photographers through the glass and wondering if it was one of them who sent it as some sick joke. If they were connected to her somehow. To that. At some point, I couldn't contain myself anymore, and I'd stormed out of my office and charged at them.

"Who dropped this off?" I'd screeched in an embarrassingly high Karen voice at the new guy. He was taken aback and looked to Matt for help, but Matt just shrugged his shoulders and looked in the other direction. He wasn't getting caught up in this. He'd been with me for almost three years. He knew better. Smart man.

"I, uh . . . I'm not sure . . . I didn't see anything." He stumbled over his words as his eyes skittered around the room, not landing on mine for more than the teeniest second. He visibly trembled.

Good.

I liked when they were scared of me.

"You don't know where this came from?" I waved it in front of his face. He shook his head while he mumbled no.

Tessa, my assistant, hadn't seen anything either. She'd been on a call with one of my producers when it came in. I told her I needed the afternoon to get my head straight and not to bother me unless it was an emergency. I'd rushed home, and within hours, the text came. At first nobody responded to the question, so she sent a follow-up:

**This is Blakely.**

Seeing her name in front of me after all these years brought so many emotions heaving to the surface. Not just what happened that summer, but who I was back then. And who I was, well, that was someone I hated. That girl. So desperate and insecure.

I've been to lots of therapy. Way too much, especially as a child. That's what happens when you have a rare medical disorder and your parents just want you to feel normal about it. To accept and love yourself as you are. I stopped going as soon as they'd allow it, but I'd tried again in recent years just to see if it could be helpful. Nothing had changed. Everyone's favorite therapy technique still seemed to be getting you in touch with your inner child. That was the overall approach they all loved to take in some form or fashion. But me?

I shot my inner child a long time ago, along with the white horse she was waiting for someone to come riding in on to save her. Both of them dead. Point blank. My therapists always looked at me with such a horrified expression whenever I said that, but it was the truth.

Finally, I quit going to therapy, and that was when I really started to heal. Because sometimes . . . well, sometimes you find out your parents were right all along and you should've listened to them when you were a kid. The best way to live your life was to learn to love yourself—really, truly love yourself—and accept yourself exactly as you were. Nothing broken in need of fixing. Perfectly whole. So, that's exactly what I'd done. Learned to love who I was and fall in love with my body.

But I could feel the fingers of the little-girl ghost reaching for my hand. The one that hated herself. The fat friend in the group. Because that's who I was back then. Every group of women friends has the one. Either the overweight friend or the ugly friend. Doesn't matter. We served the same role—making the other girls feel better about themselves. We were in the group to be the target of an insult when it was needed. Or someone to laugh at in an uncomfortable moment. And most importantly—to constantly provide the others with compliments. Tell them how good they looked. How amazing they were. That was me. Who I used to be. And I still couldn't shake her. I watched the others—Meg and Thera—respond once Blakely said who she was.

I got one too.

Omg what do we do??

On and on it went, in various versions of freaking out and emoji. I only sent one thing besides my response. The link to the article in the *Post-Tribune* because Regina Crosby was the first name I googled after I got the cryptic message. The first hit told me everything I needed to know:

> Regina Crosby paroled after twenty-five years behind bars for the brutal murder of her husband and attempted murder of her two children

It was no coincidence that we got our cards exactly six weeks after Regina got paroled. But that was the thing that bothered me the most. Regina had no idea what we'd done that summer. Nobody did. They'd never even asked us about it afterward. There wasn't a single soul outside our group that thought we had anything to do with what happened to Regina and her family. Except how did I know that was still true?

I'd kept my promise all these years, but had the others? It wasn't outside the realm of possibility that one of them had shared the secret with someone else over the last two decades. Lord knows I'd come close enough myself on a couple of drunken nights. That's a lot of time for guilt to fester and grow. Plenty of years to change your mind. Decide you need redemption. One of them could have easily broken down and told.

Or be playing us. That was always a possibility too. I didn't know these girls anymore. They were grown women. And if I was a different person, chances were they'd changed too. And I was just supposed to trust them? I couldn't do that. The only person I trusted was myself.

I'd watched the thread as they all agreed to meet, and it wasn't long until they were questioning me.

Grace? It was Meg.

Sweet Meg. That's what my mom used to call her. She loved Meg as much as I did.

I couldn't say no to her, and besides, if Regina—or someone else—really was toying with us, then I couldn't ignore that. It was too dangerous. So, I agreed despite my misgivings.

I threw a few things into an overnight bag and just started driving, heading straight out of the city. It was a little over ten hours from Miami to Atlanta, and instead of flying, I'd use the drive time to clear my head. That's what I did when I needed to think. Left the city and drove for hours. I couldn't think straight with everyone's thoughts buzzing around mine. All the frenetic energy of thousands of people constantly moving and going. Swiping and tapping. The collective anxiety of the masses. It didn't give you any space. That's what I loved about the city. The constant movement. Constant activity.

Except when I needed to be still and think.

Like tonight.

As soon as the city lights disappeared behind me, everything in my body loosened. Like getting home after a huge dinner and unzipping your pants. The relief was immediate. My foot relaxed on the gas pedal of my new Mercedes, and I shifted into cruise mode as the road wound through the green valley and toward the water. I rolled down all the windows and let the fresh air penetrate my cells. Taking a huge breath.

Just the mention of that summer was enough to make me feel dirty. Dirtier than any picture I'd ever posed in. It was hard to believe something that was supposed to be so wonderful—and had been for so many years—could turn into such a nightmare. But maybe it was because Camp Pendleton wasn't the real world and things happened there that didn't happen any other place.

Camp Pendleton was a summer camp for gifted kids and an alternate reality from our lives back home. It hadn't been my first choice. I wanted to go to fat camp, but my parents wouldn't even consider it, just like they wouldn't tolerate anything hinting at a diet. I'd seen the flyer for Pendleton on the bulletin board outside my violin teacher's classroom and came up with a plan almost immediately. It'd been a hard sell to my parents—sleepaway camp for six weeks for an eight-year-old—but they couldn't resist when I pitched it as an opportunity to make new friends. I threw in all the stuff they'd fall for, like how it would give me the chance to practice my social skills, to try new sports and activities. But most importantly, I'd get to spend time with other kids that were like me. I wouldn't be a freak when I was surrounded by other kids who were just as smart as I was and equally awkward. It'd be so much easier to make friends. That's when they finally said I could go. They were desperate for me to be around kids who weren't awful to me.

How was I supposed to know all the things I said about camp would end up being true? I planned on making it into my own personal fat camp. To starve myself the entire time I was there and do all the sports stuff I never did at school because I was always worried about people teasing me over how I looked. But I didn't have to worry about that at Pendleton. Not when everyone was as bad at sports as I was.

The magic of Pendleton happened almost the moment I stepped foot on campus. For six weeks, we all transformed from the bullied, geeky kids we were in our hometowns to regular teenagers. We went from being the outcasts at our schools—social misfits, because once you hit high school, it's no longer cool to be smart, if it ever was—to regular kids. A world where everyone was smart. Like super smart. Where we competed over IQ scores and SAT prep scores the same way athletes competed for sports trophies. In a world where we spent so much time pretending like we weren't smart so we'd avoid the social consequences of being bullied, it was incredibly liberating to take off our masks and be just as smart as we wanted to be. Our genius was celebrated, and everyone was awkward, so really it just seemed normal.

That's what I loved the most about it.

Until that summer.

The one on the card.

The one where everything changed.

# CHAPTER THREE

## *THEN*

### BLAKELY

I smiled wide as I stepped off the bus. We were finally here—senior campers! I loved camp. It was my favorite place on earth. Camp was my Christmas, and I counted down the days the same way little kids did waiting for Santa every year.

I was popular here, and being popular just might be the greatest feeling in the world. I wasn't exactly like all these other kids. I had a few friends back home. Not exactly friends. I was one of the periphery kids. The popular group always needs a backup crew, you know. They require an audience. A person that's always there so they never have to be alone, so they can maintain the image of being important, because important people are surrounded by people. We all knew they came with an entourage.

Or because they needed you. You had something valuable that they wanted.

In my case, it was my house. My dad and stepmom traveled constantly. Most of the time, my half brother, Jonathon, went with while I stayed behind. I was mostly raised by nannies, and once I hit fourteen,

I begged to be allowed to live without one. It's not like I was really on my own. I still had the cleaners and all the other staff around.

I had a house where parents are never home, and when you're a teenager, that's about as valuable as you can get. So, the kids at school used me when they wanted a place to party or hang out. I knew that. It wasn't like I didn't. My friend Emily always liked to act like I was somehow naive to them using me, but I wasn't. Besides, she was just jealous. She knew she would've done the same thing if the shoe had been on the other foot, because that's what you did. For whatever reason, you'll sell your soul to the popular kids in high school.

But here? At camp?

I got to experience what it was like to really be popular. Really, truly popular. And I loved every minute of it. I loved being queen. I spent all year watching and studying Samantha—the queen bee at my school—so I'd know what to do once I got here and it was my turn. Boys tripped over themselves trying to get her attention, and even the teachers stumbled over their words when they talked to her. It was like she was some kind of drug, and I wanted to be that intoxicating. I wanted to strip men of their words. Have women hate me, which really just meant they were dying of jealousy. That's what I told Thera last week during our phone call, and she'd laughed at me, but I'd been totally serious.

Where was my dead-mama twin, anyway? She should've been here by now. She hated when I called us dead-mama twins, even though it was true. She was so sensitive about her mom, though. I probably would have been, too, if I'd known mine, but killing her was the first thing I did after I was born, and making jokes about it was how I coped. I couldn't help myself.

Just as I was about to walk around to the other side of the buses, I spotted Thera over by the picnic tables. I squealed and raced over to greet her. She saw me at the same time and ran to meet me halfway. We both dropped our bags and threw our arms around each other. She scooped me up in one swift movement and whipped me around, my legs flying off the ground. She put me back down and grabbed my hands.

"Senior campers!" we shrieked together as we jumped up and down, twirling in circles. This was supposed to be the best year at camp. The one you dream about and hear stories about from your very first year. Getting to be the big people on campus. All the special privileges. There were so many rumors we'd always heard, and now we'd finally find out if they were true. Did we really get to stay up twenty minutes past lights-out? Get an extra five minutes on our Sunday phone calls back home? Were we able to have s'mores whenever we wanted to? And we could basically get away with anything. Pendleton's biggest threat to keep you in line was the loss of privilege as an attendee. Act out too much and you wouldn't be allowed back. But it didn't matter, because we'd never be back. This was it.

And then there were the pranks. The senior pranks were the best, as much a part of camp as the counselors. One year they drained the swimming pool. Another time they filled the senior girls' sleeping bags with rocks on the overnight campout in the woods. Once they let all the horses out of the east barn. Their favorite pranks were the ones that involved the counselors and the counselors-in-training—CITs—like filling their shampoo bottles with ketchup and writing messages on their mirrors with lipstick. Most of the CITs were barely older than us, so sometimes they even pranked seniors back. It was one of the funnest parts about camp, and I'd been creating a list of ideas all year.

"Have you seen Meg?" I asked, scanning the sea of faces and bodies swarming around us. All the usual chaos of the first day. There was no use looking for Grace yet. She was always one of the last people to arrive. All the East Coast kids were.

"Not yet, but Jacob told me she's here somewhere," Thera replied, standing on her tiptoes and trying to get a better look. Her hair had gotten so much longer since last year. It was halfway down her back and all the same length. Very Alanis Morissette, and I loved it.

There were so many kids stepping off the buses and milling around. Their backpacks strapped to them. Others dragging suitcases. Some of the younger ones looked terrified. A few were still crying. They didn't let the parents come up with the buses. They had to say goodbye at the bottom of the driveway. It was only campers and counselors at the top of the hill. Counselors were swarming the ones having a tough time. Pendleton prided itself on getting even the most nervous campers to stay.

I didn't see Meg anywhere, but suddenly, a guy stepped in between two boys wrestling over a sleeping bag to pull them apart, and my heart practically stopped. He was drop-dead gorgeous. Like movie-star hot. "Oh my God, who's that?" I asked, tilting my head in his direction and motioning with my eyes, so it wouldn't be too obvious that I was looking at him.

Thera's gaze followed mine, and her eyes grew just as wide when she spotted him. Six feet of sturdy muscle. A tennis racket slung over his chest. Brown hair, tousled and curly, falling into one of his eyes. Tanned, spirally legs. Was he one of the new counselors? An older CIT?

"Right?" I said to her with a wicked grin, and she smiled back. We always had the same taste in boys.

"Oh, I see you've spotted the new tennis coach," a voice—one I'd recognize anywhere—said from behind us.

"Meg!" Thera and I screamed happily at the same time. We whipped around.

Meg stood in front of us with the same goofy wide grin she'd worn the day we met when we were eight. The three of us were all arms, grabbing and squeezing and squealing as we danced in a small circle around our stuff. When we finally stopped, I grabbed Meg's face and kissed both her cheeks, hard.

"Ohmigod, hi! I missed you so much," I gushed. It was like this every year. Seeing each other again for the first time was one of my favorite parts. Every single year, it was the same thing when camp came to an end. We always said we'd keep in touch. We promised to call.

Write. Visit. All the things. And for the first few weeks after we got home, we did. The calls and letters were endless—so were the tears because we missed each other so much—but as the weeks grew into months, it would always trickle out until finally stopping. Our lives at home always got in the way. We couldn't be the people there that we were here. It just got too hard.

But this? I lived for this. It was the best part.

Thera hugged Meg next, then poked her in the side. "Sorry I didn't hug you right away, I was too busy looking at Mr. Yummy over there."

Meg burst out laughing. "His name is Mr. Crosby, and he's way too old for you."

Thera smacked her on the arm. "Not anymore."

"We're seniors!" I said, jumping up and down again. I never got sick of saying that. I never would. We'd earned it. Not only that: we already got special treatment, so it was going to be even better for us than the others. That's the way it worked when an entire wing of the recreation center had been donated by my daddy.

"So, who do you think he's ending up with?" Thera asked. She still hadn't taken her eyes off him.

The other thing about being a senior at camp was that it was no longer inappropriate to hook up with the CITs, and there were always rumors of seniors hooking up with actual counselors too. Guess we could add that to the list of might-be-true rumors we were trying to figure out. There was a hierarchy to camp staff, and not all of them were old. Some of them definitely were, for sure, like Glenda. She'd been the first cook they'd hired when they built the camp, and she'd never left. She was as old as the camp and looked like my grandma. We were on our third director, but he'd been here almost fifteen years now, so he was the only one we knew and who everyone associated with the camp. Those were the people at the top. The senior staff. And obviously, nobody messed with those people. Who wanted to? Stiff adults who didn't want to have any fun? No thank you.

But then there were the counselors and the CITs around our age. Some of them were barely eighteen, so once you hit sixteen, then it was free game. Technically, you weren't supposed to hook up, but you weren't supposed to do a lot of things at camp that people did. And besides, what were they going to do to me? Last year I tried to hook up with Ben Ross all summer, and Ben waited until senior week to finally kiss me. And that was it. We never got any further. That wasn't happening this year. I wasn't going home a virgin.

"He's super hot," Meg said with her classic grin, but then she quickly gave a dramatic frown. "Except I'm serious. I think he's way too old."

I shook my head. "The older, the better."

My daddy said older men were only interested in one thing—sex. That's why he kept them away from me, but that was the reason I loved camp the most—he didn't have any control over me when I was here.

# CHAPTER FOUR

## *THEN*

### MEG

I knew this year was going to be different. I leaned against the tree with my arms folded across my chest, watching Blakely and Thera saunter by Mr. Crosby on the tennis courts for the third time. They were being totally obvious that they were trying to get his attention. Blakely was laughing way too loud, and Thera was staring right at him, all dumb-founded and speechless like she'd never seen a hot guy before.

Senior year was supposed to be the best year, and everyone was all excited about it. But I don't know . . . I had a really bad feeling about this year. I'd tried telling my mom about it before I left.

"Honey," Mom said, pausing the basketball game she was watching on TV. "We go through this every single year before camp. This is all part of it."

She wasn't wrong. That's what I did. Every year, no matter what. Total meltdown mode in the week leading up to it. But this time, it was different. This time I had a secret. One I could never share, and that was easy to do when you basically lived in your room, like I did at home. It'd be almost impossible to do with my best friends. They'd probably take one look at me and know something was different.

"Please, Mom, I'm too old now. You can't make me go." I'd begged right up until last night, even though my bags were already packed. She'd had them packed for two weeks. She'd never admit it, but she needed the break and looked forward to camp. A single mom working two jobs—bank teller by day and waitress at Barney's by night—she relished not having to worry about me on top of everything else she had on her already full plate. She'd never complained, though. Not once. That wasn't her style. But she was the one who'd found and applied for the scholarship when I was in third grade because we couldn't afford the tuition. I was one of the youngest campers there. We all were—me, Thera, Grace, and Blakely. Part of Cabin Naomi since day one. Maybe that's why we were so close.

They were closer to me than most of my family, and I definitely saw them more often. Mom kept me away from my family as much as possible. We didn't even go there on the holidays. She said they were a bad influence on me. That there was a reason we lived over two thousand miles away from them. And she wasn't wrong. They were weird. And angry and violent, especially when they'd been drinking.

She'd packed everything she owned, including six-week-old me, into her 1980 Plymouth Duster that didn't have AC and drove nine hundred miles to Michigan. All because of a cute town she'd seen on a TV show, and she liked the vibe. So, that's where she decided we'd go, and we've been in Lansing ever since. She started working in the laundromat at night. I'd been really colicky, and she'd put me in a laundry basket, all wrapped up tight like a burrito—that's what she used to call me—and set me on top of the washing machine. That was the one thing that put me to sleep. It was why she'd loved the job. And she waitressed. She started out as a hostess because she was too young to be anything else at first since it involved selling alcohol. She was only seventeen when I was born, so we'd practically grown up together. She's always worked so hard to give me the life she never had.

But none of that mattered last night when my social anxiety and my secret were screaming violently at me. Mom paid me no attention. She kept her back to me while she continued watching the basketball game.

"Meg, we do this every year. You say the exact same things you're saying tonight. Have the same freak-out and then you go and have a wonderful time. By the end of the first week, you don't even call home, you're so busy with your friends and all the activities. You know you always have the best time, right?" She pointed out the obvious, but her rational questions didn't touch my irrational fear. If I could talk any sense into my anxiety, I wouldn't have any. I just shook my head at her. Maintaining my diligent stance.

"I just want to work as much as I can this summer. You know I'm trying to save as much up as possible over the next year so that I can pay my own rent and you don't have to," I said, fully aware of how manipulative I was being by playing into her fears about money and college. I'd received a full academic scholarship at Saint Thomas, but it only covered my tuition, and we were responsible for everything else. We were both determined to get me there, no matter what it took, though. She blamed not going to college on why her life had been so difficult, and she wasn't wrong.

Her back was still turned away from me, but I saw her pause for just a second. I'd hit the exact spot I'd been aiming for, but it still wasn't enough. "You'll regret not being able to see Dandelion."

She hit back with an equally heart-tugging attack. Dandelion was my favorite horse at camp. Horseback riding had always been my favorite part of going. The piece that stole my heart long before I developed a relationship with the girls, because that first summer, I was incredibly homesick. I'd never been away from my mom for even a night. I still wasn't sure sending me to camp was the best parenting choice on her part. To take your introverted and very shy daughter who'd never slept anywhere but beside you in bed and send them into the middle of nowhere in a cabin to sleep on an unrolled sleeping bag on a bunk with five other strangers? I probably wouldn't make the same choice with kids of my own.

But I didn't have a choice. And, see, that was the thing about my mom. The reason there was no use arguing with her about it. She was determined to give me everything she'd never had. She worked just as hard to send me to the private camps with all the rich kids during the summer as she did sending me to the best private schools with them during the year. She hated all the stigma placed on single mothers and spent every day doing her best to dispel them. We were more like sisters than we were mother and daughter, most of the time. But she wasn't afraid to throw down the mother card when she needed to, and she'd played it last night.

I don't know why I freaked out, because she was right. Once I got here, I always loved it. Just like she said. I had the best time. But everything was different this year. I knew it would be. Just having the secret already made everything feel weird, so there was no way I was telling them. Except it wasn't just my secret.

Something was off this year.

I wasn't imagining it even though I couldn't put my finger on what exactly it was. Usually when I got here, the moment I saw my friends, all my fears and worries just disappeared. They were gone like magic, and I was totally fine the rest of the time. The anxiety left and didn't come back until the following year. But so far that hadn't happened, and now I was starting to worry that it wouldn't. It had been almost five days.

I wanted to go home. Blakely was totally obsessed with the new tennis instructor, so that was what she'd got everyone else focused on too. She told us last night after lights-out that this was the summer she was going to lose her virginity. She and Thera had been researching it for the past couple of weeks just like it was a school science project. Thera pulled out a manila folder filled with all kinds of anatomy drawings. She'd literally mapped out the clitoris on paper and all the different pleasure-center nerves leading in and out like a complicated maze. But that wasn't the part that bothered me. Blakely told us she'd decided that it was going to be Mr. Crosby. Except that's not what she called him. She called him by his first name, Jared. She'd set her eyes on him, and that was the thing about Blakely. There was no stopping her when she got laser focused on something.

I sighed and watched as Grace kept swinging and missing all the tennis balls Mr. Crosby tossed her way, like she'd been doing ever since they started her lesson. I felt so sorry for her. She was clearly uncomfortable and kept tugging down the short skirt they made us all wear when we played tennis. Navy blue with gold letters. There was a strict dress code for everything we did here. Even down to our underwear. We all looked the same. Some people thought it was weird, but I found it comforting. I loved uniforms. I hated picking out what I wanted to wear. It was one of the most torturous things about school.

Grace hadn't wanted to sign up for the lesson. She hated sports. Practically everyone here did, but you couldn't blame us. We'd been the kids picked last for every team in gym class since kindergarten. That was why they worked so hard at getting us to try different sports while we were here. Ones we might not have a traumatic event associated with. For some reason, Blakely got it into her head that one of us needed to take a lesson with Mr. Crosby so that she could use it as a way to get him to notice her and flirt with him.

"But how come you don't just sign up for the lesson, then?" Grace had asked cautiously from her spot on the top bunk above me. Her voice was hesitant and nervous. Piss Blakely off and she might ignore you for days. Nobody wanted that.

Blakely rolled her eyes. "Because, duh, I mean, if I'm the one that takes the lesson, then that's totally obvious that I'm into him."

If that's what she was trying to avoid, then she was doing a terrible job, because Mr. Crosby looked as uncomfortable as Grace whenever Blakely came by.

"Oh hi, Mr. Crosby," she said with mock surprise every time as if she'd forgotten he was going to be there since she'd walked by seven minutes ago and said the same thing. She'd stick her chest out and do this weird cocking-her-head-to-the-side movement that I guess was supposed to be cute?

She wasn't very good at flirting, but I wasn't, either, so I didn't know why I was being so judgmental. I wished I could snap out of this terrible mood. It was going to be a long summer if I just felt homesick the entire time.

Just as Blakely and Thera were about to pass by him again, a perfectly made-up woman carrying a Kroger grocery bag breezed past them and rushed over to Mr. Crosby. She was stunning and totally out of place on the tennis court in her heels and full makeup. He noticed her right away and quickly whispered something to Grace before hurrying over to meet the woman. He put his arm around her waist and walked her over to the other side of the court. She set her things down and wrapped herself around him, giving him a big kiss. Like a huge tongue-in-mouth kiss right in front of everyone. All anyone could do was stare.

I shifted my gaze to Blakely and Thera. They'd stopped in their tracks. Thera's mouth was open in shock, and Blakely looked crushed. But only for a second. She quickly wiped the disappointment off her face, and her eyes narrowed to slits, her face pointed and calculated. She grabbed Thera's arm and turned on her heel, hurrying toward me. I raced around the bleachers and to the other side of the athletic building to meet them just as they came out of the gate.

"His girlfriend is beautiful!" Blakely gushed as soon as she saw me. And she was. As pretty as Mr. Crosby—dark hair, super fit, with big pouty lips and high cheekbones.

I nodded at Blakely, hoping this was exactly what we needed to shift the energy. Snap her back into focusing on us. That's what camp was about. Being together. Not chasing stupid boys. Especially ones that were way older and had girlfriends. Maybe now we could let all this nonsense go and get back to focusing on the things that mattered, like hanging out and being together.

# CHAPTER FIVE
## *THEN*

### GRACE

My insides seethed with anger. Fiery hot as all of them splashed around the water in their bikinis. Even Meg. She'd promised she was going to wear a one-piece with me. Solidarity and all that. But she'd shrugged her shoulders and pretended to be surprised when we all started getting ready earlier.

"Look at this?" she said in a way-too-loud voice in a super-dramatic fashion so I'd definitely hear her. "My mom packed me a bikini. I had no idea. She just loves throwing stuff in my suitcase at the last minute."

She gave me an apologetic look, but I ignored her and just kept stuffing myself into my one-piece. The classic Speedo I wore every summer. The only swimsuit I'd ever get in. I crossed my arms on my chest. Watching them from the shore. I loved camp, but it wasn't fair that I looked so different from my friends, especially since I couldn't help it.

It wasn't my fault I was big. Seriously, it wasn't. I know every fat person says that. They swear they don't eat. As if they're just miraculously overweight without consuming massive amounts of calories every day. But it was true in my case. One hundred percent.

I have a mutation in my melanocortin-4 receptor. Sounds like I'm a weird sci-fi creature, and people used to look at me so strange when I would tell them that. Back in elementary school, before I went through Mrs. Willoughby's social skills training group, it was the first thing I announced to anyone the moment I met them, even total strangers at the grocery store:

"I have a mutation in my melanocortin-4 receptor. Doctors call it MC4R. 'People with genetic mutations in MC4R—often just called MC4R deficiency—tend to gain weight from early childhood. They also have increased fat mass, an increase in lean mass, and increased linear growth in childhood. Most of them appear what we call big boned. The increased growth is in part mediated by disproportionate early hyperinsulinemia. The main clinical feature in MC4R deficiency is hyperphagia. That's an increased drive to eat and impaired satiety.' That means they're still hungry after they eat. That's what I have. Doctors diagnosed me at six weeks old."

I rattled it off like an encyclopedia because that's what I was at the time—a walking encyclopedia of facts about my unique genetic disorder. Back then, I was just a naive kid, and I'd actually believed it made me special because that's what my parents drilled into my head from the moment I could remember. They had both my siblings believing it, too, even though my siblings didn't have the same disorder.

"Only one in five hundred thousand babies are ever born with the gene missing," they'd say. "You're our special princess." Followed by a hug or a kiss. I'd beam proudly every time because they made it sound like I'd won the genetic lottery. I spent my early childhood skipping around with an imaginary crown on my head, thinking I'd been specifically chosen by God for something really unique and amazing.

Until Stephanie Adams had a birthday party in second grade. She invited the entire class, and we played the chubby-bunny marshmallow game. The one where you see who can stick the most marshmallows in their mouth while still saying *chubby bunny*. I'll never forget that moment. The one that changed everything. The instant my childhood ended.

I was only seven, but I remember it like it happened yesterday. Kyle turned to look at me with thick white goo stuck between his teeth as he grinned and pointed right at me. "She's Chubby Bunny. The real Chubby Bunny!"

Everyone had collapsed into hysterics. The kind of laughter that I was almost always left out of. That was almost always at my expense. Half the time I didn't even understand why. What it was that I'd done or said that they found so funny. But that wasn't one of those times. I understood what they were calling me wasn't good. What they said I had wasn't something anyone wanted to have.

I'd never looked at myself the same way in the mirror again.

Part of me wished I resembled a bunny because at least then maybe there was a part of me that was cute. I didn't feel like a bunny at all. And definitely not cute. Most times I felt like the marshmallow man in *Ghostbusters*, towering down the hall at my school in the same way he plowed through the buildings in New York City. That was the other problem.

I wasn't just off the growth charts in weight. My parents had given me all sorts of messed-up genetics I didn't want or have any control over. As if it wasn't enough for my weight to be off the growth charts—so was my height. I looked like a burgeoning Shaquille O'Neal, and if I had an athletic bone in my body, it just might've been perfect. But I didn't. I was uncoordinated, slow, and really clumsy. Like really, really clumsy.

I'd stopped giving people my life story about my body, though. Now I just told them I had a hormone disorder that made me heavier than most and made it really difficult for me to lose weight. Believe me, I'd tried everything to shrink these extra pounds off my body. I watched every single morsel of food I put in my mouth, but it never mattered. I might as well eat Big Macs every day and pints of Ben & Jerry's. I gained eight pounds the week I got my period for the first time. I was eleven.

Camp was my favorite place, but I hated the undressing parts of it. Baring our bodies in front of each other, everyone pretending not to look but still comparing. At least here it wasn't like gym class, where people's eyes slid over me with disgust, as if there was something wrong with me. Here, people were more accepting. That's why I loved Camp Pendleton, even with all the drama over my body. We were the geeks, the nerds, and the freaks back home. But here we were just regular teenagers. It also happened to be the only place I ever lost weight, because I didn't eat.

I did my best to eat as little as possible without the counselors picking up on it, like my mom would if I was at home. At home it was always "Grace, you are totally healthy. There is absolutely no need for you to diet. Your body is beautiful." But camp was my rules. Not hers.

She tried so hard to make me feel good about myself. She really did. Said it didn't matter what I weighed as long as I was healthy. At the beginning of middle school, when I ballooned into massive proportions, she went and gained twenty pounds just to show me she meant it. She stuffed herself that fall. Constantly eating and drinking these huge protein shakes every night before she went to bed. It was probably why I felt guilty about my low self-esteem. How could I not when someone worked so hard trying to make me feel okay? To not be alone.

Except she could always lose those twenty pounds in the same way she gained them. I didn't have a choice. It wasn't fair not to have a choice. I felt like I'd done something wrong. Like karmic punishment or something. That's what I hated. The unfairness of it all. Mom said it wasn't personal. Bad things happened to good people all the time, and there was nothing wrong with not being skinny or average size, especially if you were healthy. Thinking about my mom sent a surge of anger through me all over again. None of what she said mattered anymore, because she was a liar. I quickly shoved the feelings down and turned my attention back to my friends.

They were still splashing around next to the shore with Clint and the boys from Cabin Abraham. The boys were tossing a football back and forth between them. They were in one of the other senior cabins. We'd started plotting senior pranks with them yesterday, and that was turning into them always being around, which I wasn't sure I liked. It might not be so bad if one of the boys was looking at me like they were looking at my friends, but they weren't looking at me the same way. Even now. They were all huddled around the girls in the water, acting all goofy and purposefully missing the football to try to get their attention. No one had even noticed me yet.

Everyone was so boy crazy this summer, and it was starting to get annoying. Blakely had been that way since forever so it was pretty much expected, but Thera and Meg were as bad as she was. Thera pranced over to Clint and threw the football at his head. He grabbed her and shoved her underwater while she squealed.

At least Thera and Meg were interested in the boys our age. Blakely's obsession with Mr. Crosby was over the top. She was being so stupid about it too. Making all of us take lessons with him. Thera had hers today, and it was a good thing because we found out he was married. The woman kissing him on the tennis court that day wasn't just his girlfriend—she was his wife.

"I don't like this. It's gross," I'd whispered to Meg last night when we were brushing our teeth together before lights-out. Meg agreed with me, but finding out Mr. Crosby was married hadn't deterred Blakely at all. Instead of Blakely giving up her mission to lose her virginity to Mr. Crosby, she'd doubled down. More determined than ever.

"Why can't you just hook up with Clint? Or Sean? He's been flirting with you ever since the first campfire," Thera asked after she'd come back from her lesson and told us she'd seen the ring. She asked Mr. Crosby about it, and he told her they'd been married almost five years. "I'm all about you losing your virginity this summer, but do it with someone besides Mr. Crosby."

Thera was a lot like me—a strict moral code and a strong sense of justice. There were lines you just didn't cross. This was one of them. Cheaters destroyed families. Ruined everyone's life. Just ask my mom.

But Blakely just shook her head hard back at Thera. "No way."

"Those guys would hook up with you in a second!" I jumped in, immediately showing my support of Thera. It wasn't just that he was married. Blakely's attention on Mr. Crosby made me nervous in all these other ways too. Really uncomfortable ones that made me feel funny. It had since the first day. He was hot, but he was a grown man. Like a full-on grown man, with hair all over his chest and everything. I'd seen it poking out from underneath his polo shirt, and I didn't like it. If you asked me, Clint was way cuter than him anyway.

"They totally would," Meg exclaimed, agreeing with me and Thera.

"Exactly. That's the whole point." Blakely looked at the three of us like she was super annoyed, as if we weren't getting something important. We all stared back at her blankly, firm in our position. Maybe now that she knew we were all on the same side, she'd let it go. But instead, she just sighed like a frustrated parent. "Trying to get high school guys to hook up with you is nothing. Zero challenge. They'll put their little wieners in anything. They don't care. They're like the absolute-lowest-hanging fruit. You know what I mean?" She shook her head and then gave us a huge smile. "That's not what I'm going for. Some awful first time with someone who has no idea what he's doing or how to please a woman? No thanks. I'll pass." Her eyes filled with challenge and excitement. "I want to be with a real man." Desire filled her face. "I want it to mean something. How much more could that mean?"

"But he's married," Thera said again. Like she'd been saying all afternoon.

"Exactly! Did you see his wife? She's absolutely gorgeous. If I can steal a man like that away from her?" She grinned. Chef's-kissed the air. Then collapsed into giggles. We'd given up. At least for the night. Thankfully, he hadn't come up yet today. I was so sick of talking about him.

I pulled my suit down a final time and slowly plodded into the lake to join them. Clint and his crew had stopped playing football, and they were all huddled up, looking super serious with their heads down and whispering to each other. Clint was in the middle of talking when I walked up to their circle.

"We'll do it sometime tomorrow when they're having their morning check-in," he said, eagerly nodding his head.

I quickly filled in the blank. We'd been trying to figure out the best time to get into the faculty restrooms since Sean bought pop snappers from the canteen last night. The boys wanted to line the counselors' toilet seats with them, but we weren't sure that's what we wanted to do with them. We hadn't come up with a better idea, though.

"That's so unoriginal," Blakely said just as I slid in beside her. I put my hands on my hips and tried to look cute.

"Yeah." Meg immediately agreed with Blakely, like she'd been doing ever since we got here. "They do that one every year. The CITs practically expect it. I feel like we should try to do something different with the pop snappers."

Clint was staring back at Meg in this weird, mesmerized way. Looking at her the same way Blakely looked at Mr. Crosby—totally enamored. Everyone loved Meg this year. Sometimes they loved her so much I couldn't stand it. She'd barely paid attention to me and she'd been all about Blakely ever since we got here. It was one thing that she was suddenly so boy crazy, but being all about Blakely too? It was a bit much.

*Oh, I love those jeans. Your Birkenstocks are amazing. Where'd you get them?* Going on and on like she even cared anything about clothes. She didn't even do her own shopping. Her mom did it for her.

All the boys paying attention to Meg was totally bugging Blakely too. Blakely couldn't stand when the attention wasn't on her. She tried really hard to pretend like it didn't bother her, but she'd spent more time in the bathroom this summer than she had any other year. I'd never forgotten what I caught her doing in there when we were eleven. She might be fooling everyone else, but she wasn't fooling me.

I watched Blakely as she stared at Meg waiting for Clint's response. He was clearly flustered by her and what she'd said. Finally, he shrugged and looked sheepish. "I guess we do it because it's like tradition?"

"It might be fun to break tradition for once," I said, taking a risk and inserting my opinion into their conversation. This was why I came every year. I never would've taken this chance at my school, but camp always gave me courage, and my bravery was rewarded by a huge smile from Blakely. I beamed. Meg wasn't the only one who could impress her.

Blakely threw her arm around me and high-fived me with her other hand. "Exactly. Let's switch things up a little this year!"

# REGINA

I was always watching them. Studying. Observing. Taking notes. They didn't know I was always watching. It's because rich kids are just like their rich parents.

Totally self-absorbed. And without regard for anyone else. Especially people outside their inner circle.

See, that's the thing about rich people. They live their life without consequences. With rich daddies and trust funds to get them out of any kind of trouble they might find themselves in.

Don't like your $40,000-a-year private school?

Don't worry. We'll send you to a new one.

Got into a bit of trouble with the law?

No problem. This Ivy League attorney will get you out of it and make sure it never shows up on your permanent record.

Can't get a spot on the basketball team?

I'll build a new gym and put our family name above the door so they have to take you.

I didn't even know what I was doing at Camp Pendleton. I didn't belong there. Neither did my husband.

But that's what they didn't know.

They thought I was one of them. Born from the same diamond-studded cloth. Fed with the same golden spoon.

But I wasn't anything like them.

Not even a little bit.

And it was time they found out.

And not just who I was. They needed to learn about life. Real life. The one the rest of us lived.

I wanted them to hurt and bleed and suffer like the rest of us.

I'd tried to find my reason for living for so long. A way to move forward. Maybe this had been it all along.

My job was to be the one that showed them. Introduced them to a life with consequences. Where you pay for your actions. Where you're punished when you hurt other people.

For the first time in their spoiled, entitled lives, they were going to live like the rest of us.

# CHAPTER SIX
## *NOW*

### MEG

Thera was a good person. One of the most beautiful souls I'd ever met, and I took one look at her tonight when she ran down Blakely's sidewalk and knew that hadn't changed at all. She still had the long flowing hair—so blonde now it was practically white—which matched her long flowing skirt. Her eyes the icy, translucent gray they'd always been. Mirrors reflecting her experience back at you every time you looked at her. Losing her mom at such a young age had turned her into such an old soul.

In that moment, it was like no time had passed, and we were just long-distance friends seeing each other again at camp after another year had gone by and we'd missed each other terribly.

"Ohmigod, hi! How are you?"

"You look amazing!"

"So do you."

Our words and questions tumbled out of our mouths on top of each other. We hugged and danced in a circle just like we used to every summer when we saw each other for the first time. She'd quickly led me inside Blakely's house, chattering away about putting my things in my room and then joining them downstairs in the kitchen while we waited for Grace to arrive. I was grateful to have a moment to freshen up from the plane and to center myself again for whatever was about to happen. I had no idea what to expect. I walked over to put my suitcase in the closet and smiled again at how good it felt seeing Thera after so long.

I'd looked up whether her dad was still alive while I was on the plane. It was almost a five-hour flight from Seattle, so it'd given me plenty of time to look everyone up. I'd scoured all their social media like a jaded lover. I was so happy to see Mr. Grey was still alive. He'd always been her world.

I was shocked to find out Thera was a practicing psychic and spiritual counselor, though. It was so out of the realm of science for her, and Thera was definitely a scientist. She always had been—logical, practical, grounded in rules. Order and equations. A brilliant mathematician. She'd destroyed all the boys in the math competitions every summer at Pendleton. Built a lab in her closet when she was eight and almost blew up their house mixing ammonia. That's when her dad moved her to the basement. She won all kinds of awards when we were kids, from the junior science award to national honors. She'd already done all her science prerequisites in high school so she could go right into med school when she got to college. Talking to dead people was the last thing I ever expected her to be. It wasn't exactly scientific, but it did make sense. If I'd lost my mom when I was seven, I'd want to believe I'd found a way to talk to her still too.

But as shocking as it was to discover that about Thera, Grace's life was the most shocking. I'd choked on my glass of chardonnay on the plane when I found her Instagram. Sent the liquid straight down the wrong tube and me into a coughing fit that made the woman sitting next to me start handing me Kleenex from her purse.

"I'm so sorry. Thank you," I said in a raspy voice as I tried to recover. I hadn't seen that one coming. Grace was a supermodel now. She was internet famous. I couldn't believe it. Her Instagram had over a million followers, but it was her OnlyFans account that was the most impressive. She was Bahd Barbie, and she'd made over $2 million last year. She was number five on Forbes's list of top-fifty content creators.

I didn't go to her OnlyFans account even though I really wanted to. My wife, Claire, had access to all my social media accounts, same as I did hers, and we were completely transparent about everything, but I was dying to know how racy Grace got on there. The Grace I knew wore biker shorts underneath her uniform shorts with extra-long T-shirts hanging down. There was no variability to her wardrobe. Her nighttime outfit only included pulling a camp hoodie over her uniform. She was super self-conscious. Always changing with her back to us in the cabin and as fast as she could. Perfecting the art of being in the clothes you were taking off at the same time as the ones you were putting on. She even wore a T-shirt over her swimming suit. How'd she go from that to being Bahd Barbie?

The only thing stopping me from going to her page and signing up for her exclusive content was worrying Claire would see it and think I was trying to hook up with someone else. I had no business being on those types of sites as a married woman. Claire had a very low tolerance, bordering on none, when it came to pornography too. She thought it exploited women even if women were making the choice to do it as sort of a reverse exploitation. It didn't matter to her. All of it still fell within the patriarchal system she was vehemently opposed to. Besides that, I didn't want her asking questions about Grace, which she absolutely would. I couldn't explain without lying the reason I was looking her up after all this time had passed.

This was why I hated lying. You couldn't just tell one lie. One lie led to another and another, like an alcoholic who couldn't have just one drink. So, I wasn't taking any chances of Claire finding out about OnlyFans. It was bad enough that I was lying to her about this trip. I'd never lied to her about anything before. Not once. We told each other everything. But I couldn't tell her about this.

I'd shared about the girls years ago, though. How much they meant to me growing up and the way those summers shaped me. I'd never done that with any of my partners before her, but she was my wife. That was different. It'd only been within the last ten years that I'd finally started unmasking. Peeling off the layers of the person I'd built in order to survive. It wasn't until I met Claire and was genuinely loved for the first time in my life that I was safe enough to be who I was. I'd left out most of the details about the last summer, but she knew all my fond memories about the ones that came before and my complicated relationship with Grace. Really, my complicated relationships with all of them.

I really thought I knew Grace, and I never would've pictured her in a million years as a social media influencer. Blakely, absolutely. I'd been half surprised to discover she wasn't. She didn't have any kind of a presence on social media, and she barely posted. Like most forty-three-year-old women, she probably used Instagram to spy on other people's lives and send her friends memes. As far as I could tell, Blakely hadn't done much with her life except marry one of Georgia's most eligible bachelors. Literally. He'd been named that in all the papers. The same ones that featured their expensive wedding in the Cayman Islands a year later. She might have been missing from the majority of social media, but their wedding had made all the papers. I'd skimmed those articles, too, and they practically made it sound like an arranged marriage. Her dad and husband were the only two interviewed. They didn't even have a quote from her, which seemed odd, not to have anything from the bride, but her father had always controlled her life, so maybe he still did. Her half brother, Jonathon, was the vice president at her dad's company. That wasn't surprising either. He and his dad had always been a team. A two-person team, leaving out Blakely. Wonder if they still did?

I slid my suitcase into the closet and shut the door, surveying the gorgeous room. Light and airy. It was a mosaic of bright colors, flowers, and pillows covered in linen. It felt so strange being here. It'd been weird enough seeing Thera again after all this time, but what would it be like to see Grace and Blakely? We were still waiting for Grace to arrive, even though she was the closest one to Blakely in distance. Funny how some things never changed. Camp never officially felt like it got started until Grace arrived, and this weekend wouldn't be any different. She was supposed to be here at eight.

People always wondered how four girls could get along so well, but that's exactly why we got along the way we did and there wasn't the usual fighting among us. Because there were two dyads to the group: Thera and Blakely. Me and Grace.

Thera and Blakely were always going to be close because they'd both lost their moms. They had a connection you couldn't really touch or compete with. It transcended the bounds of ordinary friendship. They understood each other in a way no one else ever could.

And then there was me and Grace.

She was basically my only friend in the whole world besides my mom. We waited until our third summer to tell Blakely and Thera that we knew each other from back home. It'd taken two full summers to trust them enough to keep it a secret, because the camp had a strict policy of not grouping together kids who knew each other. Grace and I lived in the same rural area, and even though we didn't live in the same town or go to the same school, we went to the same karate studio. We met hiding in the back row on the first day because neither of us wanted to be there, and we'd been friends ever since.

Did we talk about Thera and Blakely sometimes when they weren't there? Yes, obviously. But it wasn't like they didn't do the same thing to us. We didn't try to pretend like there weren't alliances. It was when we started crossing party lines that things got messy and all the trouble started. That's what happened that last summer. The boundaries shifted and changed between best-friend groups. That's what the fights were always about. When somebody cheated—that's how it felt when Grace started siding with Thera over me. That's what drove me to Blakely in the first place. I'd never done what I did if Grace hadn't pushed me there first, but she'd liked to play it off like she was such an innocent victim. Was she still going to see it that way?

She never sent me a card when my mom was hospitalized with meningitis last year. It was weird that it bothered me because it'd been years since I'd even thought about Grace or the others. I had no idea what was going on in her life, so what made me think she paid attention to what was happening in mine, especially after all this time had passed? But it was like, somehow, she should've known? It was so silly.

But the girls always made me lose my bearings. They always had, especially in the beginning, when me and Grace had to pretend like we didn't know each other. The camp's entire mission was to help you live outside the role assigned to you. Break you out of your comfort zone, because it was only outside of your comfort zone that you discovered the freedom to be who you truly were. They didn't just frown upon putting kids in the same cabin who knew each other—they flat-out refused it. But you couldn't stop my mom when she wanted something, especially anything having to do with me, and she'd made her mind up that being with Grace was the only way she'd get me to go to camp, so she made it happen. Sent me to the camp filled with child prodigies where being smart was the normal and it went without saying that your IQ was superior intelligence. And unlike anywhere else, for the first time outside of your home, you could be proud of it.

That's what my mom thought was wrong at school. Why I didn't have any friends and got picked on constantly: my giftedness and social awkwardness coupled with my difficulty reading social cues. And it was true. I didn't really like being around people. They just made me so nervous, and I always forgot everything I wanted to say. It was the narrative I told her about why I didn't have any friends. Why I never got invited to parties. But it was only partially true. I couldn't tell her the real reasons the kids hated me, or how they treated me. If my mom had any idea what they did to me at school, it would've destroyed her, and I couldn't do that to her. No way. So, I created an alternative story.

I didn't tell her all the ways they picked on me—tagging my locker, shoving me down the stairs by the gym, calling me furry because of my body hair, throwing trash at me in the cafeteria, and so many other awful things. I didn't know why they chose me to torture out of all the other kids they could've picked on. They just did. Fourth grade had been the worst. It started when they cornered me in the bathroom and made Becky Phillips smell my breath. They forced us both down on the nasty hexagon-tiled floor.

"Eww!" she shrieked, wrinkling her nose and gagging while Eric Fischer held her face in front of mine, so close we were practically kissing. "Your breath smells like poop!"

"It's because she smells her dog's booty hole every day," someone yelled from behind her.

It was the kind of thing that made absolutely no sense, especially since I didn't even have a dog. But it caught on, and everyone was instantly repulsed by me. It's funny how one sentence spoken over your life in fourth grade could change things forever. Things were never the same after that, and any chance I had of finding a way to fit in was gone. After the bathroom, kids started plugging their noses whenever I came by or making gagging sounds. It got so bad that, at one point, I started believing I smelled like poop and became obsessed with hygiene. I was borderline OCD about it. Washing my hands constantly. Putting deodorant on multiple times a day. I showered before bed every night, elaborate scrubbing rituals that I had to complete, and again in the morning before I went to school with the same routine. Sprayed on perfume. Covered myself in Mom's expensive lotion. But none of that mattered. It didn't stop them. Nothing did.

I'd practice my comebacks in the mirror, but once I was face to face with anyone, all the words disappeared from my head and I just turned bright red and started stuttering. They loved it. That only made them howl with laughter.

Every kid at Camp Pendleton had horror stories similar to mine, even though we never shared them. That was the point of camp. Pretending like you were regular kids. We came to Pendleton because it was supposed to be different from the towns we came from. The schools that raised us. The ones that didn't understand our unique talents or the way we interacted in the world.

You'd think that once we'd broken away from our schools and those systems that were so mean and cruel to us, that we'd exist as this cohesive nonjudgmental whole. Like we'd be the best team and most supportive of each other. But that wasn't what happened at all. We recreated the same social hierarchies at camp that plagued our high schools. It was the strangest thing, and it always happened.

It never started out that way. But by the end of the summer? It always was. We became vicious creatures. No different from our tormentors at home. Except at Pendleton, I got lucky. At Pendleton, I was at the top. And when you've always been at the bottom, sometimes the power of being at the top goes to your head. And we were treated like royalty. That's what happened when you were friends with Blakely and her father was the biggest donor. There was a bench outside the admissions office with his name on it in gold lettering.

So, we were the stars. They treated us like celebrities, and for a bunch of social misfits, it was like a small piece of heaven. But we didn't know what to do with it when, the rest of the year, people treated us like the gum on the bottom of their shoe.

That kind of treatment turned you into different people. Made you do things you didn't know you were capable of.

# CHAPTER SEVEN
## THEN

## BLAKELY

I crouched on top of the toilet seat, clutching the bag of gummy worms in one hand and shoveling them into my mouth with the other as fast as I could. The thick sugary goo slid down the back of my throat, which was already coated with chocolate. I'd devoured four chocolate chip cookies before I started with the worms. I'd finish it off with the Cheetos.

My hair stuck to my forehead. Sweat dripped down my back. I had to hurry.

Complete focus. On the door and this feeling. This wonderful, indescribable feeling that would only last for a second. And I couldn't miss it. I had to savor it. I didn't know when the next time I'd be able to sneak away would be.

I told them I needed privacy in the bathroom. Thera was standing watch outside, even though we'd put the Do Not Disturb sign on the door. I hated sharing bathrooms. Like, didn't we pay enough money for this place to have bathrooms in our cabin? It was another important piece of the camp experience. At least that's what the brochure said.

Humiliation burned my cheeks as I tried to open the bag of Cheetos quietly. That was the hardest part about camp. Fueling my binges. But it was also my favorite part, too, because I binged so much less when I didn't have any privacy. Sure, I'd never made it through the entire six weeks, but there'd been plenty of times that I'd made it through with only a few episodes. This wasn't one of those times, though. Things were rough. I was already halfway through my stash. What would I do if I ran out before the summer was over?

"Blakely, hurry up. There's people coming from Ruth," Thera called from outside. She was standing watch and making sure nobody interrupted me. She'd done the same thing for me yesterday.

I shoved a handful of chips into my mouth, savoring the crunch. The way the pressure satisfied my teeth. One more handful. Just one more.

I jumped off the toilet while I ate it and leaned over, getting ready to get rid of everything I'd just eaten. There was no chance to lick the cheese off, even though that was my favorite part. But someone could come at any second, and I wasn't getting caught. It left the ritual feeling a bit incomplete. Almost like I'd wasted it. I quickly did my business— throwing up without making a sound, and watching for the Doritos to come up. The first thing down was always the last thing up. That's how I knew I'd finished. I quickly washed my hands and hurried to join Thera.

"Do you feel better?" she asked with concern etched all over her face. Anyone getting sick freaked her out. It was a huge trigger. It reminded her of her mom. That's how it'd started. A simple cold. Turned into a bad flu with a high fever she just couldn't shake. You couldn't blame Thera for jumping to the worst-case scenario anytime someone got sick.

I flung my arm around her shoulder and hugged her tight. She still smelled like the lake from kayaking earlier today. "I'm good. I think I just left my milk sitting out in the sun too long today, and I shouldn't have drunk it. Pretty sure it curdled my stomach." I rubbed my stomach while I talked. "That's all."

"You know you can get listeria from that, right? You should—"

I put my finger up to her lips to stop her. "Hush. Don't worry. I'm fine. Really, I am." Besides being hypervigilant about her or anyone else getting sick, she also knew every rare thing that could possibly happen to you, and if you didn't shut her up, she'd tell you all of them.

"You just looked so awful." She stared at my face, searching for any sign of illness. Guaranteed she'd grow up to be a doctor. She'd probably be the one to cure cancer, smart as she was—and the fact that it'd stolen her mom from her.

I plastered a smile on my face. "Let's go back to the fire. I heard Jerry's going to tell his getting-lost-in-the-cornfield story tonight and traumatize all the younger kids for days." I laughed even though part of me still felt like crying.

I'd seen the way Clint looked at Meg when we sat down around the campfire tonight. He came by right after Mason pulled out his guitar and started playing. It wasn't fair. Guys were throwing themselves at her this summer. There was something about her energy lately that pulled you to her, too, that had never been there before. And she wasn't bothered by any of the attention, which only made them want her more.

Clint had walked up right after Mason finished playing the latest Smashing Pumpkins song and we'd all belted out the lyrics to "Disarm"—*I send this smile over to you.* He poked her in the side and whispered something in her ear. They both burst out laughing. It was so annoying. Not that I liked Clint or anything. But still. He was supposed to want me. Not Meg. She was starting to get on my nerves.

And when people got on my nerves, I wanted to eat. That's what I did. Feelings always made me hungry. Ravenous.

I followed Thera down the path leading to the firepit, nodding and laughing at all the appropriate parts of whatever she was saying, but I wasn't paying any attention. All I wanted to do was go back to my room and tear open my stash. Lock myself in there and eat every single piece of junk food I'd brought along with me. But what would I do if I ate it all? Because I just might.

I hated this feeling. It made my skin burn.

"Actually, I changed my mind." I abruptly stopped just short of the fire. "I'm going to head back to the cabin and lay down for a few minutes, because I have a headache now and I don't want it to get any worse," I said, motioning for her to keep going and join the others.

"Are you sure? I can stay with you if you want." The concern was immediately back on her face.

I shook my head. "I won't be able to sleep if you're there. You know I always have to be the last one to fall asleep."

"Okay," she said hesitantly, like she still wasn't convinced it was the best idea. But she knew I wasn't lying about the sleep part, and her doctor mind knew it was important for me to rest if I was sick. She gave it another second before letting me go. "I'm going to come check on you in an hour, though, okay?"

"Sounds good," I said, quickly waving her off and hurrying back to the cabin before she could change her mind and try to stay with me. I burst through the door and went straight to the suitcase tucked underneath my bed. I pulled it out and listened carefully for the sound of anyone coming before opening it. My teeth ached with want, a powerful and incessant desire to chew, to swallow—get something inside me—but instead of releasing the lock and pulling out a bag of chips or another candy bar, I just rubbed the worn leather top while I tried to breathe. It took forever, but my heartbeat finally slowed. I quickly shoved the suitcase underneath my bed before I changed my mind or another craving hit.

I threw myself on the bunk and lay flat on my back, staring up at the wooden slates of Thera's bed above me. I clenched my jaw and folded my hands on my stomach. I squeezed my eyes shut like it'd help drown out the desire.

I could get through this. I didn't have to eat. It wasn't even that big of a deal. It's not like every guy at camp had to like me.

Why was I like this?

I'd sworn I'd never binge again after that first time. I'd never puked so hard in my life. I didn't even have to stick my finger down my throat to do it. I'd just eaten like a feral dog taken straight off the streets, and my body had no other choice but to reject consuming that amount of food in such a short period of time. And for a while I was just fine. I didn't do it. Just thinking about it made me feel sick to my stomach. Filled me with incredible disgust.

Until one day after school, when I was sitting in front of the TV watching my favorite episode of *Beverly Hills, 90210* and I just started thinking about the Cheetos in the pantry. It was the strangest thing. The thought popped out of nowhere, quickly followed by the strongest craving to eat them. I didn't really even like Cheetos, but for some reason I couldn't stop thinking about them until finally, I got up from the couch and dashed into the pantry where we kept all the snacks. I grabbed the bag and brought it back with me into the family room. I sat down in the same spot I'd just left and ripped open the bag. And then, it was just like I was in a trance. Hypnotized. I stared straight ahead as Brenda and Dylan fought over getting invited to Donna's party and stuck my hand in the bag, eating the chips by the handful. My fingers were covered in thick orange cheese when I finished. I went finger by finger until I'd sucked every single one dry. I was satisfied. Full. Complete.

I sat on the couch with the empty bag on the coffee table and the orange crumbs on the front of my shirt and scattered around me, and I just smiled. I should've just stayed on the couch. Finished watching the show. Gone upstairs to finish my homework. Anything but what I did.

I walked back into the kitchen like someone else controlled my body. Usually, I hated my house. It's why I spent so much time in my room. The only place with color. Everything else was in beige and creams, because my new stepmom—Daddy's latest toy pet he'd brought home and married—said she liked a neutral palette. Said it kept her mind peaceful. So, he remodeled the whole house just the way she liked it. The way he did for every single one of his girlfriends. It made the house so boring. Totally lifeless and without personality. Just like her.

But that day, I walked into the kitchen with a quiet and calm brain. As if for just a second, the storm inside me had subsided. My brain soothed. I could fit inside the house like the walls had somehow expanded enough to finally give me room to breathe. It was February, and the new stepmom's Girl Scout Cookies were on the counter. A box of Thin Mints, because she took two with her coffee. She stretched her boxes out throughout the year. Freezing them. And every afternoon, she made tea and dipped two in slowly. It was a huge production every time. Only two.

"You have to watch your figure, but there's nothing like a delicious treat," she'd say.

I took out a sleeve and popped one cookie into my mouth. It dissolved quickly, and I grabbed another. Then another. Before long I was ferociously popping them into my mouth and devouring them until there was only the empty wrapper in my hand. I was horrified at what I'd done. An entire bag of Cheetos and a sleeve of cookies.

Except now I wasn't full. Now I was something else. Something I'd never been before, and I had to have more. I didn't know how to stop it. Whatever this thing was that had come over me. This line I'd crossed that I didn't know was there until I was already over it.

I hurried to the pantry again before the shame could catch me. And I just started grabbing things and eating as fast as I could. Like I was on some sort of weird clock and had to eat as much as I could before the alarm went off. I ate at a frantic pace, like a possessed person—crackers, grapes, cheese sticks, yogurt, pickles, and more cookies. Then leftover pizza followed by chocolate ice cream. I brought the whipped-cream can up to my head and opened my mouth wide, spraying the white foam in thick swirls into my mouth. That's how I finished. Like a sundae I'd eaten. I was only missing the cherry.

I slid to the floor. So sick. So disgusted. Sour burps erupting from me. And then a wave of sleep enticed me, and I walked right toward it. A blanket of nothingness fell over me. Knocked me out immediately. I'd never experienced anything like it before. So warm. So cozy. Like love was supposed to feel. At least the way I'd imagined it'd be. Nobody had ever loved me. Not really.

When I woke, I barely made it to the bathroom in time. Explosive diarrhea like I'd only had one other time, when I got food poisoning from Hugo's Tacos on spring break. I'd never smelled something so vile. It went on and on until my body had gotten rid of all the trash I'd consumed in such a short period of time.

I took a scalding-hot shower, letting the water pummel me, and swore I'd never do it again. Just like before. Except this time, I really meant it. No more. Never again.

That was four years ago, and I hadn't stopped.

It was my dirty little secret. I lived with the fear and embarrassment of anyone ever finding out about my disgusting obsession and compulsion. What kind of a person kept a secret like that? How did you live in the world when you did such heinous things to yourself behind closed doors? Had such a filthy habit?

But then something happened, and it changed everything. Changed everything in a way that had never been the same since. I guess it's true, what they say about growing up? You pass all those developmental signs without even knowing it. Leaving your childhood behind, one step at a time. Like you never actually knew the last time you went outside to meet up with all your friends on the block to play freeze tag would be the last time. It happened that way with my secret too.

I carried it with me like this demon I couldn't let anyone else see. This darkness. Part of the shame was that I thought I was the only one living with such a beast. But then I learned I wasn't the only one living with a demon, and somehow that made it okay to have mine.

# CHAPTER EIGHT

## *NOW*

### THERA

My heart was thumping so loud in my chest. Could they see it? It felt like it was beating too hard for them not to, but Blakely was just chattering on about the dishes she'd imported from Italy like nothing was wrong, so maybe they couldn't.

"Can I get you another drink?" Blakely asked, shifting her focus to me. Her skin glowed and was practically flawless. How was it possible she looked so young? Was it real, or did she just have a really good plastic surgeon? I'd never done Botox or fillers or anything like that, but I was one of the few who hadn't. I tugged at my sweater. Her youthful appearance just made me feel even older.

"I'm good," I said. "I'm still working on this one." I raised my glass. Still half-full of the vodka soda she'd made for me when we came down to the kitchen. I wasn't a big drinker and had no idea what to say when she asked me what I wanted to drink, so I just ordered what I used to back in college. Those days seemed like another lifetime ago. All my time when I wasn't working was devoted to taking care of my dad. It'd been that way for years. I barely drank and the only reason I agreed to the first one was so that I'd have something to hold in my hands, but it was starting to take the edge off, which was good. I needed that.

I glanced at the clock on the microwave: 7:42.

Not too much longer and Grace would be here. It didn't feel right to talk about what we were going to do in response to our letters until she got here. Conversation wasn't flowing as easily as I thought it would. Or maybe it was just me. Meg and Blakely seemed to be doing just fine. Going into public got harder and harder the longer I lived such an isolated life.

Blakely's house was gorgeous, but I hadn't expected anything less. She'd paired us in separate wings, just like we'd divided ourselves in our bunks in the cabin. We could've met anywhere for this. A hotel or public space might've even been better, but she'd wanted to bring everyone to her house. No doubt to show it off. The place practically sparkled, even from the outside. Did she dust the outside of her house too? She looked so happy. Perfectly in her element as she bustled around the kitchen, serving us.

They lived in this huge house without any kids. Did it get lonely? Did they have friends over a lot? I hoped they threw parties. At least she had pets. Her two little Pomeranians followed her everywhere. There were as many pictures of them on the walls as there were of her and her husband. Hopefully, that breathed life into this place. How was it possible to be in such a huge space with floor-to-ceiling windows and thirty-foot vaulted ceilings but still feel claustrophobic and like I couldn't breathe?

*Relax, Thera. You're just way out of your comfort zone.*

And I was.

For the last six years, my life had centered around taking care of my dad. He'd suffered a stroke and had all kinds of complications afterward. The worst part wasn't what had happened to his body, though. It was the way it'd ravaged his mind. More and more of him slipped away every day. Everyone told me I should put him into a nursing home—well, they didn't tell me; they said it behind my back. No one dared say it to my face because they knew what they'd be met with. A huge angry no. After all he'd done for me, there was no way I was putting him in a home to be cared for by strangers.

Not that it wasn't hard taking care of him all by myself. It was. Way harder than I ever imagined it would be, and they were right about it being easier to let someone else take care of him. But I just couldn't do that. No matter how sick he got, I'd be there until the very end.

Still.

Didn't mean that it wasn't incredibly overwhelming and exhausting. Never mind isolating and lonely. The only people I saw on any kind of regular basis were his doctors and nurses. Shuffling him back and forth to medical appointments and physical therapy. Those were my social connections. I was practically a recluse since I didn't actually see any of my psychic clients in real life. I only met with them online.

So, to be catapulted into the real world again—and such a different world at that—felt a bit disorienting and daunting. Like I was halfway between sleep and real life. To be around so many people talking at once in the airport had been so overwhelming. I had no idea how socially isolated I'd gotten or how good it would feel to be in a room full of women who used to be my closest friends. On some level, they still were. What's that they say in *Stand by Me*? There's nothing like the friends you have when you're twelve? Or something like that. They found a dead body lying next to the railroad tracks, and we found one at camp.

I took a sip of my drink. Then another. This might help. I needed help, especially if we were going to talk about Regina. I didn't know whether others thought about her, but I still did all the time. Just like I thought about them. Didn't matter how many times I pushed the memories down, they popped back up.

There was no way we could've predicted that she'd snap. Nobody saw that one coming. If we had any idea she was already in such a fragile mental state with a history of her own sexual abuse, we never would've done it. I would've worked harder to stop it, even though I did try talking Blakely out of things more than once. Not that it made it okay, but we weren't monsters. How could we have known what Regina was going through? She and Mr. Crosby had seemed so happy. They looked like the perfect couple. They held hands when they walked together, practically skipping along, and she never looked depressed. I didn't ever even see her without her makeup on. But if I've said it once, I've said it ten thousand times—you never know what's going on behind closed doors, and there was all kinds of stuff going on at home when no one was watching. Not to mention her past trauma.

There were two opposing sides with Regina, and public opinion was evenly divided. No matter how diametrically opposed each side was to the other, they were fired up and opinionated about their position. Everyone equally loud and convinced they were right, with lots of supporting evidence to back up their points.

One side believed in the insanity defense presented by her attorneys. They claimed that the combination of postpartum depression and sleep deprivation coupled with her posttraumatic stress disorder pushed her over the edge. And who wouldn't be? Individuals could only handle so much before they broke. So many people could put themselves in her shoes, and lots of them would've done exactly what she did to her husband.

And then you had the other side, who were just as convinced about their position and believed she was a sociopath. Pure evil. Their arguments were equally compelling and had just as many facts to support them. The way she'd buckled her kids into their car seats to drive them to the camp. How she'd lied to the security guards at the gate to gain access to the property. They'd said she appeared fine. That it seemed like every other day when she stopped by to see her husband. Or how she made notes in her planner about hurting him in the days leading up to his murder.

We all picked our sides, and I fell on the side of wearing her shoes. I knew trauma could break you. Dismantle your insides. Pull your sense of reality right out from underneath you. Twist you and push you into doing things you never thought you were capable of doing.

It wasn't that she'd stabbed her husband 117 times. As awful as that was, nobody really blamed her for doing it, especially after what he'd done. Lots of people thought he deserved it.

Except there was the problem with the kids—Jaylen and Jordan. Nobody understood why she tried to hurt them. That's where she lost all compassion and support. Mothers didn't hurt their children, no matter what, and she'd broken the cardinal rule of motherhood.

Her lawyers didn't spin it that way, though. They claimed she tried to kill the children to punish Mr. Crosby, since she said they were the only things he cared about and she wanted to hit him where it'd hurt the most. But her story didn't really make sense because she killed Mr. Crosby first. He was already dead when she went after the babies. They argued time wasn't linear in her fragmented mind. To her, it didn't matter that he was already dead. All of it was connected.

I've never forgotten what she looked like that day. Never will. Blood-splattered face. Wild eyes. Hair gone. Because the first thing she'd done when she heard the news was shave her head. Why hysterical women shave their heads, I'll never understand. But she'd tied a bandanna around her bald head like she was going into some kind of real battle. Who knows what else she would've done that afternoon if she hadn't been stopped.

Part of me always knew this day would come. You couldn't get away with doing what we'd done, even though we were good kids and good kids weren't supposed to get into trouble. They didn't do bad things. But we did. We did a terrible thing and eventually you have to pay for something like that. You just couldn't get away with it. It was too big. Things that bad didn't go unpunished.

What did they think would happen when Regina got out?

I'd been waiting for this. On some level, even though I'd never acknowledged it.

Because the truth?

If a group of teenage girls had done what we did? I might've wanted to hurt us too.

# CHAPTER NINE

## *NOW*

## MEG

I gulped down the rest of my wine while Blakely took Thera upstairs to show her the dogs' closet. Apparently, the two dogs had enough outfits to warrant their own walk-in closet. They even had their own bedroom, complete with a huge king-size bed in the center, but Blakely said they never slept in it because they always slept with her. She wasn't lying when she said they were spoiled. I told them I had to use the restroom and would wait down here, but really, I just needed a minute to breathe. To calm my nerves and get myself together.

We'd been sitting in the kitchen for the last hour, having drinks and waiting on Grace to arrive. We shared all the customary stats: marriage, job, kids, friends, et cetera. It was starting to get that elephant-in-the-room feeling that I hate so much. I walked over to the island and refilled my wineglass. I knew seeing Blakely would bring everything from that summer heaving to the surface, but I wasn't prepared for the way my insides curled at seeing her again. She'd greeted me with a huge smile and a gushing hello, like no time had passed, but I jumped back the moment she touched me. My reaction was totally involuntary, and I tried laughing it off, but she had to have noticed.

I'd been triggered ever since I got the letter. It was just like when I found out I was pregnant three years ago. Becoming a mom cracked me wide open and sent a flood of memories I'd long buried and forgotten to the surface. That summer being one of them.

The only way I'd recovered from what happened had been to take those memories and bury them so deep inside me that even I couldn't reach them. Our psyches were built to protect us, and I'd worn that armor right up until the point my daughter shattered it. That's the first time the door to that summer had opened. This felt the same way, and I hated feeling this way.

Powerless. Terrified. Frozen.

I didn't like thinking about Mr. Crosby. I'd never wanted him to take an interest in me. Never. I thought it was a bad idea right from the start. Same as Thera. Send me in next? Ask to get a private lesson? It should've been Blakely. It always should've been her. I only did it because she wanted me to. It was her plan. All of it was, and we just went along with her like lemmings.

I couldn't believe I was ever that foolish and naive. Or so easily influenced by another person. But I so desperately wanted to be liked and accepted back then. I wanted to fit in. I would've done anything to fit in, especially that summer, when I realized how different I was from my friends.

Back home, I hadn't cared about being liked anymore. I'd gotten so used to not being accepted by people and them treating me poorly that I sort of expected it. I didn't even try fitting in at my school. Not like I had in elementary and middle school. I'd embraced being the outcast and grown purposefully antagonistic toward people at my high school because I was so over it.

But something happened at camp, and it wasn't just to me. It happened to all of us. We transformed into these completely different people. I didn't recognize myself sometimes. But there was nothing more intoxicating than fitting in when you'd always stuck out. And once you'd tasted it? Well, you'd practically do anything for it.

So, eventually I said yes to the lesson.

How was I supposed to know I'd be a good tennis player? Sports hated me and I hated them equally back. Balls zooming by my face had always made me nervous. And I was just like everybody else—always picked last in gym class. I didn't know what to expect, but I certainly never expected to smack the ball the way I did or to position it so perfectly on the court. Mr. Crosby was immediately impressed. He'd jogged over to me halfway through the lesson and double high-fived me.

"I didn't know you were a tennis player, Meg. Why haven't you signed up for the team?" he asked. His eyes were lit with the surprise of discovering I could actually play. He was even more gorgeous in front of your face. Perfectly symmetrical features. Long dark lashes. Plump lips begging to be kissed. And he smelled good, too, even though he was all sweaty. No wonder Blakely had such a crush on him. I could feel her watching us from where she sat on the bleachers. Her eyes daggers into my back.

I shrugged and giggled nervously. "I just play for fun," I said, even though I'd never touched a racket or hit a ball a day in my life.

I didn't know why I said it. The same way I didn't know why I agreed to join the team or have more private sessions with him. I should've just said no. All of this would've been avoided if I'd just never gone. But I didn't. I went because it'd been a long time since I'd been good at something other than drawing and playing the piano alone in my room. And I couldn't lie—it felt really good that he wanted me. I was never the girl picked first. I just had no idea it would make Blakely so mad or that she'd get so jealous. But nothing Blakely ever did with Mr. Crosby made sense.

# REGINA

Stupid little girls masquerading as women. I told Jared working at the camp was a bad idea. I told him we shouldn't go there. But he didn't listen to me. He never listened to me. He acted so shocked when it started happening. When the girls started vying for his attention and his affection.

"What are you so surprised about?" I asked the first night he'd come home, looking all downtrodden and sad, talking about how a couple of the campers seemed like they were trying to flirt with him and he was so worried about how other people might perceive it.

I knew my husband was gorgeous. Like pull-your-panties-down-and-break-all-your-rules-on-the-first-date kind of gorgeous. Why do you think I married the man? Got him walking down the aisle as fast as I could after he slapped a ring on my finger and before he could change his mind. He was the kind of prince you dreamed of when you were a little girl.

If you were into that kind of thing.

Which I was.

So were all those girls fawning over him. It'd been that way ever since we'd walked on the Pendleton campus for the first time, but he'd been too blinded by all the other glittering lights and the smells of rich people to notice. This was going to be a huge stepping stone for him.

He was a former tennis pro with a torn disc in his shoulder that had permanently sidelined his career, but it made him a great coach. One private schools and camps paid lots of money for. Having such a talented and accomplished coach made parents feel better about sending their kids away for long periods of time to be raised by other people. It was easier to justify doing it if you were giving them the best possible experiences. Things you'd never be able to provide for them on your own.

Camp Pendleton hadn't even been taking applications at the time. Jared only got the interview because he joined the same running club as the dean, and not even on purpose. It just happened that way. Jared had no clue the dean was on the team. They'd gotten a chance to talk on one of their runs when the dean rolled his ankle and Jared helped him finish the race. He supported his weight and walked with him seven miles to the end. The dean had practically given him the job when it was over. All Jared had to do was fill out the application and complete his background check. He was over-the-moon excited when he got home that night.

He'd opened a bottle of wine and twirled me around the kitchen. "I'm going to make so much money training private clients on the side."

But I would've rather stayed poor and found another way to make it to the top than have him working at the camp. I had a bad feeling about it from the very beginning.

Privileged white girls. I told him that's all the camp was full of. That his brown skin would stand out among their whiteness, but he didn't listen to me. He liked to pretend racism didn't exist. I was the one that pointed out the way they followed us around at Nordstrom's like we were going to steal something.

"You're the white person in this relationship, remember?" he'd say whenever he'd had enough of me. "Why don't you let me decide what I think is racist?"

That would shut me up, but I wasn't wrong. At least not that time. See, the biggest problem with those girls wasn't that they were every kind of privileged and white, even though they were. It was that they were so damn smart.

Except never in my wildest dreams did I ever imagine how it would play out. But what they did to him? Well, that was the reason they had to pay.

# CHAPTER TEN
## *THEN*

## BLAKELY

I hurried to get my spot next to Thera around the campfire. I'd just finished three king-size Snickers in the bathroom and was still feeling pretty good. It was team-building night leading up to Olympics week beginning tomorrow. They started out Olympics week the same way every year, by having all the teams meet their coaches and get to know each other. We competed in competitions all week long—the mythology bee, math competitions, science projects, a film festival, and all kinds of outdoor sporting activities ranging from water balloon tosses to kickball matches.

They always tried breaking up the cabin groups so that you got to know more people outside of your usual friend group, but the four of us stayed together no matter what. They constantly threatened to separate us if we didn't do a better job at connecting with the other campers on our team, but we knew that was a lie. All I had to do was call my daddy and let him know they'd split up me and my friends into different teams, throw in a few cries for good measure, and he'd be on the phone with the director as soon as we hung up. And, no doubt, we'd be back on a team together quicker than they'd split us up. Staff knew their threats were empty.

Olympics week was one of my favorite weeks at camp. We made it our mission to win gold every year. Sometimes we were successful, but sometimes we weren't, and I absolutely hated losing. A lot of your experience depended on your coach. We were still waiting to find out who'd been assigned to us when Mr. Crosby came out of the dark, waving a purple flag.

"Oh my God, is he going to be our coach?" I whispered to Thera. That would be perfect. Like the universe had smiled down on me from heaven. Olympics week followed a completely different schedule from our usual one, which meant he'd be with us every day from after breakfast until the evening. He was going to be all ours, and I couldn't wait.

"I think so," she gushed. Just as excited as me. Our team was us, Cabin Ruth, and all the boys from Cabin Cain. Pendleton used to be a Bible camp owned by some huge church. Everything had been changed and remodeled except the names of the cabins. All of them were named after important people in the Bible. I always thought it was weird they named a cabin after someone that had killed their own brother. Like wouldn't it have been better to name the cabin after the brother who died? I swear that's why all the boys in that cabin ended up being wild too. Like you couldn't be assigned to it if you weren't high strung and hyperactive. The ones that were always getting in trouble at school. They could be so difficult to wrangle. Not to mention super immature and annoying, but none of that mattered. We were going to have to find a way to work with them if we wanted to win.

"Hi, everyone!" Jared waved the purple flag again. Each team was assigned a color, and we'd gotten my favorite one. Even more perfect. "Looks like I'm going to be your coach this year. Now, most of you I already know or I've met, but just in case, I want us to go around the circle and introduce ourselves. First by saying your name, and then a fun fact about yourself that other people might not know. I'll go first." He cleared his throat and looked around the fire. "I'm Mr. Crosby, but you can call me Jared. I teach tennis. Obviously," he said, motioning at his clothes. He was still in his tennis shorts and polo shirt with the camp logo. "So, you all know that I play tennis, but what you might not know is that I'm also a dad." He grinned. "I have twin boys—Jaylen and Jordan—and they're only three months old. Feels like I haven't slept since they were born, but they're my entire world."

He was so adorable, the way he was smiling and beaming over being a dad. You could just tell he was totally proud of them. Too cute. I grabbed Thera's hand and squeezed. She squeezed back. Just as excited. This was going to be so much fun.

We went around the circle, with everyone introducing themselves and giving a fun fact like he'd instructed, but I couldn't pay attention to anyone else except Jared. I loved how he genuinely listened to everyone when they talked and the tiny smile that was always pulling at the corner of his mouth. After our introductions, he went through all the boring rules and expectations for our behavior, like they did every single year. Stressing, like always, how important it was to include everyone and that the goal was learning how to be on a team. To have good sportsmanship and all that.

But he was wrong. He knew it, and I did too. So did everyone else.

The goal was to win. He was only saying that because he had to. He used to be a professional athlete. I've never met a professional athlete before, but you didn't get to that level of success without loving to win at all costs and being extremely competitive. It was just another thing we had in common, because there's nothing I like more in this world than winning.

I settled into my seat and grinned at Meg. She knew it too. We had one of the only former professional athletes as our coach. It was definitely going down. His hair was wet, like he'd just come out of the shower, and the glow from the fire made his face even more golden. He looked like a delicious piece of candy, and I wanted to eat him up.

He stood slowly. "Okay, well, I'm going to let you guys do your thing. I'm going to head home and snuggle those babies I was telling you about. Besides, I know this is when all the good campfire-story stuff starts happening, so you don't want me here for that anyway." And then he winked. Right at me. My stomach flopped.

"You should stay," I blurted out before he could leave. "You're going to want to hear my Shamu story."

"Your Shamu story?" He raised his eyebrows. Curiosity instantly piqued.

"Yes, I was there the day Shamu killed the girl—her trainer—in the water." It was such a tragic story, but for some reason, I liked telling it. People felt sorry for me when I told them that I lost my mom, but they didn't feel any pain themselves. Just pity for me, and I didn't like it. Something about their pity always made me so uncomfortable. When I told them about the whale swallowing its owner while we ate . . . that one hit everyone differently. It hurt them, and part of me liked making them feel bad, but I wasn't trying to make Jared feel sad. I was just trying to get him to stay awhile longer.

Grace quickly started rattling off all the facts about what happened. "It wasn't Shamu. The original Shamu left Sea World in the seventies after a bitter dispute between Sea World, and they just kept naming all the other whales Shamu after that. They didn't want—"

I cut her off. "I know that. It was actually at Sealand, and it was a whale called Tilikum. They ended up moving him to Sea World and calling him Shamu afterward. That's when he killed his second trainer. I'm talking about the first trainer he killed." I shook my head at Grace to shut up, because if you didn't make her be quiet, she'd go on forever. She wouldn't stop talking until she'd spouted off every potentially related and relevant fact she knew about what happened.

"You were there the day she got killed, or actually *there* there?" Jared asked. Instead of leaving, he'd sat back down. My plan was working.

I nodded slowly and dramatically. "*There* there." Every eye around the campfire was glued to me, including his, even though some of them had heard it before, since I told it almost every year.

"What happened?" he asked next.

"Tell us!" somebody else exclaimed from the other side at the same time. Telling stories around the campfire was as much a part of camp as the senior pranks and Olympics week.

"Okay, so there's this place that's just like Sea World in Canada, and it's called Sealand. Something terrible happened there . . ." I paused and dropped my voice low so they all leaned in even closer, hanging on my every word. Jared too. "They used to have these eat-dinner-with-Shamu nights that you could buy, so of course my dad got us tickets. We always went to see my mom's grave on her birthday, and then afterward my dad would plan an elaborate trip somewhere to cheer me up." This was the part of the story that really got people. The gut puncher, always. I never left out the part about my mom. "Since she died, everyone was so obsessed with taking me on all these magical experiences on her birthday or other important days. Like Disneyland would make me miss her less or something." It was bizarre. It'd felt like being on drugs to walk through all the Disneyland rides after I'd thrown flowers on the top of my mom's grave just hours before. It'd never made much sense to me and hadn't that day, either, but that wasn't important to the story. I continued, ratcheting up the tension in my voice. "My dad got us the VIP experience, so we had our own staff member assigned to us, and we sat at one of the tables right in front of the water. In fact, I was signed up to have my own private meet and greet with Shamu and his trainer, Keltie, after the show."

There were audible gasps around the fire. God, I loved camp. There was no place better.

"Anyway, so it's totally great, right? Like the two of them are swimming around in front of us, they're doing all their regular tricks. He's flipping his tail. Spitting out water"—I wrinkled my nose—"which was kind of nasty considering we were all eating, but whatever. Everyone was loving it. And then they did the part that they do in the regular show where they lay down on the edge like they're totally exhausted and taking a nap together. You know which one I'm talking about?" It was one of the most iconic parts of their act. If they'd been there before, then they'd seen it. "Keltie is laying with her hands folded underneath her, and her head laying on the side of his face like she's resting her head on his cheek. It's super sweet. And then—suddenly!—he grabbed her ponytail and jerked her into the pool. At first, everyone thought it was a joke. Like he was being funny, but the moment he flung her back . . . man, you heard her neck snap. She was miked, so everyone heard it. That's when everyone in the place just started screaming. It was total chaos." A few of the girls to my right put their hands on their ears. That happened every year when I told the story. There were always people that couldn't handle it.

My Shamu story was as famous in our circle as bigfoot, and I was proud of that. Jared was hooked. Just like everyone always was when they heard it for the first time. His eyes were huge, and his face was filled with curiosity. It was the best story and even better because it was true. Mostly, anyway.

"Wow, Blakely, that's quite the story. That must've been so traumatic for you." His eyes were filled with a mixture of awe and concern.

I nodded. "It was, but even though I'm young, I've been through a lot in my life. It's made me so much more mature than other people my age." I held his gaze. It felt like he was looking into my soul, connecting with the intimate parts of me. He forced himself to look away.

"I'm not sure exactly where to go after that . . . Anyone else have a story they want to share?" His eyes circled the fire.

Jennifer raised her hand. No doubt she was going to share how her aunt won the lottery twice in one year, but I didn't listen. All I could do was stare at Jared while he listened to her. My body buzzed with electricity and energy.

He knew my name. Jared knew my name, and unlike the other girls, I still hadn't taken a lesson from him. But he knew who I was. That meant something. And the way he'd looked at me?

There was no denying the connection or the attraction.

# CHAPTER ELEVEN
## *NOW*

## MEG

It's not like Blakely actually physically killed Jared. Was the one to hold the knife in her hand and stab him 117 times. That kind of annihilation was all about rage. That's what the forensic psychologist said at the trial, anyway. You didn't want to just end someone's life—you wanted to destroy it. Like I said, she wasn't the one that did that. She got in the room before I did, though. It was only a few seconds—maybe a couple more—before I got there, but we didn't tell anyone that part of the story. Not even the other girls. Blakely was with Mr. Crosby when Regina burst through the door. Regina had come around the back. That's why I'd missed her. I was standing watch at the front entrance. The screams were the first thing that alerted me something was wrong.

To this day, I still hear that scream in my nightmares. And to this day, I still couldn't tell you who made it. It was like nothing I'd ever heard before, so I couldn't identify it other than to say it sounded more animal than human.

You couldn't just toy with people's lives. It wasn't right. How many times had I said that to Grace back then? I couldn't say it to Blakely, though. I didn't have the courage to stand up for myself or anyone else back then. Plus, I was too scared of my own secrets. Because that summer was also the summer I figured out I was gay, and I would've done anything to keep people from finding out. Absolutely anything. It was pure survival.

While we watched the same scenes over and over again from *I Know What You Did Last Summer*, I fell in love with Jennifer Love Hewitt. I imagined myself as her boyfriend in all the kissing scenes. Not because I wanted to be a boy, but because I wanted to be the one kissing her. The flood of desire I felt was shocking, but at least I knew I wasn't broken. I'd been pretending to like boys since the second grade. I'd started making out with them at camp the year before because everyone else was doing it, but I'd never actually liked it. I hated their thick clumsy tongues and the way they'd try to wrap theirs around mine. And the way that they smelled—yuck! It wasn't like they didn't shower. They just all had this same cottage cheese scent that I hated. So repulsive. But I pretended it was amazing and that I liked it. I flirted just like everybody else because that's what you did.

Grace, Thera, and Blakely were mesmerized by Freddie Prinze Jr. and Ryan Phillippe. They had massive crushes, and I acted like I did too. Swooning and squealing over all the appropriate parts because it was the nineties in the rural Midwest and nobody was openly gay. There was no greater form of social suicide than anything hinting at homosexuality, which was probably why it took me so long to figure out what I was. Anything besides straight was never an option, and we lived in regimented heterosexualism. It was as compulsory as high school.

I was so afraid of my friends finding out and thinking I wanted them. Like somehow because I liked girls, that meant I liked *all* girls. But they were my best friends. Grace was like a sister to me. I didn't even picture any of them that way. The freedom we had in the cabin would be gone, and I couldn't lose that. So, I kept my mouth locked tight about being into girls.

You should've seen Blakely's face tonight when I told them I was married to a woman. Complete shock. She'd erased it quickly, but not fast enough to hide her real reaction. I could tell she and Thera wanted to know more, which only added to the weird tension in the room. It's probably why they went upstairs to see the dogs' clothes. We needed a break from the awkwardness of everything for a minute.

But they were coming back now. They were all giggles and squeals as they thundered down the stairs. The dogs followed behind, prancing into the kitchen with them and twirling circles, begging for the treats sitting on the counter.

"Seriously, Meg, you should see all their outfits. I swear they have more clothes than me. I'm not even kidding." Thera laughed, coming to stand beside me, laying her head playfully on my shoulder and wrapping her arm around my waist.

"Oh stop," Blakely said, waving her off with a smile. "It's not really all that bad." She glanced out the window behind me. "Any word from Grace?"

I shook my head. "Nothing." The mention of Grace quickly brought us crashing back to reality. Their smiles disappeared instantly. So did their laughter. It was way past eight, and Grace still wasn't here. Maybe she'd changed her mind and wasn't coming.

"Did y'all watch any of the news on the trial?" Thera blurted out.

Clearly, she couldn't take it any longer either. Good. We had to address what was happening. There was no point in talking about anything else or pretending we were here for anything more than figuring out what we were going to do about the letters. This wasn't any kind of a high school reunion or girls' weekend.

Blakely and I shook our heads in unison.

"You never even read about the trial?" Thera asked in disbelief, and we shook our heads again. "I don't know how you did that. I wasn't able to stay away. I had to know what happened to Regina. I followed all the news reports. Read anything I could get my hands on."

Blakely shrugged. "I just figured she'd go to jail forever. People don't take kindly to mothers that try to kill their babies."

"And I'm pretty sure I was still in the phase of pretending it never happened," I said. The trial hadn't made national news, so it was super easy to do, especially back then.

"Well, apparently, Mr. Crosby's crimes triggered a posttraumatic stress reaction in Regina where she thought she was attacking her former abuser, when she was really stabbing Mr. Crosby," Thera explained. "They called in all kinds of forensic experts on PTSD, and they all said the same thing."

Blakely rolled her eyes. The same dramatic eye roll she'd had since we were kids. "Oh, come on. That's what she said? She couldn't come up with a better reason than that for being a crazy psycho killer?"

"If what she said was true, it might actually make sense," I said. I didn't want to get into it and make it a whole thing, because arguing with Blakely was one of my least favorite things to do. But I wasn't afraid to stand up to her anymore. Had she grown any emotional maturity over the years?

Thera nodded her agreement. "According to her defense team, it was a similar situation. She'd been molested by a former coach, and when she found out about her husband, it triggered all of the repressed memories and emotions about what happened to her." She paused, making sure we understood the implication. I looked away, fully aware of what she meant. "Are we just not going to talk about this?" Her words hung in the already tense air. "Isn't that what we came here for?"

Blakely placed her hand gently on top of hers. "Of course we are, Thera, but I think we should wait for Grace before we do. Otherwise, we'll just be repeating ourselves."

"And if she doesn't come?" I asked. She'd really pulled away from all of us that last summer and she'd only said two things in the text thread, so I wasn't sure she had any intention of showing up. I wasn't sure I blamed her.

"She'll come," Blakely said definitively, like she didn't have any doubts about her loyalty. "She has to. We promised."

# CHAPTER TWELVE
## *NOW*

### GRACE

I kicked the tire. Unbelievable. It was still going to be another twenty minutes before my roadside assistance showed up with a spare. Apparently, my Mercedes didn't have one in the trunk. Who knew.

I let out a deep sigh. Maybe this entire thing was a bad idea, but I was only twenty minutes outside of Atlanta, and I'd come too far to turn around now. Might as well see this thing through. Settle it once and for all. My sixteen-year-old self had been at war with adult me for the last seven hours. I wasn't sure how much more I could take. Maybe the flat tire was good so it'd give me a chance to refocus before I got to Blakely's.

They had to know who I was, didn't they? What did they think? I hated that those were my first thoughts. That I even cared. But all this had resurrected my teenage self, no matter how hard I tried to keep her buried. What would they think of how I looked? Even after all these years, that's still what I cared about. And I *hated* that I did! My fat phobia was so deeply ingrained in me, even after all this time. Every time I thought I'd gotten rid of it, it reared its ugly head. And here it was again.

I walked to the front of the car and leaned against the hood.

For so many years, I'd desperately tried to lose weight. I worked all through college to save enough money for liposuction. My parents flat-out refused to support me in it, like they'd always refused to see my large body as anything but beautiful. They'd been that way from day one and never wavered. They hated my obsession with my weight. Always had. They paid for my college tuition, but they wouldn't pay for my surgery, so I worked my ass off to pay for it myself. Before then, I'd done so many things to lose weight—the grapefruit-only diet, fasting, Special K, Atkins, the South Beach Diet, the Master Cleanse, and every other fad diet to hit the market. Plus the trainers and the gym memberships, the body wraps—I'd done all of it, and none of it had ever made a dent on the scale, at least not more than a few pounds. Liposuction had been this magical cure dangling like a carrot in front of me since fourth grade when I learned they could suck the fat out of your body with a big straw. Once YouTube arrived, I watched all the live videos of the procedure. I was obsessed.

Liposuction left me bruised and broken. I woke from surgery in that fancy recovery hotel swollen, distended, and looking like a cartoon character. I muscled my way through it, though. And for a few weeks, I looked great. Felt great too. The forty pounds I'd always dreamed of losing were gone, just like that. But I wasn't prepared for the fat to grow back so quickly, and it didn't grow back in the same places they'd taken it from. It spread and grew around the empty pockets, giving me even more dimples than before. Different stretch marks added to the ones that were already there. I went from being at my absolute highest to a devastating low, and that's how it was for the next two years, as I went under the knife again and again. Having fat sucked out and moved around. Put in different places in my body. I was convinced, like I'd been all my life, that there was this mythical thin person inside me, whom I was actually supposed to be. But no matter how hard I tried, she just slipped further and further away.

"It loses its effectiveness over time." My doctor had warned me that second time. She hadn't been wrong. I was bruised. Things sagged.

Hurt. I was covered in scars. Nobody talked about the scars you got from plastic surgery.

I was wrecked. Devastated. And alone. Because even in the moments where I had the body I wanted, I functioned like a broken person. I was needy and desperate. Incredibly insecure with every person I dated. My personality was so repulsive it pushed them away. I'd just finished my last cosmetic procedure, and I lay curled on my side on the bed, where I'd been immobilized for hours, when out of nowhere the thought came: *What if you just loved yourself?*

It was such a foreign thought, I literally looked up at the ceiling as if someone was up there and had dropped it into my head. Loving myself as I was had never been an option. Not once had I even considered the possibility that my parents were right. That I was perfect the way I was.

Whenever I go live or do any interviews, people always ask me how I got to be so confident. It's the most common question I get. They ask about my confidence like there's a specific formula to follow and if they just take the exact same steps as me, they'll get there too. But there wasn't any formula. Gaining my confidence was really quite simple.

I'd lived with suicidal hate for so long that the moment I tasted what it felt like to have an ounce of love for myself, I chased that shit like it was heroin. I'd never stopped.

Do you know how freeing it was to live in a world where you didn't give a fuck what people thought about you? Especially as a woman? There's no better feeling on the planet. At least I haven't found one yet.

The way I loved my body now was indescribable. Every single roll and fold. But I didn't even think about it like that anymore. I proudly threw myself in front of the world. Right in front of the camera. Straight in their faces, where they couldn't ignore me, and I'd spread my legs. It was the most liberating thing I'd ever done, and the first time I filmed myself I almost came on camera. Okay, maybe that's being a little bit dramatic, but it was absolutely amazing.

Once I switched to OnlyFans, I made more money the first month than I did at my engineering job in a year. Within two years, I was making more than all my friends with Ivy League degrees. Not that I didn't have an Ivy League degree too; that's where I'd met them in the first place—at UPenn—but I didn't need to use mine anymore. I bought my own house five years ago, and I've almost paid it off already. People didn't believe I was making that much money until I bought it. Then they figured out I wasn't playing around.

Turns out, there was a whole world of people that loved the way I looked—big and curvy, back to how I was before all my surgeries—and the world was finally beginning to change. Slowly realizing that there wasn't just one type of body that's attractive or healthy. We'd been let out of our cages, and we weren't going back in. You couldn't make us.

There were still so many people that looked down on the way I made a living, though. For every adoring fan, I had ten haters. Would my old friends look down on me too? Think they were better than me because I'd taken my genius and my advanced degrees only to become a social media star? And not just any social media star. One that revealed all of it on camera. I didn't consider myself a porn star. I never had sex with myself or anyone else on camera. But still . . . would they think I'd wasted a beautiful brain?

Except, from what I could tell, nobody had really done anything spectacular with their life except me. What a surprise. All the child prodigies that everyone thought were destined for greatness were mostly mediocre. Blakely married a rich man. Shocking. Not that I ever thought that was an important life goal, but it still made me cringe. I expected to see Thera with a Nobel Prize or lots of humanitarian awards, but she didn't even have a LinkedIn profile. I couldn't tell where she worked or what she was doing with herself because she wasn't on social media. Only her dad, and he rarely posted about her. Meg was the only one who'd stayed along the traditional pathway—gone to college and grad school, gotten a job, and gotten married. Living in the suburbs now with two kids and a mortgage. But she wasn't supposed to be average. None of us were. We were supposed to be spectacular.

I'd never fully understand what happened that summer. How I got swept up in all that. How do you just go along with something you know is so wrong? That's what bugged me the most. Was there a moment where I could've stopped it? I didn't even really know how it all got started.

I spotted the lights of the tow truck finally heading down the interstate. How would I have reacted that summer if I was the person I am now? What would I have done if I wasn't already in such a disturbed place because of my mom's affair? If that summer had just been like every other summer—if that piece was missing—would I still have gone along with them? Been so easily swayed? Or silenced?

The questions plagued me. All I wanted to do was go back in time and rewind. See who I might've been if I'd still been me. Because that was the thing. I didn't know who I was that summer. Coming out of the grocery store and seeing my mom kissing a man that wasn't my father two weeks before leaving for camp sent me there in a state of shock. Nothing felt real. And when nothing's real? Well, then, you can pretty much convince anyone of anything.

And maybe that's exactly what happened to me.

# CHAPTER THIRTEEN

## *THEN*

### THERA

"Did you see the way he was looking at me today during the mythology bee?" Blakely whispered as we made our way back from the bathroom. She'd had me post up outside to watch for anyone coming again. Her stomach was really bothering her this summer. I was starting to get worried about it, even if she wasn't. She just kept saying she was fine, but I didn't know. It wasn't normal. She giggled. "He kept giving me these little side-eye glances, and then he'd do that tiny smirk he does when he wants to smile but he's trying hard not to. It's so cute!"

"Yeah, he was totally staring at you the whole time," I lied, because really, I hadn't noticed. He'd seemed pretty focused on judging the competition, but I couldn't say that to her. Yesterday, when she asked if I noticed the way he brushed against her shoulder when he walked by us at lunch and I told her that I hadn't, she'd been pissed off at me for the rest of the day. She'd said she hadn't been, but she'd barely talked to me. I hated when she ignored me.

She grabbed my arm. "I think I'm going to finally do it." Her eyes were wild. Lit with excitement.

"Have sex with him?" I asked in disbelief. That was a big jump. I wasn't sure how she was going to go from barely speaking to him to having sex. How would that even work? That was super bold, even for Blakely.

"I mean, if he wants to right away, I'm definitely not going to say no." She giggled. "But I feel like we probably need to work up to that, you know? I'm just finally going to tell him that I see the way he looks at me. I want him to know I'm into him too. It's not like he can come out and say anything first because he's got to be so careful, you know? A wife. Kids. And . . ."

Her voice trailed off. But yes, I knew. She was a minor, and he was an adult. "It's like every time we're in the same space together, there's this incredible energy between us. It's so strong. Can you, like, feel it just by being around us?"

I nodded. Not as eagerly this time. Truthfully, he seemed kind of annoyed with Blakely. That was the one thing I noticed when they were together. She was so obvious about trying to get his attention. This morning she even stopped to tie her shoe in front of him, making this big dramatic production of bending over to do it. I'd caught his face as he tried to quickly move around her, and he looked so uncomfortable. The same way he looked uncomfortable whenever she volunteered. And she volunteered to help him with everything. She was the first person raising her hand for things, no matter what.

"I'll get the balls, Jared."

"Can I help you with that, Jared?"

"Do you need anything, Jared?"

And it was the way she said his name. All breathy. Every time she talked to him, she batted her eyes and puckered her lips. Stuck her chest out. Honestly, I was a little embarrassed for her, but I couldn't say that to her. No way. Once during camp in fifth grade, I caught her throwing up after the ice cream social and she got so mad when I told my dad she was sick that she didn't speak to me for six days. It was like I was dead to her. I was never going through that torture again.

Meg and Grace met us on the way to the cabin. They were coming back from kitchen clean-up duty.

"Yuck," Grace said immediately. "Why is everyone such slobs?"

"My hands are all wrinkly and gross." Meg joined in, stretching them out for us to see the wrinkles. Everyone was assigned a night of kitchen clean-up, and nobody got out of it, even Blakely, and she could pretty much get out of anything here. But they made us all do it. Part of the family and team-building experience.

"Guess what?" Blakely interrupted them. She didn't wait for them to respond. "I've decided tomorrow is the night I'm finally telling Jared I know what's going on between us. I'm making things official."

Grace wrinkled her forehead. "What do you mean?"

Blakely looked at her like she was ridiculous not to know what she was talking about. "Eventually, one of us has to make the first move and acknowledge what's going on between us, and he can't be the one to do it. He's got way too much to lose, so I've decided I'm going to be the one to cross over that line."

"How are you planning on doing that?" Meg asked next, like she couldn't wait to hear.

Blakely let go of me and grabbed her hand instead. "Come on, let's go back to the cabin. We definitely can't talk about this here, and I'm totally dying to tell you, but I don't want anyone overhearing." They raced toward the cabin, and we ran after them. Blakely shut the door tight behind us once we were inside and even locked the screen door. She checked all the windows to make sure nobody was outside, listening to us. Sometimes the boys from Cain liked to creep around our cabin and eavesdrop. "Okay, so there's only three weeks left for me to make it happen, so I've got to start."

"Totally, or you're going to run out of time." Meg eagerly nodded her head in agreement.

I shot her a look. Was I the only one who thought this was a terrible idea?

Blakely clapped and squealed. "That's what I was telling Thera like two seconds before y'all came up. He's been totally flirting with me all week and I want to let him know that I've noticed." She giggled again. "And not just noticed, but that he can do more than flirt with me. He can do whatever he wants. Did you see him take his shirt off today down by the lake?" She fell back onto her bed dramatically. "Oh my God. Could he be any hotter? He has like a full six-pack."

He was stunningly gorgeous. So was his wife. The one person Blakely kept forgetting about. But I couldn't. Every time Blakely brought him up, that's all I thought about. His wife and twin boys at home. It was one thing to go after an older man. But a married one?

"Right?" Meg said, jumping onto the bed next to her. "He's perfection. The way he swipes his hair off his forehead when he gets all sweaty." She fake fainted onto the bed, and Blakely caught her. They collapsed in giggles.

I looked at Grace, studying her closely, trying to gauge what she was thinking, but I couldn't tell. Something was weird with Grace this year. Like she was here with us, but not really. And she had this slightly angry edge to her, too, that she'd never had before. She was usually so mellow.

"What's the plan?" Meg asked, and I wanted to tell her to be quiet. To stop encouraging Blakely.

I glanced at Grace again. This time her face was wrinkled in the same disapproval as mine. Okay, good. She didn't like this either. Maybe she could talk to Meg.

Blakely sat up. The two of them knee to knee on Blakely's bunk, like me and Grace weren't even there. "Here's what I'm thinking," Blakely gushed, her eyes wild with excitement. "He always goes back to the athletic building before he goes home every night. I think he's the one responsible for locking everything up or something, so I'm just going to be waiting for him in his office when he gets there."

"Oh my God. Are you really? What are you going to say? What are you going to do when he comes in?" Meg sounded as excited as Blakely was, but she had to act that way. I hadn't noticed the way he was with

Blakely, but I'd noticed the way he was with Meg. Everyone had. If there was anyone he liked, it was her. She was the one he paid the most attention to. But I didn't think it was because he liked her like that. It was all about the tennis. Turns out, Meg was like this super tennis star, and he was pretty obsessed with making her into a better player. He even talked her into joining the tennis team. Blakely was obviously pissed, but Meg had quickly spun it.

"Think about how much time I'll be able to talk about you with him. I'll totally pump you up. And you'll be able to see him so much more than you would, because you can come with me every day," she'd said. This was before we knew he'd be our coach for the Olympics. Blakely hadn't been convinced, and Meg had been trying to work herself back into Blakely's good graces ever since.

"So, here's what I'm thinking," Blakely said. She pulled Meg close, and they started whispering. Giggling in between whatever they were saying. Grace turned around and rolled her eyes at me. She climbed up on her bunk and pulled the book she was reading out from underneath her pillow. I stood there for a second longer, staring at Blakely, so animated and lively. Trying to figure her out, like I'd done so many times in the past.

Dad had been over the moon when he'd learned about Blakely that first year. He couldn't believe that I'd matched in a cabin with another girl that had lost her mother. He'd been so excited and adamant to send me to camp. He desperately wanted me to have friends my own age. Someone that wasn't him.

That was the thing. I wasn't bullied like the others. But there's something worse than being bullied, and that's being invisible. Which I was. People didn't know what to do or say to me after my mom died, so they just left me alone. And for some reason, once I got on the outside, I stayed there. I never got back in. At least when you were bullied, you knew you were alive. Being ignored was like being a ghost, and that's exactly how I felt most of the time at my school.

It broke his heart.

Meeting Blakely had changed all that.

"There's someone like you, sweetie!" he'd gushed the first week I called home that first year and told him about her.

But I wasn't sure we were all that much alike, even though we'd both lost our moms. Maybe it was because I had mine for seven years and she only had hers for two minutes and thirty-eight seconds. There was no bigger hole you could have than losing your mother when you were still a little girl. I didn't care what anyone said. Children weren't supposed to grow up without their mothers. Whatever that thing moms do, whatever it is that they put inside you, my mom did to me before she passed away. She was one of the best moms in the world, and I wasn't saying that just because she was gone and that's what you're supposed to say when someone passes away. It was true. I carried her with me still. Blakely didn't have anything to carry. She didn't even have a picture of her mom holding her. Her mom died during childbirth. She'd hemorrhaged after pushing Blakely out, but that wasn't what had killed her. She'd thrown a blood clot that had traveled straight to her lung, killing her almost instantly.

We both have holes in our hearts now, but hers is bigger. Much bigger. And, I don't know, there's just something different about her. She was missing something else, and as I stared at her again tonight, I couldn't help but have that feeling I'd get sometimes. Like in sixth grade when she shoved little Elliott underwater and held him down until he started choking. She just laughed and said it was a joke, even though the poor thing was terrified. Last year, she tripped Meg so she could beat her in the hundred-yard dash during Olympics week. She pretended like she hadn't. Even said how sorry she was about it to her afterward. But I saw her do it. And this? What she wanted to do with Mr. Crosby? She was messing with his life. He had a real life with a wife and children. Like maybe she was a little bit more broken than me. She might even be more broken than all of us. My only hope was that he'd reject her and this whole thing could be over. Except what would happen if you rejected Blakely?

I wasn't sure I wanted to find out.

# CHAPTER FOURTEEN
## *THEN*

### MEG

I stood outside the building, waiting for Blakely. Why did I say yes to this? She'd run back to the cabin because she forgot the camera. Grace brought her Polaroid this year, and half the screen door was covered in our pictures. Those dumb boys. God, why did they encourage Blakely? And why had we brought them into this in the first place?

She made it sound like she wasn't all that interested in Mr. Crosby. Acted like it was the other way around and Mr. Crosby was the one throwing himself at her. That's what she said when we were hanging out with the Cabin Abraham boys yesterday. Clint and his crew were the only other group of campers that had been here as long as we had. His clique was just as close as ours.

The four of us and the boys had all been sitting by the watercoolers, taking a break after kickball, when she brought it up. She stared at Mr. Crosby. He was working hard trying to calm down one of the younger campers, who couldn't kick the ball when it came across home plate. The girl had gone into full meltdown mode. Throwing herself on the ground, kicking and screaming the way little kids do. All snotfaced and angry. He'd been patiently working with her for the last ten minutes. She'd stopped throwing things and kicking, but she was still crying.

Blakely pointed at him. "He's totally into me, you know."

"Yeah, right," Clint said. Jacob snorted. He was sitting next to Clint on the dirt, drawing circles in it with a stick.

Blakely smiled and shook her head. "Seriously. He totally is. You should see how he flirts with me. It's constantly. Like he can't even help himself. He's had a thing for me since the first day."

Clint and Jacob looked back and forth at each other. Neither of them appeared convinced. Mr. Crosby's wife was around all the time, and the two of them seemed very much in love. We weren't the only ones who'd noticed. They couldn't keep their hands off each other, and they were always smiling.

"It's true," she continued. "He's been all about me since the first day. I'm going to hook up with him for fun. Me and Meg have been talking about it for two days now. Right, Meg?"

I smiled and nodded at her, just like I'd been doing for weeks.

I just wanted this to be over with. Despite what I told Blakely, there was no way Mr. Crosby was hooking up with her, or any other girl here, for that matter. He was totally committed to his wife and his kids. They were all he talked about during our lessons, besides tennis. You couldn't feel that way about somebody and cheat. No way. Hopefully, once she saw that, she'd move on to somebody else.

"I'm hooking up with him tonight. We already have a plan," she said, nudging me in the side. I gave a nervous laugh back. Grace gave me a dirty look. She'd been mad at me all day. Said I was ruining camp by being so caught up in all Blakely's drama, but Blakely was a force and she knew it. Nobody wanted to make her mad. What would happen if we did? She was the boss around here. The only reason we were treated so well by everyone was because of our association with her.

"I'm not trying to piss off Blakely." Those were my exact words to Grace last night after everyone else had fallen asleep. She didn't say anything after that because she understood how awful Blakely could be if you were on her bad side, but she'd been pouting all day.

Thera was acting just as childish as Grace, like I'd somehow stolen Blakely away from her, but that was never my intention. I didn't set out to be in the center of the drama. It just happened that way. I couldn't help that Mr. Crosby liked me or that Blakely thought I was her partner in all this, instead of Thera.

"You're going to hook up with him tonight?" Jacob's already large eyes grew even bigger. "Just how do you think you're going to do that?"

"Easy. I'm going to meet him in his office when he's closing up for the night." She crossed her arms on her chest and gave a satisfied smile. She sat back in the grass, stretching her legs out and looking like a demure cat.

Clint grinned back at her with a challenging expression stamped on his face. "I don't believe it. I want to see proof."

"Just how exactly am I supposed to prove it happened?" The question had no sooner come out of her mouth than you could see the realization hit her. She snapped her fingers. "I know exactly how I can!" She grabbed my arm again and pulled me closer to her. "Meg will take a picture."

"I'll take a picture?" I whipped around to face her. So did Grace and Thera.

She nodded eagerly. The plot forming in her mind while she spoke, making it up as she went along. "Yes, Grace brought her Polaroid this year, remember?"

We'd played with it a lot during the first week of camp, but I'd forgotten all about it until the moment she brought it up at the water-coolers. We hadn't used it much lately because it'd gotten kind of boring, and especially not with the Olympics going on. Staff took plenty of pictures to send home to our parents this week, so we didn't have to worry about it.

Blakely had never even asked if I wanted to go with her and take the picture. She just assumed I'd say yes.

And now, here I was, standing watch and waiting for her to come back with the camera because she'd forgotten the most important part. What was I supposed to do if somebody came by? What would I say if they asked what I was doing hanging outside Mr. Crosby's office door like some creepy stalker chick? I'd already seen him go inside. What if he came out before she was back?

My head hurt. I just wanted to bolt. I didn't want to be a part of this, but I couldn't tell her no and I couldn't stop her. Not when she had her mind made up, and she had her mind made all the way up on this one. At least this might end her obsession, because there was no way he was hooking up with her. Not tonight or any other night.

I spotted her hurrying back through the darkness, but this time she wasn't alone. Thera and Grace were with her too.

She was still smiling when she got to me. She'd been like a little excited kid all day. "Here's what I realized"—her eyes darted around, making sure nobody was coming—"you're going to be inside with me so you can take the picture, and that means there's not going to be anyone outside watching the door. There has to be somebody watching the door, because what if one of the other counselors comes by and wants to get in the building or something? Somebody's going to have to distract them." She pointed to Thera and Grace. Neither of them looked thrilled to be there. Grace looked angry, and Thera looked like she was going to be sick.

"Can you please go fast?" Thera asked, clutching her stomach. "This whole thing makes me nervous. I don't want to get in trouble."

"You're not going to get in trouble. You're not doing anything wrong," Grace said. "We're just standing here."

"Right," Blakely said, agreeing with Grace. "Stop being such a baby," she snapped at Thera, then turned to me with the excited smile back on her face. "Are you ready?"

# REGINA

Those little snots ruined my life. I loved my husband. Really, really loved my husband. In that all-consuming, there-will-never-be-another, will-do-anything-for-you kind of way. Our love had been a passionate fire from the very beginning. That's why it was so devastating when the news broke. Delivered by one of the police officers that knocked at the door to seize his computer. That was the day my world changed forever.

I've spent so many sleepless nights awake in my cell, lying on the cot and staring at the water spots on the ceiling, wondering what would've happened if I'd never opened my door that day. If I'd known what was coming and refused to let the police in without an attorney present. Asked for a warrant. I'd never been in any kind of trouble with the law before and had no clue you could even do those things. I just let them walk right into the house like they were entitled to be there and gave them access to everything inside. I didn't know there was anything to hide. I had no idea what was going on. All they said was that there'd been an incident down at the camp with one of the girls. I thought they were referring to some kind of accident. Like one of them had gotten hurt or someone was sick.

We lived in the faculty housing slightly off campus. On the other side of the highway, so that when Jared wasn't working, he could feel like he'd gotten away from the kids. And believe me, when you worked with other people's children, you needed a break from them, especially those high-maintenance ones like those camp brats.

The officers ransacked our house, and I just kept holding my babies—one in each arm—and crying, "What are you doing? What's happening?" They just kept telling me to sit down and be quiet, as if I'd done something wrong, too, or been a part of whatever mess he'd gotten himself into. But I had no clue what was happening.

I never wanted him to work at Pendleton. Rich people were trouble. I knew that in a way that he didn't. I'd spent the first ten years of my childhood having them treat me like trash because I grew up poor in a single-wide trailer on the southeast side of Austin. We didn't even have our own phone and had to use the neighbor's or run down to the pay phone at the grocery store whenever we wanted to make a call. Back in those days, we had no cable either. We jiggled the antenna covered in tinfoil every night, trying to get a signal so we could watch the two channels that actually came in. Food stamps paid for all our groceries, and my mom worked miracles, stretching every last ounce of food out until the end of the month. Living off Spam sandwiches. Bologna and cheese on white bread. Tomato soup that was really just ketchup packets mixed with lots of water. But no matter what, we never went hungry.

None of that mattered, though. Everyone in town still looked down their noses at us—at our hand-me-down clothes and Goodwill tennis shoes. They didn't care that my parents were two of the hardest-working people you'd ever meet or that it wasn't their fault they ended up poor. My dad's father had died when he was ten, and by twelve, he'd dropped out of school to help his brother take care of the farm for his mother. They thought the farm would be theirs after Grandma Pearl died, but the farm was already in foreclosure and had been bought by the bank almost immediately. So, my parents and uncle's family watched in utter disbelief and devastation at what they thought would be theirs getting bought out from underneath them.

I'd never forgotten how the community treated us. It didn't matter that eventually my mom earned her nursing degree and worked at a thriving clinic with one of the top doctors in the state. Or that Dad got his real estate license and discovered he was amazing at selling commercial properties. We'd gotten out. Moved all the way across state when I was eleven and starting fifth grade. But I'd never forgotten. Not how they'd treated me, or my roots.

That's the one advantage I had over Jared as he pined after the wealthy—I knew rich people couldn't be trusted. The other thing I knew about rich people? They protected their own. If you were outside the family, that's exactly where you'd stay the moment anything threatened the family.

And somehow, he'd crossed them. At least that's what I thought happened until the officer turned around as they were leaving and announced they'd already taken him in for questioning, down at Pendleton. That's all I heard, even though he kept talking. Filling me in on the next steps.

I stumbled backward in my mind. What was the police officer saying? What was he implying? That my Jared had touched one of those girls? That he'd returned their attention?

No.

I shook my head.

Harder.

No.

He wouldn't do something like that. I twirled aimlessly around the kitchen. Running my hands along the countertops, trying to still my racing heart. Slow my thoughts down so I could think. There had to be some kind of explanation. And then the other officer spoke, shattering the last piece of my denial:

"I'm sorry, Mrs. Crosby, but there's been a report filed against him."

# CHAPTER FIFTEEN
## *THEN*

## THERA

I gnawed at my fingernails while I watched for anyone coming down the path, but it was impossible to see when it was pitch black. I had a flashlight, but it was pointless because I couldn't turn it on since we weren't supposed to even be here. Grace looked as anxious as I felt. She'd been shifting back and forth ever since Meg and Blakely went inside. We hadn't said a word since. Neither of us really wanted to be here. This wasn't a prank. There were pranks and then there was whatever we were doing.

Part of me had hoped Blakely wouldn't go through with this. That she'd miraculously grow a conscience about it, but that didn't happen. The moment Mr. Crosby appeared from behind the tennis courts today, she got that look in her eyes. The one she gets when she's plotting something. She'd skipped inside the athletic building with Meg in tow.

"This is a bad idea," I said right before she left us, but she'd blown me off and gone in without looking back.

Blakely never cared about what anyone else thought. She only thought about herself. Everyone just felt so sorry for her because her mom died. And her dad ruled the world, so she got away with anything.

She wasn't worried about getting caught tonight. But what about me? Totally different story. My dad wouldn't be angry with me. Not like Meg's mom would be if we got caught. She'd be furious. Especially since it might mess with Meg's college scholarship. But my dad? He'd just be disappointed in me. That's way worse than mad.

I looked at Grace, but she still wasn't looking at me. She'd switched to angrily kicking the rocks at her feet. We shouldn't have been doing this. Nothing about it felt right. It made my guts twist, and my guts were always right.

"Listen to your gut, Thera. Your gut never lies." That's one of the things Mom said to me. She might've even written it in one of the letters she wrote for me before she died. And my stomach was twisting and turning like I was about to squirt diarrhea down both legs.

How long was this going to take? It already felt like we'd been standing outside forever. God, I missed my dad. I almost told him what we were planning and how much I didn't want to do it when I talked to him on the phone last night. He'd understand. He always understood when I was upset and knew exactly the right thing to say to make it better. Well, except when it came to my mom. Sometimes he made me really mad when he acted like our experiences with her were the same.

Dad said resentment was like drinking poison and waiting for someone else to die, but he could say that stuff because he was an adult. And yes, he'd lost his wife. His best friend. She was his soulmate. His one and only. That's why he'd never dated. Still didn't. It didn't matter how many times my grandparents and all his friends tried to set him up with women—and there'd been some good women over the years. He refused.

Him and my mom had known each other almost their whole lives. Since kindergarten, when he'd pulled her pigtails sitting behind her at circle time, and she'd turned around and smacked him in the face. He'd been her best friend from that moment on. More like a brother to her than anything else. All the way up until they were teenagers, and then he claimed he looked at her one day and everything changed.

He'd never had eyes for another. Still didn't.

"Your mama's got my heart forever, bug," he said unapologetically any time I tried to push him to date.

He could put her passing into a nice, beautiful package. He didn't have the same anger. Not the kind like I did.

But those were the parts of me I shoved down. Nobody wanted to see or hear that. That's the other thing you learned when you lost a parent so early. Even though everyone says they want you to tell them how you feel, they don't really mean it. They're lying. Everyone wants you to be okay, and they definitely don't want to hear any sad or dark parts. They want to talk about my mom dying like God needed her as an angel. Really? Like I'm pretty sure I needed a mom more. But, of course, I didn't say that. It'd make people mad. Hurt their feelings, and I hated that. But that's why Dad and I were different.

He got to have his time with Mom. Decades. And sure, I got way more time with mine than Blakely, but still. It was barely any.

I could never tell my dad the truth. Not that I hated God, even though I should. I didn't believe God even existed. I was an atheist. I didn't know what that'd do to him, especially when I was the one who'd brought him to church in the first place. He leaned on his faith to get him through everything now. The women at church loved it. They swooned over him. Everyone wanted to bring us meals. Clean the house. Take him for a walk around the block like he was a new puppy. Even the married ones, but nobody seemed to mind. I guess there was a free flirting pass since he's a widow.

I lived in a world without God, and sometimes that got scary. A world without God was just like you'd imagine it to be—dark. Real dark. But he didn't know that. Nobody did. And I couldn't tell anyone that. Ever. That was fine, though, because I'd gotten really good at acting okay.

I straightened my hair and strained for the sounds of anyone coming through the woods, but it was still quiet. Only the wind. A few rustling noises. Grace was starting to look sleepy. We'd stayed up way too late last night, talking about the plan for tonight.

"This is so stupid," she said, finally breaking the silence.

"Right? And I hate the way Meg just acts like everything Blakely says is so brilliant. Like really, Meg? We know you're lying because Blakely is acting like the biggest idiot about all this." For a second, I felt guilty for talking bad about them and worried she might tell Blakely, but she quickly agreed with me.

"I'm *so* over Blakely always wanting attention too," she said, rolling her eyes. "That's the only reason she even brought the boys in on this, you know? So that as many people as possible could know what she was doing and be watching her. It's totally working too. She has everyone eating out of the palm of her hand. Did you see the way Jacob was looking at her yesterday when she walked by after lunch? He was practically drooling. So was Sean. What if they tell someone about tonight? Sure, we might be able to trust Clint, but we never even talk to those guys. We have no idea if they'll keep quiet about everything. Has she thought of that?"

Of course she hadn't. I quickly realized that I hadn't thought about it either. We didn't know if we could trust those boys not to say anything. What if they'd already told other people? This was all so stupid.

Suddenly, Meg burst through the metal door, practically knocking me over and sending me flying backward. Blakely was right behind her. Smashing against her back to get her to move faster.

"Run!" Meg yelled without looking at me or Grace as she took off into the night. Blakely raced past her.

I grabbed Grace, and we sprinted after them through the forest. We all ran as fast as we could back to the cabin. Feeling our way through the darkness. Doing our best not to trip on any of the rocks or get hit in the face with branches. We barreled through our cabin door and slammed it shut behind us. Grace and I giggled right along with them. We might not agree with what they'd done, but that race was exhilarating.

"I can't believe you did that!" Meg squealed. Her hair was wild and everywhere.

Blakely jumped up and down, clapping her hands. "Did you get the picture? Did you get the picture?"

"I did," Meg said, pulling out the Polaroid from her back pocket. She was still breathing hard. Her cheeks flushed.

"Let me see it." Blakely snatched it from her hands and twirled around while she talked. "Oh my God, it's perfect. Clint's going to die when he sees it." She beamed proudly.

The excitement drained from my body as quick as it'd come. I was afraid to ask, but I had to know. "How'd it go?"

# CHAPTER SIXTEEN
## *NOW*

### GRACE

It felt so weird being in the same room with all of them again, and I took another sip of my wine as I eyed the stone-tiled kitchen. Of course Blakely was rich. I would've been shocked if she wasn't. Looked like she went from a rich daddy to an even wealthier husband, if this ginormous house was any indication of things.

The girls had all been in the kitchen when I arrived, but they'd flocked to greet me as soon as Blakely opened the front door to welcome me inside. Marble floors lined the entryway, but it was the huge spiral staircase opening into it that was the most impressive. The wall offsetting the stairs was lined with professional photos of her and her husband in gold frames. Also, ones with what I could only assume were her dogs in cute outfits. We'd all hugged awkwardly before I followed them back inside and into the kitchen.

"Let me catch up," I said, grabbing a bottle of red wine from the island and filling one of the glasses sitting next to it before raising it up. "Cheers." I quickly tapped all their glasses before taking a drink. "Sorry, I missed all the small talk. Anyone want to fill me in on the last twenty-six years?"

Everyone laughed, which finally relieved some of the tension in the room, and Blakely was more than happy to bring me up to speed. "Let's see, both me and Meg are married. She's got kids, I don't. Well, not human ones anyway," she said, pointing to the floor where two Pomeranians twirled circles at her feet. The same ones in all the pictures. "Thera spends most of her life being the world's best daughter, because how could she possibly be anything else?" She beamed at Thera, and Thera blushed. But it was true. Thera was one of those people just naturally born good. "And you." She shifted her eyes to me. She'd just had her eyelashes done, and she batted them at me. "Little Miss Social Media Star."

She caught me off guard. I hadn't been expecting that, and she knew it. How was it possible that she still knew exactly how to make me lose my footing, even after all these years? I took another sip of my wine like I wasn't fazed, though. "Life's had some surprising plot twists," I said with a grin.

Thera cleared her throat like she was nervous and about to give a presentation. "Okay, so we have so much stuff to get caught up on and could probably talk all night, but we should discuss why we're here first." She eyed the table. We all had our hands wrapped around our drinks like they were our emotional support blankets. "I was thinking—"

"I don't think we do anything yet," Meg interrupted, like she couldn't keep her opinion to herself a second longer. Her cheeks were rosy, and her forehead gleamed with sweat. "It's not like anything has happened. All she's done is write a stupid note saying she's going to make us pay. It's a pretty vague threat too. Maybe she's just messing with us to see if we'll do anything. Also, let's not forget she just got out of prison and she's on parole. I'm pretty sure she has to check in every day and get permission to leave the state."

Thera shook her head. "We have to do something." She stuck out her fingers while she went down the list she'd probably been keeping in her head for days. "First, we have to find out where she's living. And like you said, Meg, can she leave the state? Second, once we track her down, someone should talk to her face to face. Get a feel for where she's at. See if we can't nip this in the bud now. I'm not sure who that person should be. That's probably something to decide tonight. We—"

Meg interrupted her again. "No, that's so unnecessary, Thera. It makes it into a potentially bigger problem than what it already is. We leave it alone. See if anything else happens. There's no rush to jump to any conclusions."

"What do you think?" Blakely turned to me like I was the deciding vote.

I just shrugged. "I guess it all depends on what she means when she says she's going to pay us back."

"It doesn't mean anything," Meg snapped, her voice slightly slurred. She was on her second drink, and that was just since I'd arrived. "And what does it matter? What's she actually going to do to us? Tell? Who's going to believe her? And even if they did, technically we didn't—"

"God, Meg. Please. Don't start that again. You know exactly what we did." Thera's voice sounded just like it did the day in the bathroom when we were washing off the blood and Meg slapped her to be quiet. Thera looked like she was the one who might want to slap Meg this time around if she kept going down that path.

Meg shook her head. "Doesn't matter. It was twenty-six years ago."

"Of course it matters," I jumped in. I couldn't help myself. "None of us would be here if it didn't." Meg shut up then, and I gave her a few more seconds to get herself together before I continued. This was already too much drama. "We don't even know if the notes are from Regina."

Thera balked. "Who else could it be?"

I cocked my head to the side. "Seriously? It could be anyone."

"But nobody knows what we did," Thera said, like the matter was settled.

This time I was the one to give her a strange look. Was she sure about that? "Nobody's said anything to anyone? Not after all this time?"

We all eyed each other.

I was skeptical of every single person in this room. Sure, we knew each other once. We spent every summer together since we were eight years old, but did that mean we really knew each other? Just because Regina was recently released didn't mean she was the one to send the letters. It was perfect timing if any one of us in the group had decided to fuck with us.

We were at the age where everybody went off the rails. I'd always thought the stories about midlife crises were a myth, but I'd watch people do the most bizarre and shocking things from out of nowhere the closer they inched to forty. And then, once we passed it? Marriages dropped like flies. People left their spouses. Stable jobs of twenty years. Had affairs. Deconstructed from religion. Bought expensive cars. Boats. Houses. Got tattoos. Piercings. You name it. It was all going down.

Maybe one of us was bored and decided they wanted to stir things up a bit. There was one other thing I knew about housewives—and I didn't have to look any further than Blakely's sparkling countertops and perfectly manicured nails to know she wasn't the one paying the mortgage—and that was that they got bored. With all that time on their hands, they needed to find something to keep them busy. And Lord knows, Blakely needed constant stimulation and attention.

I sat staring at Blakely, waiting for her to speak. She'd been entirely too quiet so far.

Despite all the years, she still looked the same. Young. She could easily pass for thirty. Had she invited us all here just so she could show off? You could usually tell the sort of life someone led by the lines on their face, but her smooth face was misleading. She'd lived anything but an easy life, even though she was old money rich. She'd basically raised herself once her dad remarried. Blakely hated her stepmom, and her stepmom equally hated her back. If her stepmom had been one of the billionaires trapped in that bizarre submarine incident, she would've done exactly like the stepson—she would've gone to a concert while her stepmother was running out of air. She probably wouldn't have posted about it on social media like his dumb ass, but she would've done it.

She was nervous. I could tell. Her eyes didn't show it. Those were lit up with excitement. Wild and bright. They stayed that way most of the time, and she kept smiling whenever her eyes landed on one of us, but I paid attention to her left hand, tucked behind her thigh, slightly hidden. The one where she rubbed her forefinger into her thumb over and over again whenever she got nervous. I couldn't help but smile as I watched her do it. The top part of her thumb had been soft and silky from rubbing it so many times when we were kids. I couldn't imagine what it looked like now.

"You guys, none of that stuff matters." Blakely finally jumped back in to the conversation. Her eyes went around the room connecting briefly with each of us before she spoke again. "That's not why you're here."

Everything came to a screeching halt. What did she mean, that's not why we were here? A pregnant pause filled the space after her sentence.

"I'll explain everything," she said, gathering up the bottles of wine from the counter. "Can we go outside in the backyard to talk about it, though? It's way more comfortable out there, especially now that the sun's gone down."

# CHAPTER SEVENTEEN
## *NOW*

### THERA

Blakely grabbed me on the way out of the kitchen and pulled me back inside. "We'll be there in a sec," she called to the others. "Thera's just going to help me grab some more glasses and ice." She turned around to face me as Meg and Grace headed through the sliding glass doors and out to the backyard. She dropped her voice to a hushed whisper. "You have to help me."

"What?" I asked. I couldn't have heard right. It sounded like she said *help*. She couldn't have said that. But then she said it again. This time more desperate.

"Please, Thera, you have to help me." Her nails dug into my biceps. "You're the only one I can really count on." She sounded frantic. The happy and put-together woman she'd been seconds ago was gone that quickly.

"Help you?" My brain searched for clues. What had I missed?

Her eyes darted around the room. Her pupils were huge. Was she on drugs?

"He's a bad man. A really bad man, Thera. I need you to know that. You have to trust me. Do you trust me?" She couldn't get the words out fast enough, as if any minute someone or something would stop her. But nobody was here. It was just us, and I was totally lost.

"Who's a bad man?" I asked. "What are you talking about? You're not making any sense."

"Phillip. And my dad. They're both terrible people. I need you to help me. Help me tell them." She pointed behind us, where Meg and Grace were awkwardly waiting for us to join them on the patio.

"Tell them what? I don't understand." She'd just been so calm and put together. How did you go from that to this so quickly?

"I can't tell you everything right now because it would take too long and they're waiting on us, but he makes me sleep in the yard. Sometimes he locks me in the shed. Starves me for days. Controls absolutely everything I do. I promise I'll explain all of it as soon as we get outside with the others." She jerked her head up and switched to her happy singsong voice, calling out to Meg and Grace, who'd finally settled into the chairs, "We're almost done, girls. We'll be there in a second!"

She dropped her voice low again as soon as she'd said it. She let go of my arms and grabbed both my hands. Hers were slippery with sweat. She was definitely manic. "I'm just so nervous. I don't know how they're going to react when I tell them what I did, and now I feel like this whole thing is a mistake. Meg seems drunk, and Grace acts like she doesn't even want to be here, but I know I can count on you, Thera. You've got to help me tell them. I just really need your support. More than I ever have before." She looked like she was going to burst into tears at any second, and she rarely ever cried. Not unless it was something really bad. "I can't do this if I don't have you behind me."

"Blakely, I'm sorry." I gripped her hands and peered into her eyes. "I don't know what you're talking about. What's going on?"

"Everyone was always afraid of my father. You know that. But it was so much worse than what you think. Than anyone thought. He's nothing like your dad. He never was. He only cares about himself and money. That's it. I always tried telling you that, but you just looked at me like I was a spoiled brat. You always thought I was such a spoiled brat. You probably still do."

"No, I didn't." I shook my head even though there were times I did. It was impossible not to, with the way she acted sometimes.

"It's okay," she said quickly. "That's not the point. I don't even care. He's evil. Always has been. That's the most important part for you to know. Want to know why?" Her eyes were lit with fury. "You see all this?" She twirled around, pointing to her incredible house. "My husband, Phillip, is loaded, and my daddy wanted in on it. Just like everybody else. But guess what my daddy had that nobody else did?" She stabbed her chest with her finger. "Me. I was part of their business deal. I mean, not on paper, but my daddy dangled dinners with me as a bargaining chip and forced me to go on the dates. That's why I married Phillip. He made me do it." She narrowed her eyes to slits. "And then once I married him, you know what happened? Phillip turned into a monster like literally on our wedding night. I'm not even kidding. He locked me in the bathroom and made me sleep there all night because he was mad about something I said at dinner. A few weeks later I woke up tied to my bed, and he kept me that way for almost two days because he didn't like the way I looked at one of his business partners the night before. The worst part? I went to my daddy and told him everything, but he didn't even care." She snorted. "He didn't even act surprised. It was like he already knew Phillip was a terrible person, but that didn't matter to him."

"I don't understand." I just kept saying it over and over again. How did this have anything to do with the notes? With all of us? What were we doing here? This was supposed to be about the notes. Not her. Or had it always been about her? Had she set this whole thing up? Maybe Grace was right to be so paranoid.

"Just, please. When we go outside, promise that you'll support me? Promise you'll stand behind me? Promise?" Her fingernails dug farther into me. Desperation clung to her voice.

"Blakely, I don't even know what I'm agreeing to. How can I promise you anything? You're not making sense." I pried myself out of her grip and rubbed her arms, trying to calm her down as I looked into her eyes.

"I'm sorry. I'm so sorry. I just had to tell you first before I tell the other girls. I need you on my side. You're my best friend." She said it like she'd said it that summer. The visceral memory of it hit me like a real force. "I need to know that you're going to love me no matter what. The others can hate me, but please, promise me that no matter what, you'll still love me."

"I'll always love you, Blakely. Nothing changes that."

"Promise?"

"Yes, I promise," I said even though I had no idea what I was agreeing to or what she was about to tell us. She just looked like she was going to fall apart on the spot if I didn't tell her.

She let out a deep sigh. "Okay, then, as long as I have your support, I can do this. Let's do this."

# CHAPTER EIGHTEEN
## *THEN*

### BLAKELY

Clint snatched the picture from my hand before I even got a chance to tell him what happened last night. Jacob looked over his shoulder. Both of them gawked at the image. Meg had captured the perfect shot of me and Jared. I still didn't know how she did it. She hadn't wanted me to show it to them. At first, she hadn't even wanted to give it to me. She wanted to keep it, like it was hers or something, but it wasn't hers. It was mine. I'd done all the hard work. Taken all the risks.

"Oh my God," I'd gushed when I first saw it last night. I was still out of breath from running so hard to get back to the cabin. "Look how his hand is brushing against my thigh." But Meg didn't look at the picture. She just wrinkled her face and looked irritated. "I can't wait to show Clint and the boys."

"You can't show them that," she snapped and immediately snatched the picture back from me.

"Can I see it?" Thera piped up from behind me. She'd been quiet ever since we got back to the cabin. Both her and Grace. They probably felt left out because they weren't inside with us when it happened. I could always tell when Thera was upset. She was terrible at hiding her emotions. I felt bad. I needed to do a better job including her, but Meg just had such a better in with Jared. If we got caught doing anything in his office, she could just make up some stupid story about tennis.

Meg frowned. She hugged the picture against her chest and shook her head. Her brown eyes pointed and focused. "No. I think we should just get rid of it. This was a bad idea."

"It's not your picture. Let her see it." I grabbed for the Polaroid, but she jumped back, keeping it out of my reach. Anger surged through me. "What's wrong with you, Meg? Give her the picture."

We locked eyes. Like two dogs trying to establish dominance, but she was no match for me. I was the undefeated champion of stare-downs. She dropped her head and reluctantly handed Thera the picture.

Thera frowned as soon as she saw it and quickly passed it to Grace, but Grace barely looked before giving it back to me. She was in one of her pissy moods again tonight, and unlike Thera, I had no clue how to make her feel better.

"You can't show Clint or anyone else that picture," Meg repeated.

I turned around and shook my head at her. "Of course I can. That's the entire reason we did it. To show them. They're not going to believe it otherwise."

"Yeah, but they're going to think something happened." Meg pointed at me and the picture. "That makes it look like something happened between you guys."

"Exactly!" I giggled, proudly waving the picture in the air and dancing around. "That's the point."

Meg shook her head. Adamant. "What if someone else sees it? That could really get Mr. Crosby in trouble."

"I don't get it. What exactly happened again?" Grace asked.

I batted my hand at her. "Oh, nothing, it's just like I said before— he's definitely into me. That's for sure. But he was too afraid to do anything. You should've seen how nervous he was. Like he was all shaky and sweaty. Totally stumbling all over his words. But I thought it was adorable. He reminded me of a little boy." I squealed. Still excited over it. That Meg had captured the shot. Meg glared at me while I talked, but that didn't bother me. I was used to people being mad at me. I lived in a home with people that hated me. "Anyway, I had to make the first move, or it was never going to happen, so I just went for it. I still can't believe I did that." I put my hands up to my mouth, giggling.

"You can't show that to Clint. You can't show that to anyone," Meg said, doubling down. She sounded like a broken record.

"Can you stop being such a baby about this, please?" I asked her. "It's not that big of a deal."

"Yeah," Thera said, coming to stand next to me. "It's just a senior prank. That's the point of senior summer."

I took a step back, surprised at her sudden support. She looked so upset seconds ago, and I thought she'd be on Meg's side for sure, especially since she'd been against my relationship with Jared since the beginning. Her change of heart was totally surprising, but I liked it. I definitely wanted her on my team.

Meg crossed her arms on her chest. "You can't mess with other people's lives like that."

I rolled my eyes at her and looked at Thera. At least she agreed with me on this one. I could always count on Thera when things got bumpy. "They already know what we were doing tonight, so it's not like the picture changes anything. We might as well show it to them, and then this whole thing can be over," she said.

"No, just no. I don't want to do anything that might get Mr. Crosby in trouble." Meg glared at me and crossed her arms on her chest. Her forehead lined with determination.

How many times was she going to say the same thing? So annoying. I looked at the others. "Is that how everyone feels? You think we shouldn't do this?"

"Of course we have to show them. Otherwise, why'd we go through all that trouble to do it?" Thera said quickly, agreeing with me and shooting Meg an irritated look to show she really meant it. That's what best friends were for, and I was glad she was on my side, even if it'd taken her a while to come around.

Meg went to bed all angry, and she was still mad this morning. She made this long, drawn-out production of saying she wasn't going, after I announced that I was meeting Clint down by the canoes to show him the picture. Grace stayed behind with her. I was pretty much over Grace's attitude too. I didn't know why she even bothered coming to camp this year when she spent most of her time acting like she didn't even want to be here or be a part of anything we were doing. The two of them packed a picnic and were going to take Meg's favorite horse out for a ride, so they'd probably be busy all afternoon. Good. I needed a break from them.

I shifted my focus back to Clint and Jacob. They were still staring at the picture in awe.

"Told you he was into me," I said with a smug grin. God, I loved winning. I turned to Thera, and she wore a matching grin.

"He definitely wants to bone you," Clint said, with his eyes all big and horny.

"Totally," Jacob agreed with the same eyes, except his were pointy and squinty.

I just smiled at them like it was nothing, even though I still couldn't believe we'd pulled it off. I'd never done anything like it before, but I was acting like it happened all the time. Where'd I find the courage to just be so bold with a man? I'd surprised myself.

I reached my hand out for the picture, but Clint pulled away, holding it behind his back.

"Oh no, we've got to do something with this," he said, shaking his head. His dark hair flopping in his face and covering his eyes. "We can't just let it go to waste."

"What are you talking about?" I asked, instantly annoyed with him.

"This is too good not to do something else with it. Didn't your little friend say the other day that we needed to switch things up this year? Do something different?" He gave me a wide grin with his crooked yellow teeth. He was kind of cute until he smiled. "Nobody's ever done anything like this."

"You didn't do anything. This was all me. That's my picture." I reached for it again, but he jumped back before I could grab him. The grin hadn't left his face. "What are you doing? Give it back to me. Give me the picture."

He shook his head. Jacob burst out laughing and moved to stand next to him, throwing his arm around Clint's shoulders. "Nah. We're going to take care of this next part."

"Give me the picture! It's mine!" I yelled.

"Give it to her!" Thera yelled at the same time as me.

The boys just shook their heads; still laughing. Thera lunged at Clint and grabbed him by his shirt, clutching the blue fabric in her fist. "That's not yours. Give it back to her!" Her face was furious and red-faced in front of his. Nostrils flaring.

He rocked his head side to side, mockingly. "*Give it back to her,*" he mimicked in an exaggerated whiny voice. Jacob just kept laughing like it was the funniest thing he'd ever seen, and I wanted to smack him. Hard.

Thera shoved Clint, and he fell backward, tumbling into the dirt, but he quickly scrambled back up. Before we had a chance to do anything, they took off running. We chased after them for a few yards, but they were way faster than we were, and we lost them in the woods almost immediately.

I stopped in the middle of the clearing, hunched over and breathing hard. "What are we going to do?" I asked, looking over my shoulder at Thera.

She was bent over, too, and breathing just as hard as me. "I don't know, but we've got to figure something out because we can't let them keep that picture. Who knows what they'll do with it."

# CHAPTER NINETEEN

## *THEN*

### MEG

I sat outside the admissions office, nervously swinging my legs. My sweaty thighs stuck to the aluminum every time I moved. I didn't want to be sitting, but it'd look weird if I stood, and this whole thing was already weird enough. They'd been calling everyone in all morning. Anyone that had a class or private lesson with Mr. Crosby, which was practically half of camp. I couldn't believe this was happening. It all started with Blakely and that stupid picture. Why'd Grace have to bring her camera with her this year anyway?

All the counselors were huddled outside the door trying to pretend like they weren't snooping. Eyeing the door and paying careful attention to everyone coming in and out. The head swimming coach, Elizabeth, stood in the center of the circle with a small group of people around her. She looked like she'd been crying. Her best friend was hugging her and speaking to her in a hushed whisper.

This wasn't part of the plan, but for some reason, Clint thought it would be so funny to tape the picture of Blakely and Mr. Crosby on Mr. Crosby's computer. Blakely agreed but only because she said she'd use it as an opportunity to get the picture back from him, which followed no logical reasoning and made no sense. But none of her thinking about Mr. Crosby was rational. She'd literally gone boy crazy.

Blood pooled in the back of my head. Throbbing, making my head ache even more. I hated getting in trouble. I didn't want any part of this, but I'd helped her do it. I'd helped her sneak to the other side of camp and into Mr. Crosby's office again last night. I wasn't even the one that was supposed to go with her. It was supposed to be Thera this time, but Blakely changed her mind at the last minute and asked me. I should've said no, but she was just so mad at me from challenging her about it yesterday. She acted like it meant I wanted him or something. When she asked me to go with her, she looked at me like she was daring me to say no.

She claimed she was trying to get the picture back.

"You don't understand how much I need that picture. It means so much to me," she cried.

"But . . . how are you going to get it? Isn't the plan to tape the picture on his computer?" Thera had asked before we left. I was glad she was the one to ask the question and not me. That might've been the reason Blakely picked me at the last minute. She didn't like Thera's questions, even though she'd been the one backing her up yesterday when I hadn't. The boys taking the picture had brought Thera crashing back to reality, though. She hated getting in trouble even more than I did.

Blakely nodded, affirming their plan.

"Then, how are you going to get it?" Thera asked the most obvious question next. "Are you just going to wait until Clint puts it up there and just yank it off?"

Blakely shrugged. "I don't know. I'll figure it out once I'm there. Worst-case scenario I don't get it tonight and it gives me a reason to go back to Jared's office by myself and talk to him about it. I'll tell him the boys were doing a senior prank or something."

It was a terrible idea, and I looked to Thera and Grace to back me up after she'd said it. But they both refused to meet my eyes, so I'd left it alone too. Why bother? Nothing was changing her mind at this point, anyway.

We all walked across campus together in the dark, meeting the boys halfway at the CITs' cabins behind the stables. I breathed a sigh of relief to see the CITs were having their own party so they wouldn't be the least bit worried or concerned with whatever trouble we were getting into. And maybe this would finally be it, I thought as we traipsed down there. Blakely would get her picture—the ultimate memento of the summer, that's what she was calling it—and this would be over. She could recreate whatever fantasy she wanted with the picture because it wouldn't hurt anybody.

At the last minute, right before we were supposed to go inside, Blakely had turned to Thera. "You know what? I'm taking Meg in with me. I feel like you should wait outside with Grace again."

Thera looked devastated. She stopped walking like she'd actually hit a wall. Even though she'd switched her opinion on how she felt about the picture and Blakely's relationship with Mr. Crosby way too many times to count, the fact that Blakely had picked me again over her hurt.

I'd been so proud and happy. It didn't matter that I didn't agree with what we were doing either. I mouthed "Sorry" to Thera, even though I really wasn't, and hurried inside after Blakely.

Now I felt like an idiot, and the only thing I was wishing was that I hadn't gone. Blakely was acting so weird last night, and she wouldn't give me a straight answer on anything. It didn't make any sense.

"You told the dean what really happened, right?" I whispered to Blakely, long after lights-out. I'd waited until after second bed check, the one they were really serious about, before tiptoeing over to her bunk. The others were asleep. Thera snored above our heads while we whispered beneath her.

Blakely nodded. "Of course. I told him it was just a senior prank. That we were just trying to have some fun."

The thing nobody counted on was them locking the door for the night and not being able to get back inside to get the picture or

Elizabeth being the first one back in the office instead of Mr. Crosby. We didn't have any idea the two of them shared a desk. She'd been the one to find the picture, and she'd flipped. She'd bypassed Mr. Crosby and gone straight to the dean. Since Blakely was the one in the photo, she was the first person the dean questioned.

I'd nodded at her. "Right. Right. But you told him about the picture. What actually happened with the picture . . ." I dropped my voice even lower, even though everyone in the cabin already knew what happened with the picture. We'd all been there.

"He didn't ask about that."

"He didn't ask about the picture?" She shook her head and looked innocent. Sweet. Except I knew when someone was faking it, and she was definitely faking it. "That's pretty much the most important thing, and for obvious reasons. Everyone's going to think something happened between you guys."

She shrugged. "You should've heard how personal he was with all his questions. I mean like he wanted to know did I have a boyfriend at camp or one at home? What does that have anything to do with anything?"

"You told him nothing happened with Mr. Crosby, though, right?" I pressed, refusing to let her change the subject or not give me a straight answer.

"I told him I had a crush on Jared. It's like whatever . . ." She rolled her eyes.

It wasn't *whatever*. This was a big deal.

It felt like an even bigger deal now that I was sitting outside the dean's office, waiting my turn. What would happen if I just left? Right as I considered bolting, the door opened, and the dean stuck his head out. "Come on in, Meg." He motioned to me.

I got up slowly and moved to follow him into his office like a dog with its tail tucked in between its legs, even though, technically, I hadn't done anything wrong. I hadn't gone into the office. I didn't put the picture on Mr. Crosby's computer. All I'd done was watch.

I'd never met the dean in person before, even though he was a permanent fixture around camp. He reminded me of a principal. He looked just as stern.

"Take a seat." He motioned to the upholstered chairs in front of his huge desk. I slid gingerly into one of them and wrung my hands on my lap, doing my best not to look terrified.

What did he think of the picture? By now, it felt like everyone had seen it. Clint showed it all around camp before they put it in Mr. Crosby's office. Blakely pretended to be upset by all this, but she loved the attention. Everyone had been treating her like a celebrity all day, thinking she hooked up with Crosby.

Except that was the thing.

It hadn't gone down like she said it had, and it certainly wasn't anything like the picture suggested it was. I should've ripped that thing up and thrown it away the second I got a chance. Why couldn't I stand up to Blakely? Why'd I always give in to her?

Dean Morris put his elbows on the desk and folded his hands. He gave me another serious look. "I'm sure you know why you're here today, Meg," he said sternly, giving me a long stare-down to make me even more nervous than I already was.

I nodded slowly. A huge lump growing in my throat, getting bigger by the second.

"I want you to know that we take instances like this very seriously." I gulped. Would he send me home? Could this go on any kind of my permanent record? Would I lose my scholarship to Saint Thomas?

He hadn't taken his eyes off mine yet, and all I could do was stare back. Waiting. Shaking my legs. I had to pee.

"As I'm sure you know, at Camp Pendleton we screen all of our staff very, very carefully. We make sure that the people we have working with you children are safe. That's our number one priority here at camp— your safety." He cleared his throat. "You would let me know if anything had happened that made you feel unsafe, right, Meg?"

I nodded at him again.

"We're calling in lots of the campers today to chat. I'm sure you've heard. Like I said, we take instances like this very seriously, and we've never had anything like this occur before. I can assure you of that."

There had to be someone besides us that had messed with a counselor in all these years, hadn't there? The camp had been around for almost twenty years or something like that. Blakely couldn't have been the first one to have a crush on one of the counselors or do something so immature. No way.

"I noticed that you've been doing private lessons with Mr. Crosby in the afternoons and that you're a member of his tennis team. I know these questions are going to be hard for you to answer, and I want to let you know that you're safe in this room with me. Do you understand?"

I nodded.

"Could you speak up?"

"Yes." My voice was quiet and small. I didn't mean for it to be, but I felt anything but safe with him sitting there in his huge office chair, peering down at me like he was some kind of judge in a courtroom.

"I know this is probably overwhelming for you, and I want you to know that I'm here for you. We all are. Has Mr. Crosby ever done or said anything to make you feel unsafe?"

I shook my head. My voice was gone as quick as I'd found it.

He cocked his head and raised his eyebrows at me. "Are you sure about that? I'm just going to be honest—you look scared, Meg. You don't need to be scared."

He wasn't wrong. I was terrified. Terrified of what would happen if I told the truth. Scared of what would happen to Blakely if I told. How it would change things with us. In the group. I was afraid of them telling my mom what I'd been a part of. That they'd take away my college scholarship if I got into any kind of trouble. There were so many things I was scared of. My stomach was a ball of roiling nerves. But there was one thing I wasn't scared of, and that was Mr. Crosby.

I cleared my throat. "I'm not scared of Mr. Crosby. He's a good coach."

"Yes, I understand he's a good coach. It's why sometimes it's hard for girls to come forward and talk about these kinds of things, especially when it's someone they love and care about that's also the one hurting them. That can be very confusing. I imagine you must be very conflicted."

I had to look away. His gaze was making me sweat. My thighs were sticking to the seat again, like they had been in the waiting room. I wanted to get out of here. I needed to get out of this room. I felt dizzy. Lightheaded. I gripped the armrests.

"Are you sure he's never done anything to make you feel uncomfortable? Take your time. There's no rush." He did that thing again where he got silent and just stared at me.

"No," I said again. Just like before.

"What about any of your friends? Do you know of any incidences with Mr. Crosby that have made them feel unsafe?"

I shook my head again. I didn't know why I couldn't talk. *Just speak, Meg. Open your mouth and tell him the truth.* But I couldn't. I didn't know the truth anymore. Not really. I'd watched through the office door window as Blakely had gone in there that night to talk to Mr. Crosby. Her back had been toward me the entire time. I hadn't seen her face. Only his. At first, it was utter surprise. Even though I couldn't hear anything they were saying, I didn't need to. There was no mistaking he was shocked to find her coming into his office late at night. Then, it'd quickly switched to what looked like concern. Why was he concerned? What did she say to him?

She hadn't told me. All she'd said was that he was worried his wife would find out about his feelings for her. But he'd pushed his chair away from his desk, farther from her. And maybe I'd seen fear? Something else? I didn't know. It all happened so fast, and I was so nervous. Plus, I had the camera, waiting for the right time to take the picture.

"Make sure you get the perfect shot." That was the last thing Blakely said to me before going in.

I'd watched it all through the blurry Polaroid camera lens. Had I missed something? Was that possible? My mind felt like it was playing tricks on me. Suddenly, I couldn't trust my own mind. My own memories. What was wrong with me? I knew exactly what happened, didn't I?

But it all happened so fast. One minute she was in front of him, talking. He was nodding his head, listening to her. Then, shaking his head. When suddenly, she stepped into his space and tried to sit on his lap. Like she was about to straddle him.

That's when I snapped the picture.

"Meg?" Dean Morris's voice broke into my thoughts. "You would tell me if there was anything going on with Mr. Crosby and one of your friends, right?"

"Yes," I said with as much earnest sincerity as I could put into my voice.

"Okay, great." He finally relaxed his hands on his desk. Pushed himself back from it in the same way Mr. Crosby had pushed himself away from Blakely. "So, then, I'm going to ask you again—has there been any inappropriate behavior between any of your friends and Mr. Crosby?"

"No."

He smacked the desk and I jumped, my blood pressure skyrocketing. "You're lying to me, Meg. Do you know what happens when people lie? They can't be trusted anymore. And when they lie to protect other people?" He shook his head like he was slightly disgusted with me and raised his voice. "Well, it's pretty much a guarantee that someone gets hurt. You don't want anyone to get hurt, do you, Meg? You seem like such a nice girl. Someone that really cares about others. But I guess I was wrong about you."

I immediately burst into tears. I couldn't help it. I hated when people were mad at me. Hated it even more when they raised their voice at me. I didn't know what to say. What to do. I wanted to go home.

"Can I call my mom?" I cried, doing my best to stop the tears, but that only made me cry harder.

He gave me a clipped nod. He'd started out as my friend, but now he was irritated with me. I'd made him mad somehow. I didn't mean to. "Certainly. You can call your mom as soon as our conversation is over. I just need you to start being honest with me."

"I'm telling you the truth." I pulled my shirt up to cover my face. I didn't want him to see me cry. I was telling the truth, wasn't I? The truth was nothing had happened. Blakely tried. She'd done exactly what she'd set out to do, and the moment she'd tried to sit on Mr. Crosby's lap, he'd flung her off like she'd burn him. He threw her so hard she fell backward onto the floor, landing on her butt.

Mr. Crosby had pointed at the door. I hadn't heard anything else they'd said to each other the entire time, but I heard the last part. You couldn't miss it.

"*Get out of here!*" he'd screamed.

I took deep, hiccuping breaths into my shirt, trying to calm myself down. It wasn't working, and Dean Morris still wasn't letting me leave. What did he want from me?

He cracked his knuckles. Then stared at me for what felt like a really long time, and all I wanted to do was disappear into the floor. I didn't look up until he finally started talking again. "Well, Meg. See, that's where we have a problem." He opened a drawer on his desk and made a long dramatic production of pulling something out. A small square glossy Polaroid picture. I knew exactly which one he held in his hands. He didn't have to show me, but he did. He slid it across the desk. "Then, what's going on in this picture?"

I didn't need to look down to see it. I already had. Mr. Crosby pushed Blakely off. That much I was sure of. I'd seen it with my own eyes. But that's not what it looked like in the picture. Not at all. It looked like she was getting onto his lap and he was trying to put his hand up her uniform skirt.

# CHAPTER TWENTY

## *THEN*

### GRACE

I grabbed Meg and pulled her into the bathroom with me, slamming the door behind us. I put the Do Not Disturb sign on the door and checked underneath both stalls before saying a word. You couldn't trust anyone right now.

"Blakely made it sound like something happened with her and Mr. Crosby," I hissed at her. "And now someone else is saying that he messed with them too." I couldn't believe what was happening.

It was the third girl to come forward in the last two days. Dean Morris had been calling everyone into his office. One by one, they interviewed all of us, starting with Cabin Naomi. The entire camp was buzzing with stories and rumors. There was no way to know what was true or not. Their stories were similar to Blakely's. They'd taken a private lesson with Mr. Crosby or they'd been down at the tennis courts, and he'd flirted with them. Then, he'd tried to slip his hands underneath their tennis skirts. He liked making them sit on his lap in his office.

The entire camp was obsessed. Who would be the next girl to come forward? That's what everyone wanted to know. And how many victims had there been in such a short time? There were all kinds of rumors that the only reason he was at Pendleton was because he'd been kicked out of the school he worked at before. Everyone was talking about it, even though none of the staff had actually said or confirmed anything.

The only thing we knew for sure was nobody had seen him anywhere on campus, and Olympics week had officially been canceled.

I'd never seen Meg so worried. She'd been a wreck ever since she came out of her interview with the dean a few days ago, and it'd only gotten worse. Especially after this morning, when they'd called us all in to the chapel for a special assembly and told us they were halting all regular activities. Would they be sending all of us home? Closing down camp? As awful as everything was, and as much as I hated what was happening, I didn't want to go home. I wasn't sure I ever wanted to go home.

It'd been four weeks, and I hadn't called home once. Mom started calling when I didn't, but I refused to take any of her calls. I hadn't answered any of her letters either. I didn't want to see her. I didn't want to talk to her. I wasn't sure I ever wanted anything to do with her again, except she was my mom, so that was going to be tough. Meg's voice interrupted my thoughts.

"I mean, is it possible something did happen?" she asked. Her face was twisted with confusion. Her eyes searched mine for understanding.

"What do you mean? With Blakely and Mr. Crosby?"

She nodded.

"Are you serious right now?" I cocked my head to the side, eyeing her with disbelief. It was like fourth-grade summer all over again, when everyone was obsessed with playing Bloody Mary in the bathroom. All the girls were saying they'd seen Mary's ghost appear in the mirror, and eventually, we'd both said we saw her, too, even though we hadn't, no matter how many times we tried. I grabbed Meg, pulling her close. I wanted to shake her. Just like I wanted to shake everyone right now. But I didn't. I just stared deep into her eyes, trying to reach her with the truth. "You know what it's been like all summer with Blakely. She's obsessed with him. And you were there that night. Christ, you're the one who took the picture, Meg. You said he rejected her. Not the other way around."

"I just, I don't know . . . there was something that police officer said today about how girls sometimes pretend they, like, wanted something so that they don't have to see themselves as victims. It got me thinking . . ." Her voice was hesitant and unsure. She let it trail off.

It hadn't seemed like it was going to be all that serious until the police officers arrived. Everything changed then. There were two of them. One short and stocky, wearing the traditional uniform, and another as tall as his partner was short, dressed in regular clothes. Whatever was going on, they were the ones handling it moving forward. Even if you'd met with the dean already, you had to be reinterviewed by them.

I eyed Meg, trying to figure out why she was acting so ridiculous and going back on everything she'd said before about the situation. What was wrong with her? What was wrong with everybody? I stepped even closer to her, completely invading her space, so she had to pay attention. "Blakely wanted Mr. Crosby, and he rejected her. That's how this whole thing started. You know that as well as I do. But somehow, it's gotten all twisted up, and now the police are involved. Someone has to set them straight, and there's nobody better to do that than you."

"Me?" Meg pointed to herself like she was in complete shock, as if she wasn't the person who made the most sense.

"Yes, you," I said, slightly annoyed. "Blakely's not going to confess and say she made it all up, and I told them what you'd told me, but I wasn't inside the building. You were there with her that night. You can tell them nothing happened and end this whole thing."

"That's what you told them?"

"Of course that's what I told them, because that's what happened."

"We don't actually know what happened." She eyed the door like she wanted to leave and was plotting her escape.

"Did you talk to Blakely today?" I fingered her chin and lifted her head up. "What'd she say to you?" I wanted her to look me in my face. Right in my eyes and tell me what was going on, because she was the only one there that night, and she'd told me afterward nothing happened between Blakely and Mr. Crosby. That the picture was misleading. She regretted taking it. Felt bad about being part of the entire thing. That's the last thing she'd said before she went into her interview. Something happened to change her mind. "Did Blakely tell you to lie?"

"No." She jerked her head away from me and looked everywhere but my face while she talked. "I thought I knew what happened, but I don't know . . . I'm just saying that officer made some good points today. He said that even if a girl wanted to hook up with one of the staff members, it was still wrong because they were older and it was an abuse of power. He kept saying that over and over again. How it was an abuse of power. And girls our age didn't really know how to consent. It flipped me upside down, and now none of it makes sense."

"He's a detective, Meg. He's supposed to be able to get in your head. That's what they do. But you've got to be stronger than that. You know what really happened. You were there."

"Do I?"

"Of course you do. Blakely's had a *huge* crush on Mr. Crosby since we got here, and Blakely absolutely hates being rejected. Why are you defending her?" Meg refused to make eye contact.

"I'm not. I'm just confused."

"You know he didn't touch her."

"I wasn't there."

"Yes, you were! You were right outside the door. You're the one that took the picture."

She smacked her hand over my mouth. "Be quiet! Someone is going to hear you."

I pushed her hand off me. "You told them the truth about the picture, right?"

"Of course I did," she said, but I could tell she was lying. Meg was a terrible liar.

My heart sank. "I thought we were on the same side."

"There's no sides. I just don't think we should jump to any conclusions." She turned away from me, still refusing to meet my eyes.

"So, what? You're saying this whole time Blakely's been trying to get Mr. Crosby's attention that he's actually been interested in her instead of ignoring her? That even though you were there when she tried to plop herself on his lap and he practically threw her off, he somehow hurt her?"

She shrugged. She looked like she was going to cry, and Meg rarely cried. "I don't know. This is all just so confusing. I don't understand any of it. Wait until you talk to the police. You'll see what I mean."

This time I was the one to shake my head at her. "No, I won't, because I know the difference between reality and fantasy."

"You weren't there."

She kept stressing that point, but it didn't matter. I'd talked to her about it that night, and even if Blakely lied about it, Meg always told the truth. She might not be clear on the details anymore, but I remembered all of them. She said nothing happened.

There was a knock at the door.

"Hurry up," a voice—one I didn't recognize—called out. "You've been in there forever."

"One more minute!" I yelled back.

"What about the other girls, Grace?" Her face crumpled like she was about to burst into tears. That's the part that was really bothering her. Same as it was me. "Why would they say he'd done something to them if he didn't?"

"I don't know . . . ," I admitted, even though I didn't want to. I couldn't make that part make sense either. I'd racked my brain for plausible scenarios and came up empty. It kept me up half the night. "Maybe Blakely told them to say that because she didn't want to get in trouble for lying? Or they wanted attention too . . . Except if she didn't want to get in trouble, then why wouldn't she ask us to do it? But she didn't ask us. She hasn't said anything about it other than being shocked. She acts like we haven't been there for all of it. Like we don't know she's lying."

"Or maybe she's telling the truth." Meg finally burst into the tears she'd been holding back. "Maybe those other girls are too."

# REGINA

Everyone wanted an explanation for my behavior. For me to put those thoughts—those terrible moments—into some kind of logical narrative that they could understand. All the investigators. The police. The judge. My attorneys. My own mom was the worst.

"I just don't understand, honey. Tell me why you would do something like that. Please." That's what she'd beg while we waited for my trial, like I was purposefully keeping it from her.

How could you hurt your babies?

That was the other question everyone wanted to know, and I didn't have an explanation for that one either. Anyone asking those questions has never lost touch with reality. Your thoughts aren't linear.

And believe me. My behavior was as abhorrent to me as it was to other people.

I spent my first three years inside on suicide watch, locked in the mental health unit, because I kept trying to kill myself. I couldn't see any way to live after what I'd done.

The next few years were just as dark as the first three, even though they moved me into the general population.

I didn't get out of bed if I didn't have to. I ended up in the mental health ward two other times, and I wasn't there for a vacation. I'd ripped the tube out of my throat twice before they finally had to sedate me so they had a chance at saving me. I still didn't know if I wanted to be alive most days.

Believe me: no one wanted an explanation for the things I'd done more than me. But I couldn't explain why I believed killing my children would punish my husband when he was already dead, except that it made perfect sense to me at the time. Just like everything else I did.

Jared loved his boys more than life itself, and I just wanted to annihilate him for hurting those girls. I felt strong enough to rip the skin off his body with my bare hands too. That's what I remembered the most—the white-hot fury pumping through my blood.

Finding out he'd sexually abused teenage girls unleashed the rage I'd kept buried inside me for over two decades—tucked away in the corner of my unconscious. At first, I'd been in disbelief when the police officer told me there was an official investigation opened against him. But then there was another girl. Followed quickly by another. They all said the same thing. Told the same story.

"You can't deny this is happening, Regina." That's what the detective had said in the interrogation room down at the station. "Your husband is abusing these girls at camp, and we need you to think of any information that might be helpful in bringing him to justice."

Jared became someone else in that moment. My abuser. Their abuser. And every other sick pervert who'd put their hands on a child. I knew exactly what those girls were going through. I used to be them.

My parents couldn't afford day care, so they'd enrolled me in all the after-school programs at the Salvation Army, and staff walked us down to the YMCA every day. It didn't take them long to recognize I was a talented gymnast. I started clubs and private training through scholarships when I was eight, competing in and winning meets in the division two years ahead of me. That's when all the real trainers came crawling. How our family met Saul, and he talked them into being my private coach. Promising all of us the moon. And he delivered. I was one of the most decorated gymnasts in the country by ten and made the Olympic trials at twelve. Saul was like a second father to me, and I spent more time with him than my own family.

It happened so quick that first time. One minute we were standing there in the middle of the gym talking about my dismount and, mid-sentence, he just reached down and put his two fingers between my legs. My body turned to ice. Alarm bells shot off inside me, exploding at the top of my head and shooting all the way down to my toes, but I couldn't move. I could barely breathe. I just stood there on the mat.

Big man.

Big hand.

Tiny me.

And he just kept talking. Talking and talking like his fingers weren't there. On that private spot. Massaging. Making my body feel funny when I didn't want it to. *Stop it!* I wanted to scream at him. Just as I was going to—when the words finally got to my mouth—it was over.

His hand gone. But he was still talking. Would he ever be quiet? *Shut up.* That's what I'd thought.

We finished practice like it never happened, and by the end of the day, I'd convinced myself it hadn't. Some strange slip of the hand that I'd made into something else. But that wasn't the last time. And that wasn't where he stopped. That was the moment I split into two people—me, the talented and decorated gymnast, and me, the girl who was being raped by the coach helping her earn all the medals. When I found out about Jared, it was like the two of them finally met for the first time. Crashing together in a fierce tornado, and all they wanted to do was hurt him.

Sometimes I still did when I thought about it. Most of those days were a blur. Fragmented and disjointed. But I clearly remembered that rage. I'd never forget that part. So powerful it'd obliterated the love I felt for my own children. And believe me when I tell you, my baby boys were my whole world.

Those pieces—what I'd done to Jaylen and Jordan that day—were the most muddled and the hardest to retrieve. If it hadn't been for the trial, I might not have even remembered any of it. Part of me didn't want to remember, and maybe it was my psyche's way of protecting me. Because when I tell you I loved my sons?

I *really* loved my sons.

It physically hurt me to think about hurting them. Made me sick to my stomach, and all I wanted to do was jump straight out the window.

I didn't remember putting them in the car. I remembered the drive to camp, but nothing about them being there with me or in the back seat. There was no recollection of me leaving them there, either, when I went into the building to find Jared.

That was the one brief moment I recalled. Busting into the building and finding him there with that girl. The one in the picture. The one they showed over and over again at the trial. Their most tangible piece of evidence against him.

I had no memory of leaving the building or taking my babies down to the lake.

I'd flinched over and over again during the trial as I listened to the counselor who'd found me down there describe what it was like. How I'd left Jordan lying on a blanket on the sand and was holding Jayden underwater. She testified that I kept yelling at everyone to get away from me and that I was baptizing him to get the evil off him. I was still screaming it when they pulled me off him. There was a bloodstained handprint in the middle of Jordan's white onesie where I'd grabbed him. That's the picture the prosecution showed the jury over and over again. Evidence that I was a monster.

Some days I agreed with them. Maybe that's what happened when evil men squirted themselves inside you. They ruined you forever.

# CHAPTER TWENTY-ONE

## *THEN*

### THERA

I lay on my bed feeling queasy. The others had gone down to the cafeteria for breakfast, but I'd stayed behind because the thought of food made me even more nauseous. I wanted my dad even though I'd just talked to him last night. We'd all been required to call our parents, even the kids that usually had nothing to do with them while they were here.

"Did that man hurt you, Thera?" Dad asked me the same way Dean Morris had asked me. Just like the police officer who interviewed me again yesterday did.

"No, Dad, he never touched me," I told him, just like I'd told them.

"You would tell me if he did, right? I know lots of girls think they can't tell anyone when something like that happens. They think they'll get in trouble if they say anything, or their abuser says they're going to hurt them if they tell. Did that bastard threaten you?" He kept going without giving me a chance to respond. "If he threatened you, bug, I want you to know that I won't let him hurt you. I'll protect you no matter what. He's not getting anywhere near you, but you have to tell me the truth. Just let me know what happened. Did he touch you? Hurt you in any way?"

"He didn't. I promise, Dad. I'd tell you if he did." And I would. I could tell him anything, but I had to keep what we'd done a secret. I didn't want him to think badly about Blakely, and I hated hurting him in any way, even if it wasn't about me.

He continued ranting. "They finally fired him. Did they tell you that? I don't know why it took them three days to do it. They should've let his ass go immediately. You don't give someone like that the benefit of the doubt. You just don't. Do you want me to come get you?" He rarely swore in front of me unless he was really mad. He'd done it three times already, and we hadn't even been on the phone five minutes.

I'd told him no, that I was staying. Plenty of kids had already left. Parents had started picking up their kids the moment the news hit, whether they wanted to go home or not. But it wasn't like Mr. Crosby was just roaming around campus. No one had even seen him since the day they found the picture in his office.

I was committed to staying. As awful as this was, I couldn't leave my friends yet. They needed me, especially Blakely. She was a wreck over this. It was the first time I'd ever actually seen her cry. Blakely didn't cry. Over the years, she might've gotten a few tears in her eyes. One or two might've even slipped out. But a full-on cry? Never. Not until last night.

"He's going to be so mad at me," she'd sobbed while I held her on the bed. "This is all my fault. I never should've hooked up with him."

*Tried to hook up with him.* That's what I wanted to say, but she didn't need to hear that. She needed me to hug her. Hold her. Make things better for her. I had my dad, but Blakely had nobody. She was all alone in this world.

"It's going to be okay. It's going to be okay," I said to her over and over again while I hugged her and she cried into my chest. I ran my hands through her hair, trying to soothe her.

"I just want one more chance to talk to him, you know? Tell him that I'm sorry. I really want to tell him I'm sorry. This wasn't supposed to happen. I never even got to tell him goodbye." She'd really started sobbing then. Gut-wrenching sobs, like the ones I'd cried when my mom died. She really cared about him. And she wasn't wrong. In some twisted way, this was her fault, even if she hadn't meant for any of it to happen.

She'd eventually cried herself to sleep in my arms on her bunk. That was where we spent the night. I'd barely gotten any sleep because she was a terrible sleeper. Constantly turning. Flipping and flopping. Every time I tried to sneak away to my bunk, she grabbed me and pulled me back close.

"Don't leave," she'd begged. "I need you."

So, I stayed. I'd been up since four, watching her sleep. Maybe after Mr. Crosby was officially gone, this would all blow over. There was still two weeks left of camp. We could salvage this. We had to salvage this somehow.

I loved my dad, but I dreaded the thought of going home and back to my life as a nobody. I was important here, especially to Blakely. She needed me. Your first heartbreak was always the hardest. At least that's what they said. I'd never been in love before. I could help her get through it. And once we did?

Then things could get back to normal. I could—

The door burst open, interrupting my thoughts and sending me sitting straight up in my bed. Grace, Meg, and Blakely came barreling inside the cabin.

"Oh my God! Mr. Crosby's here! Like actually on campus. Jacob saw him being let in by Will at the staff entrance behind camp. The east gate. He's headed down to his office. He must be here to clean out his things." Blakely's eyes were wild. She raced over to my bed and yanked me up. "Come on, we have to go. You have to get up. We just came back here to get our shoes. We have to run." She motioned to Grace and Meg. Her body was practically vibrating. "What are you just standing there for? Get your shoes!" She screeched at me as she searched underneath the bed for hers.

I leaped up from my bunk. Adrenaline surged through me. "He's here?" I eyed the room like he'd be the next one to come bursting inside.

Grace nodded. She looked as scared as Thera. "Yes, Jacob and a couple other people saw him drive in a couple minutes ago."

"This is my chance, we've got to go, come on!" Blakely hadn't stopped shrieking. She'd found her shoes and was hurriedly putting them on. Meg and Grace were doing the same. Both of them tying the laces as fast as they could.

My Nikes were next to my bed, where I always left them, and I quickly slipped them on, just like everybody else. "What do you mean? What are we doing? Where are we going?"

"We're going down there," Blakely said with a tinge of annoyance in her voice, like I should've already known the plan. "We have to catch him before he leaves. This might be my only chance to ever talk to him again, and I have to tell him I'm sorry." Her eyes circled the room. Irritated we weren't ready. "Hurry up! We have to go. We have to run or we're not going to be able to catch him."

I glanced at the others. They looked just as nervous. But Blakely didn't give us any time to think or respond.

"Come on." She reached out and grabbed my hand, pulling me out the door with her. She whispered her orders out of the corner of her mouth while we speed walked across the campus. "Don't look obvious. Just act totally normal. Nothing out of the ordinary. We're just going down to the lake. That's what we say if anyone asks. Grace," she hissed without making eye contact, "stop looking so obvious. You look totally scared." Grace looked mad for a split second, but quickly rearranged her face. "Once we're past the firepits, then we have to run. Meg, you go first because you're the fastest. If you see him, see if you can stall him. I just need a minute with him. Only a minute. Let's go."

"But Blakely, what if—"

She cut Meg off. "We don't have time to talk about this. We just have to go. This is probably my only chance. I just want to tell him I'm sorry. Please. We have to hurry. Just a few more steps and then we're running." She was working so hard to hold herself back from bolting.

She owed Mr. Crosby an apology. I couldn't deny her that. Maybe this would be the thing to make it right. If she apologized, then maybe the others would too. There was a chance we could save this. I picked up the pace and sprinted as soon as we hit the trees.

# CHAPTER TWENTY-TWO

## *NOW*

## THERA

Blakely's backyard was as beautiful as the inside of her house. A large kidney-shaped pool was the center point, with exotic flowers in pots all around it. Lush landscaping behind it that must've cost a fortune to keep green during the summer months. She led us over to a set of chairs around a small firepit. The fire was already burning. It reminded me of camp, and I couldn't help but wonder if she'd done it on purpose. Then I noticed the drinks already arranged on the table, along with the fruit and charcuterie plate filled with all kinds of deliciousness, and knew this was where she'd planned to talk all along.

"I thought we might be more comfortable out here," Blakely said, pointing to all the chairs surrounding the table. She took a seat at the head, like it was a business meeting, and waited for us to get comfortable. I wasn't the only one that wasn't hungry, because nobody else grabbed any of the food, either, even though it looked amazing. She waited a few more seconds and then let out a slow, deep breath. "Okay, I just want to start out by asking you all to just try to be understanding and to please not be mad at me." Another breath. The smile she'd worn since we got here finally disappeared from her face. "Please don't be mad . . ."

Her eyes shifted everywhere but us. Up. Down. Left. Right. Back to center. Like she was waiting for us to tell her that wouldn't happen, but nobody was willing to promise that. The air was thick with tension. We just stared back at her, waiting for her to continue.

Her voice shook when she finally spoke again. "I'm the one who sent the letters. It wasn't Regina. It was me."

Nobody moved. Nobody breathed. All of us just stared at Blakely. At the words that had just come out of her mouth.

Suddenly, Grace sprung to life. "I knew it!" She slammed her hand on the table so hard it made all the drinks wobble. "Something about this didn't feel right from the very beginning. I knew it!" She jumped up like she was going to leave, even though she'd barely gotten here and hadn't given Blakely a chance to explain what she'd done.

Meg looked just as horrified and shook her head at Blakely. "I lied to my wife to come here, Blakely, because I thought it was some sort of emergency. What's going on?" She slid her chair back from the table and eyed the sliding glass doors leading into the kitchen like she was thinking about leaving too. I was still trying to wrap my head around everything Blakely said in the kitchen. She sounded out of her mind.

Blakely held up her hands. "Please, just give me a chance to explain myself before you leave. Please." She searched Meg's and Grace's faces imploringly, but neither of their expressions softened. "I'm sorry. Really sorry to do that—to lie and bring you here under such false pretenses—but I didn't know what else to do. I needed your help, and I didn't know how else to get everybody here on such short notice. I knew if I tried to plan some sort of a get-together, it would never happen—"

"So, you told us that the person we destroyed—the one we're responsible for putting away for over twenty-five years, bringing all that back up—because you wanted us to see each other again?" Meg looked almost as angry as Grace. I'd never seen her so furious. "I really thought we were in trouble. Real trouble. I was actually scared. I have a family and kids to worry about."

Blakely's eyes filled with tears, and she glanced at me for support, because I was the one who always had her back even when she did messed-up things. Today wasn't any different. I meant what I promised in the kitchen, so I nodded at her and gave her my most supportive look. I had no idea what was going on, but she wouldn't have contacted us like this if it wasn't serious. Gratitude passed through her face at my nonverbal acknowledgment and gave her the courage to keep talking.

"Believe me, I didn't want to do this. I wouldn't have done it if there was any other way. I just didn't know how to get all of you to my house, and I was running out of time." The tears she'd been holding back spilled down her cheeks, but she didn't let that stop her. "I've just been so scared, and I didn't know what else to do or who I could trust. I needed help—I . . . I still need help. I didn't know who to call. The truth is that you're the best friends I've ever had. Even after all these years have passed. And we promised. Do you remember that?" She paused for a second to look at each of us. "We promised we'd be there for each other no matter what. So, I just sent the letters, hoping you'd come, and then I could explain everything else once you got here. I didn't know what else to do." She was crying openly now. She struggled to gain composure, but Grace had no patience for any of it.

"What are we doing here, Blakely? That's all I want to know," she demanded. "You literally just keep saying the same things over and over again, but you haven't explained a single thing. You have two minutes to tell us or I'm out." She pointed to the house.

Blakely quickly nodded. She swallowed hard. "I did something terrible. Like really, really terrible, but only because I didn't have any other choice. I never would've done it if I had any other choice. I swear. It was the only way to save myself. He was going to kill me. I had no other options. None. You have to believe me. I didn't know what else to do, but now I'm in trouble. I'm really in trouble." She buried her face in her hands, and her shoulders shook with sobs.

"What are you talking about? Who was going to kill you?" Meg asked, but her question only made Blakely sob harder.

I jumped in, holding up both my hands. "Can you just give her a moment, you guys? Please back off. Just stop and give her a second to get herself together so she can at least try to explain." They each flashed me an angry, annoyed glance, but they stopped firing their questions at Blakely long enough so she could talk without being interrupted.

"I'm not a bad person. You know that, right? I'm not," she choked through her sobs. "You don't know what it's like. How awful it's been my whole life. The terrible way I've been treated. It started with my dad. He's a total sociopath. He doesn't care about anyone but himself. Least of all me. Never has. But everyone thinks he's just *so* wonderful. This poor widowed man raising his daughter alone. How I was so lucky to have him." She snorted. Her voice shifting from devastation to anger in an instant. "But he hated me from the moment I was born. I used to think it was because I killed my mom, but I think he hated me period. He always wanted a son. Not me. That's why he was so different with Jonathon. Do you know they never even brought me with on the family vacations?" She eyed their faces, but they were still set in stone. She pointed to me. "Thera knows. She's been to my house when we were kids. She saw how they treated me. Anyway, that summer we got back from camp? That's the summer he met Phillip at a golf charity event and learned his biotech start-up was killing it. There's nothing my daddy likes more than making money, so of course he immediately wanted in. But that was the problem—so did everybody else. Everyone was vying for a piece of the pie, and my daddy didn't know what he was going to do to set himself apart from the others. That was until the day Phillip stopped by the house and saw me." She paused. Her eyes traveled around the table just like they used to travel around the camp-fire right before she told one of her famous stories. The most powerful déjà vu feeling hit me. Grace and Meg still looked mad, but they were listening as intently as I was. "My daddy offered me to him. Forced me to go out with him, even though I was only nineteen and he was almost forty. It was so disgusting. He was like this dirty old man, but my dad didn't care about any of that."

"Blakely, what?" Grace asked like she was annoyed and not at all moved by anything she'd just said. "What are you talking about?"

"My dad. He basically offered me to Phillip as part of their business deal." She gave a disgusted snort. "And then Phillip? Well, he was about as wonderful as any thirty-nine-year-old man into a teenage girl might be. He controlled me from the moment we were married and practically turned me into his servant. And not just when it came to sex. All things. He treated me like a dog. Even made me sleep outside to punish me. Sometimes he doesn't even let me eat. Once he kept me locked in the closet for three days."

"That's your husband, right?" I asked, just to be sure, because it sounded so unbelievable.

Blakely nodded, sniffling. "I'm a prisoner in my own home. That's why we're out here. There are cameras everywhere in there. There's not an inch of space not covered. Out here too. Just not as many, and they never pick up the audio. But inside? He can see everything I do. Hear everything too. And if I don't follow the rules, then he punishes me." She started shaking, and I reached across the table to grab her hand. Her palms were still sweaty like they'd been in the kitchen. "He controls all the money. The accounts. My trust fund. This estate." She motioned around us. "I don't have any credit cards. I don't even know how to get into any accounts or how much money we have in them. He's got all the passwords, so he controls it and I have no access to any of it. He monitors everything I do. Who I talk to. Where I go. If I'm even allowed to go anywhere. Most of the time I'm not. I'm stuck inside the house." She sniffled and wiped her nose on the back of her sleeve. "The worst part? My dad knew this was exactly what was going to happen too. I told him how Phillip was treating me after we first got married, and he didn't even act surprised. Or like he cared." The mention of her dad quieted her remaining sobs.

She'd always hated her dad. As good as mine was, hers had been bad. I just never knew how bad. What an awful man. I squeezed her hand again.

"I started planning to leave Phillip about a year ago. Taking small cash-back withdrawals out whenever I went shopping or got groceries. Only twenty dollars at a time so he wouldn't notice. Stashing the money in the linen closet because it was the one place where I could do it undetected. I got a volunteer job at the library. He's never let me work. This was the first time he even allowed me to volunteer, and it was only because he got put on the spot at one of the city council meetings. Otherwise, he never would've let me do it, but it would've looked bad if he said no, so he didn't have any other choice. It was the most freedom I've had in twenty years. I used the library computers to do all my research and start setting things up for myself. Planning my escape. I was going to take a bus to Nashville and disappear. Start over somewhere else, where him and my dad would never find me." Her voice started quivering again. "But none of that mattered. No matter how careful I was—and believe me, I was so careful—he found out what I was planning. I still don't know how, but he did. Just like he finds out everything."

Grace interrupted her before she could go any further. "Look, Blakely, your husband sounds like a real asshole. So does your dad, and I'm sorry all that happened to you, but bringing us here like this to help you? Under these pretenses?" She shook her head just like Blakely. "That's just not cool. It's manipulative and hurtful. Bringing all that up just to benefit you? It's—"

"No!" Blakely interrupted her. "It's not like that. You don't understand."

"You're in an awful situation. I understand just fine, but I don't like being lied to. I definitely don't like being played."

She burst into tears again. "He was threatening my babies. He killed one of my babies. He was going to take James Bond too."

"Oh my God, he murdered your children? That's when you go to the police. You don't call your best friends from camp," Meg yelled. She jumped up and joined Grace.

"I don't have any kids. I already told you that. I can't have children," Blakely said in between sobs.

I got up and walked around the table. I crouched beside her and put my hand on her back. "It's okay," I said, rubbing small circles while she cried. "It's going to be okay. You're going to be okay. Whatever this is. We'll get through it." Meg grabbed a napkin from the table and handed it to her. Blakely wiped her eyes and blew her nose before continuing.

I glanced at Grace. She'd finally softened some. You couldn't hear that and not be moved.

"I can't have kids. I don't know if you know that, but it's impossible for me. Of course you don't know that. You haven't seen me in twenty-six years. Why would you know that about me? I'm sorry, I didn't expect to get so emotional. I had a whole speech planned of everything I was going to say, and now I'm just rambling." She took another gulping breath and tried to calm down. "Like I was saying, I can't have kids, and you know how bad I always wanted to be a mom, remember?" She was asking all of us, but her eyes searched mine, and I hadn't forgotten. It's all I'd wanted, too, and I hadn't gotten it either. But we'd talked about it constantly. "Remember when we used to play that silly game MASH? All the kids we'd have? The house we'd live in? I got none of it. Well, maybe the mansion, but who actually cares about that." She let out a bitter laugh. Grace gave an irritated sigh, like she'd had more than enough backstory. Blakely noticed her irritation, too, and sped up. "I have three dogs—Camille, Winston, and James Bond. I know—super-weird name, but whatever. They're my babies. I know everyone always says that, but it's really true for me. Don't laugh or judge, but I actually feed them three meals a day. And when I say feed them, I mean, on the stove or in the refrigerator, raw-food-only diet. They eat better than I do. They have outfits. Groomers. Playdates with other dogs. They sleep right next to me every night. See, the thing about Phillip? He knows how important they are to me. That they're my entire world." She reached over and petted the one that was lying by her feet. I couldn't remember his name. "I don't know how he found out that I was leaving him, but he did. Maybe he was having me followed while I was at the library. I don't know." She wiped her nose on the back of her hand. "The only thing I do know is that two weeks ago, I woke up to Camille's dead body next to mine on the pillow. He laid her there so she would be the first thing I saw when I opened my eyes. He put her favorite pink bows on her ears, just to make her look extra cute and hurt me even more. Tucked her little paws underneath her, the same way she did when she was sleeping." She gulped. Swallowed hard. Clearly trying to keep it together and not start sobbing all over again. "For a second, I thought I was still dreaming. Then, I thought she was asleep. But when I tried to move her, she was so stiff. And cold. That's when I saw the note he left next to her body. It said"—she interrupted herself with a sob—"it said, 'If you ever try anything like that again, James Bond is next and I'll do it in front of you.' I just . . . I just didn't know what else to do. He left me no other choice."

"If he's so controlling, then how'd you get all of us here? He just kept you completely isolated until now and then suddenly decides it's okay for you to hang with all of us? Is he watching us now? Listening?" Grace asked, eyeing the backyard the same way I'd just done.

I scanned it again like I had any idea what I was looking for. There were plenty of lights and sprinklers, but I didn't see anything that looked like cameras. Of course, I'd never seen any security cameras outside of department stores, so I probably wouldn't have been able to recognize them even if I had seen them.

Blakely frantically shook her head. She looked desperate. The same way she'd looked when she came out of Mr. Crosby's office all those years ago. "I already took care of it."

Meg raised her eyebrows. "What do you mean you already took care of it?"

"I don't have to worry about him anymore. He's gone."

"What are you talking about? He left?" Grace looked bewildered. "That doesn't make any sense. He kept you like a prisoner all these years, and then he just decided to leave?"

Blakely shook her head. I kept rubbing her shoulders, trying to keep her calm. She cleared her throat. "That's not what I mean." She let out a deep whispered sigh and said in a barely audible voice, "He's dead."

Meg backed up even farther from the table. She brought her hands up to her face. "What did you say?"

"I said he's dead. Phillip is dead." She said it again. Louder this time.

Meg's face went white. "Why is your husband dead, Blakely? Why is your husband dead?"

She was about to ask the question again when Blakely cut her off. "Because I killed him."

# CHAPTER TWENTY-THREE
## *NOW*

### GRACE

Thera stumbled backward. Meg put her hands to her ears like she could unhear the news. But all I could do was stare at Blakely. "That's why you brought us here? You killed your husband?"

She stared right back at me like we were the only two people in the room and nodded slowly.

"Why? Why would you do that?" Meg's face was contorted in horror and disbelief.

"Because he was going to kill my other babies. Probably kill me. It was the only way I could get free," Blakely said in the softest voice. She sounded like a frightened little girl. "Afterwards, I just didn't know what to do. That's why I needed all of you."

"What? All your rich celebrity friends weren't available?" I asked, not affected by her meekness and the damsel-in-distress act she was trying to project onto us. "They couldn't help you with this?"

"I don't have any friends." Tears welled in her eyes, and for a second, she looked ten years old again. Thera was clearly moved. Always a sucker for anyone's emotions. But I didn't move a muscle.

"You don't have any friends." I scoffed at her. "Please. I saw your Instagram. Read the article in *People* on your wedding. Ninety-two guests flown out to the Cayman Islands for the weekend? I think you could've asked one of them." I was furious. How dare she bring us into this?

"Are you kidding me? Those people don't care about me. They're all Phillip's friends. Or Daddy's. None of them actually give a shit about me. And the rest of my Instagram? Anything you see on social media? It's all fake. Everything is staged with photographers. All of it. There's not one picture I post without his permission. He controls every single thing I do. I told you that. Every single thing. Please, I just wanted you to help me. I didn't know what else to do."

"What did you do?" Thera asked in a soft, quiet voice. Finding her voice again.

"It was the same thing he'd done with Camille—"

"*No!*" I yelled over the top of her talking. "I don't want to hear any of this! Nothing. How could you? What were you—"

"Grace, calm down." Meg interrupted me before I could continue.

I whipped around to face her. "Calm down?" I glared at her. "Really, Meg?"

"I understand why you're mad, but try to have some compassion," Thera said.

I balked at her. "Are you that stupid?"

Meg grabbed my arm. "Hey, be nice." She warned me like she was scolding a small child.

"She's just implicated us in the murder of her husband, you know that, right?" I pointed at Blakely. "We know somebody's dead, and we know she killed him. So, even if we don't agree to help her—" I glanced at Blakely, quickly shifting my focus to her again. "Which, by the way, what exactly are we helping you with?" I didn't give her time to answer before I turned back to Meg. "Either way, she's gotten our hands dirty. You don't see that? You're just going to know about a murder and keep your mouth shut?"

The question was out before I thought about what I was saying. Everything stilled in the room. Because we'd already done that once. Blakely had just given us another secret to eat. But guess what? I was full.

"I can't believe you." I shook my head at her. "This is a new low. Even for you."

"I needed help," she cried, throwing her hands up in the air. "Why is that so terrible?"

"You screwed with my life again. You did that once, and I'm not going to let you do it again." The others stared at me like what I was saying wasn't true, but they knew it was. "This isn't a group decision. We're not teenagers anymore." But none of them had moved. They all stood staring at me like we were exactly that. Like we'd grown backward in the last hour. That was the thing about being that young. What your friends thought about you was more important than anything else in the world, and being excluded from the group was the most painful thing you could experience. But that wasn't who we were anymore. At least I wasn't. "We're all grown women," I said, making loaded eye contact with every single one, talking slowly to make sure my point wasn't lost on any of them. "We get to make our own decisions. We don't have to do things as a group anymore. We're separate people."

But my words just bounced off them without landing. I cocked my head to the side. "We don't make decisions as a group anymore. We are forty-three-year-old women. Are you kidding me?"

"I think we have to hear her out," Thera said reluctantly. Of course Thera would hear her out. Thera was her best friend. We tried to pretend like all our friendships were equal, but they weren't. That was the biggest lie. It was Thera and Blakely. Me and Meg. When it came down to it, that's how the sides always divided. Except for that summer, because Meg had something to prove. I'd always wondered why she suddenly went boy crazy that summer, because that'd never been her personality. But no wonder. For a second, it tugged at my heart, because she wasn't wrong. We all would've rejected her, because that's what you did to gay people in the nineties, especially teenage ones. She'd felt so bad that Mr. Crosby responded to her. She'd never wanted him to.

So, once again, it was me against them. Just like before.

Blakely reached over and grabbed my arm. "What about what we promised?"

"Are you serious right now?" But I didn't have to look any further than her face to know that she was. "We were fourteen years old! You can't expect us to keep some stupid promise we made when we were in middle school!"

But she did. It was written all over her with the same earnestness that was there when we'd made the promise.

# CHAPTER TWENTY-FOUR

## *THEN*

### THERA

I took a step back, trying to get my heart to slow down and my breathing to relax. I hated the sight of blood. Literally hated it. It reminded me of needles, which reminded me of my mom, which reminded me of everything I tried not to be reminded of. That's when she'd whimper. The only time. When they'd stick her with needles over and over again, trying to get a vein. Her veins were so beat up they'd just automatically collapse. Squirt blood everywhere. She was always covered in bruises in various shades of healing.

Grace stood in front of the campfire, holding the needle up with a big grin on her face. She'd sneaked it out of the arts and crafts room this afternoon. She was so proud of herself. Blakely was next to her, smiling just as big as she was. Meg couldn't have been more ready either. She loved this kind of stuff. Anything hinting at a ritual. Especially one where we had to pledge ourselves to each other for life.

Blood sisters.

It was the summer of eighth grade, and everyone was doing it this year at camp. They were doing it back home, too, but none of us had friends close enough to do it with.

The girls at camp were always obsessed with who was best friends with who. It was a constant competition for friendship, like having a best friend was a special kind of trophy and who you matched with was important. For the last two years, it'd been the necklaces. The broken half—each bestie with one—that, when you put the two broken pieces together, spelled "best friends." But becoming blood sisters meant you'd taken your friendship to a level above being best friends. That's what we were all doing this year. Our small cabin groups becoming tiny covens.

Everyone was pricking their fingers. Then touching them together to mix their blood, the symbol of ultimate loyalty. And I loved the symbolism. I just didn't want to actually poke myself with the needle. I'd never made myself bleed before. At least not on purpose. It was a huge safety pin, and it felt like we were going to have to press really hard. I wasn't the only one scared. We all were, even though we were excited too.

"I got the needle, you go first," Grace said, handing it to Blakely, which only made sense since she'd been the one to suggest we do it in the first place. Blakely giggled nervously. If we were going to go through with this, we were going to have to actually push this thing through our flesh.

"Which finger do we use?" Blakely asked.

"You do the pointer finger. That's how everyone does it," Meg said with authority, rubbing her fingertip like she was getting ready to go next.

Blakely took the needle and started poking it into her skin, but she wasn't actually pushing or applying enough pressure to draw blood. "I can't do it."

"You're going to have to really push," Grace instructed. "It has to be hard enough to break the skin."

Blakely squeezed her eyes shut as she jabbed it into her finger. She opened them and jerked back. "I did it!" she squealed. "There's blood! See that?" She held her finger up, and there was a small bead of blood not much bigger than the tip on the pin.

"I think you're going to have to do it bigger than that," Grace said, giggling.

"No, look, I can make more. I can make it squirt out." She gripped the tip of her finger with her thumb and forefinger on her other hand, squeezing and working it. The bead grew bigger and bigger. She gave us a satisfied grin and held out the pin. "Who's next?"

Meg had gone next. It took her all of three seconds. "Nothing to it," she said, but she had a high pain tolerance. Meg took one look at me and knew there was no way I was going to be able to do it on my own. "Want me to do it?"

I nodded, too scared to speak. I felt dizzy. Sick. I closed my eyes and turned my head away.

"Ready? Three. Two. One," she counted down, but before she got to one, she'd already pressed it through my skin. It went right in. A sting like a shot. She massaged my finger and brought the sweet release of blood to the top, just like Blakely's.

We stood in a circle around the fire, all of us holding our pointer fingers up, giddy and giggling, and bleeding.

"How do we do this? We just go around and touch our fingers together and then say the vows we wrote?" Meg asked.

I nodded. "I'll go first," I said.

I held my finger up to Meg, and just as she was bringing her finger to mine, Blakely yelled out, "Stop! I have an even better idea." I froze midgesture. We stared at her expectantly, wondering what she could possibly be thinking.

"Let's drink it. That's what you're really supposed to do anyway. That's what the Vikings did when they created the oath," she said.

"How are we supposed to do that?" The thought of poking myself even harder made me dizzy all over again.

She motioned for us to come closer, and we hovered around the fire. Tonight was the first time we'd sneaked out of the cabin and into the forest after our counselor was asleep. The shadows danced behind the trees. Lots of rustling. The wind whispered. There could be other people out here in the woods, for all we knew. And not just other kids. The counselors and CITs too. They were supposed to throw some killer parties down by the water.

Meg wrinkled her nose like she'd been totally on board with the plan up until this point, and I was with her. At least I was until Blakely explained herself.

"Listen, it makes total sense. Everyone else usually just rubs their two fingers together, right? And mixes their blood. They become one and all that. That's super great, but listen to this—if we drink the blood, then we actually have each other's blood inside us. We become one for real. All of us. Forever." She looked around the circle, but she didn't have to convince me.

I clapped. "Okay, that's super disgusting, but I actually kind of like it."

Everyone else agreed too. We were all on board.

Grace raced back to the cabin to get one of the Styrofoam cups we'd stolen from the kitchen. We didn't have a knife, so there wasn't a way to cut ourselves any deeper. Instead, we pricked our fingers multiple times and squeezed and dripped them into the cup. One by one we went around, over and over again, so that we'd have enough blood for everyone to drink. We needed more than just a taste so I added some water to the mix, and Blakely stirred it with her finger.

Once we were finished, Meg held up the cup. She wore her most serious expression. The fire danced behind her, casting all sorts of eerie shadows on her face and making her eyes glow. She raised the cup like she was giving a toast. Her other hand held the vows we'd created earlier today. She read from the script in a booming voice: "We're here tonight to take a blood oath. Binding our friendship from now until eternity. Say after me: Our souls are eternal. There is no beginning and no end. With this covenant of blood, I pledge myself to my sisters for eternity. No amount of time or space shall ever sever our connection."

We repeated after her in strong, clear voices. Word for word. Just how she'd said it. Just how we'd written it earlier today, like wedding vows to each other.

Meg continued, "I promise to always love you. Always support you. And always protect you."

Our words echoed hers.

"I will keep your secrets forever. You are now blood of my blood. Flesh of my flesh."

We gripped each other's hands. It was so much more meaningful and powerful now that we were drinking the blood and not just touching our fingers together. Nobody had done this yet. We were the first. This was serious. The air was electric, practically buzzing around us.

"I promise that no matter where I am or how old I get, I will always be there for my sisters. I will defend them and fight for them at all costs. No matter what. Even if it means my life. I will die for my sisters."

There was no greater demonstration of your love than being willing to die for it, and I'd never felt so connected with my friends as we chanted those final words together.

"Bound for eternity." Meg gripped the cup with both hands and raised it to her lips, taking the first sip. She passed it to me next.

"Bound for eternity." I brought it to my mouth and swallowed, making sure to save enough for the others. The mixture was thick and hard to swallow. I hadn't expected that, but I forced it down. Wiped my lips before passing it to Grace. She plugged her nose like she was taking a shot.

Blood tasted just like it smelled, but it wasn't that bad. I kind of liked it.

# CHAPTER TWENTY-FIVE

## *NOW*

### GRACE

I stormed back to my room. Why had I even bothered to come? I knew this was a terrible idea. I didn't care what stupid promise we made to each other when we were teenagers. I started throwing my things back into the suitcase. I'd seen enough. They could do whatever they wanted to do. Only a few seconds passed before there was a knock at the door.

"Can I come in?" Meg's voice called out meekly.

"It's not locked," I snapped back at her.

"I know, but I wanted to give you space if you needed it," she said as she came in the door. She walked hesitantly across the room and stood next to the bed. "I think we should listen to what she has to say. She sounds like she's really in trouble."

"Really, Meg? Is she in trouble? What do we know about her? Maybe she killed her husband on purpose and she just wants us to help her hide the body. You ever thought of that? She sent all of us those cards, bringing up all that stuff, to lure us here? That seems pretty manipulative and vindictive to me, so sorry if I'm a little skeptical of anything that has to do with her. You don't even know her."

"Come on, Grace. You know Blakely."

"Do I?" I raised my eyebrows at her. "Do you? Have you been in touch?" She shook her head and mumbled no. "Yeah, me neither. And I don't know what you've been doing these last two decades, but I've been doing quite a bit of changing. I'm not anywhere near the person I used to be then, and thankfully, for me, that's a good thing. But that girl I was? She's gone. So that's how I know that Blakely could be anyone now. Because guess what?" I gave her a long dramatic pause so she wouldn't miss my point. "I am too."

"I think there's a part of us that never changes, no matter how old we get. The essence of who we are—our soul—never changes."

"You're saying we've seen each other's souls?"

"Yes."

I snorted. "I'm not listening to another second of that. You can save that shit to post on Instagram."

Meg grabbed my arm to stop my frenzied packing. "I understand that you're upset."

"Upset?!" I shrieked. "Of course I'm upset. Blakely just implicated me for a second murder. Two!" I held up two fingers in her face. I shook my head. "I can't even believe this. I never should've come."

"She didn't implicate us in anything. That's not what this is about. She doesn't even want to give us any details unless we want them. That's what she just said after you left. She's actually really worried about getting us in trouble and doesn't want us to do anything we're not comfortable with."

"She said that because I was pissed, and she was backpedaling, but I bet she planned on giving us all the gory details before." I turned on my heels and stomped into the bathroom across the hallway. She followed, shutting the door behind us, but I didn't care if Blakely heard me. Besides, weren't there cameras in every room anyway?

"We don't know what she did or what happened," Meg said, sticking to her story. She sounded just like she had that summer. I couldn't take another minute.

I started tossing all my toiletries back into the bag. I'd only washed my face and freshened up before I went to meet them, but the bathroom looked like a team of dancers had gotten ready in it. Stuff was everywhere. Why was I always such a slob? I talked while I packed. "You can't be that ignorant or naive, Meg. It doesn't matter. We know someone was murdered."

"But we don't really know anything. Not really. Just that she said she did it, but . . ." She shrugged. Her eyes were innocent and big in the mirror as she watched me.

This time I laughed. "Now you're just pulling at strings. Silly, ridiculous strings." I patted her patronizingly on the shoulder. "For being so smart, you're acting pretty dumb at the moment. You know exactly what she did." I pushed past her.

"So, you're just going to leave?" she asked, like she couldn't believe it.

"Yes." I shook my head definitively, so she wouldn't miss there was no mistaking that was exactly what I was doing. I should've done it twenty-six years ago.

"But how can you just leave her when she needs us the most? When we promised to be there for each other? We promised, Grace." She paused, giving me a deep, imploring look.

"Oh my God, Meg. I don't need you to throw that in my face too. We were teenagers. Just kids. I already told you, we don't even know each other anymore. And maybe we never did. We always said camp let us be our truest self. The one place where we could let our guards down and just be ourselves. But you know what? Camp might've been the fakest we ever were."

Her face crumpled. "Don't say that. Don't ruin what it was for us just because you're mad. We were our most authentic selves. That's what made Pendleton so special."

"Really? Then how come you never told us you liked girls?"

She backed up like I'd slapped her. And I'll admit, it was a pretty low blow, but guess what? It was the truth. We weren't safe enough for her to tell us who she really was. Yes, it had been nothing like it was right now. Coming out could cost you everything, even your life. But we were supposed to be her closest friends. You trust your best friends with your life. At least you should. Wasn't that what we promised too?

Her lower lip trembled. But not because she was sad. Because she was furious. Meg always cried when she was mad. "Fuck you, Grace." She took a step closer to me. "You think you're better than all of us now because you have millions of people following you on Instagram? Like that makes you somebody?" She sneered at me. "You think any of those people actually care about you? How many real friends do you have? When's the last time you were in a relationship? Like a real relationship? You think you're successful because you've figured out how to take your clothes off for the camera?"

She was just trying to hurt me back. I reached for her, but she wouldn't let me touch her. "Look, I know I shouldn't have said that, but it's the truth and you know it. If you'd really felt safe and comfortable with us, then you would've told us who you really were. But you didn't. Because we weren't safe. And you knew you couldn't trust us." I stood there, gazing into her eyes. "You can't trust Blakely. You know that as well as I do. And this? This stunt that she just pulled? That only proves my point more. Now move out of the way, because I'm getting out of here."

# CHAPTER TWENTY-SIX
## *NOW*

## MEG

This time I let Grace go. I didn't follow her. I walked across the hallway and into my room rather than going back outside to join Thera and Blakely. I couldn't face them yet. I slowly sank onto the bed. Still stunned with everything that had happened in the last ten minutes. There were so many things I'd been prepared for this weekend. So many conversations I thought we might have, but I'd never seen this one coming. Not in a million years.

I wanted to be mad at Grace for throwing that in my face, but she wasn't wrong. I couldn't tell them who I really was. It's why I'd followed Blakely the way I had. I couldn't risk doing anything that would make me stand out from my friends. Nothing that would draw attention to my sexuality or make anyone think I was gay. That was my biggest concern. It was one of the reasons things with Mr. Crosby were so confusing. Part of me had wanted him to like me. I liked his attention, even though there was nothing sexual about it. All of it was weird and twisted. Fraught with so many raging hormones and constantly changing emotions that made it almost impossible to think clearly about anything that happened, especially that fateful afternoon in his office when Regina attacked him.

Would I ever know for sure what happened in there? I'd replayed the scene so many times. But everything was so twisted and distorted. That's what happened when other people put their hands in your mind and moved things around. Add on that I was so young—we all were—and impressionable, and I couldn't say anything for sure. Not anymore. Especially not after all this time had passed. Not when I'd spent over twenty years not thinking about it.

All I knew was that Mr. Crosby was already there when we went inside the office so Blakely could apologize to him and say her good-byes. She'd been so desperate to do it. At first, I didn't believe her when she said he was on campus. I thought the same thing then that I did now—how could anyone let him do that? It was appalling that they'd let him step foot on the campus again given the charges they filed against him. They said he was there to clean out his office after he'd officially been fired, but was there really anything in there that he needed that somebody else couldn't have picked up for him? They did everything wrong back in those days, especially when it came to sexual assault and teenagers.

We'd run down to the office as fast as we could. I clearly remembered that. Blakely and I got there first. Way ahead of Thera and Grace. I'd run so fast I could barely breathe and almost dry heaved at the door.

"Watch for me! Don't let anyone know I'm in here with him," Blakely whispered frantically. She didn't even bother turning around to see if I was on board with the plan. Just barged her way inside the building and took off for his office before I could say or do anything.

One minute I was standing there, struggling to breathe, and the next minute there were those awful screams.

I ran in as soon as I heard them, abandoning my post immediately. Regina was attacking Mr. Crosby with the knife, and Blakely was doing her best to pull her off him.

I'd thought Blakely was the one that needed my help. What if I'd had it wrong all along? Was it possible Blakely had been the one to kill Mr. Crosby? That Regina had shown up at the same time and was fending Blakely off? But I'd seen it with my own eyes. I'd watched Regina mutilate him. But could Blakely have started it? Did it really matter if she had? My memory was so fuzzy. All the corners frayed.

I shook my head at myself. Grace had just gotten under my skin. Made me doubt myself and my friends all over again. Grace might've changed a lot in the last twenty years, but her mistrust of people hadn't. There'd been something off with her that summer, and I'd asked her what was wrong multiple times, but she always just said everything was fine. It wasn't until my mom brought her up in one of our phone conversations that I'd started putting the pieces together.

Grace's mom reached out to mine because she was worried that Grace hadn't contacted her all summer. My mom was immediately worried too. She knew how close the two of them were, so she'd asked me about it, but I had no clue Grace had even been ignoring her mother. My mom explained that two weeks before camp, Grace had discovered her mom having an affair with her twenty-five-year-old yoga instructor. And by discovered, she'd actually caught them kissing.

The news hit me hard. Same as it'd done to my mom. I could hear it in her voice. The Howards were the perfect nuclear family we measured ourselves against. So many emotions pummeled me—disbelief, denial, anger, rage, hurt, betrayal, and then a deep overwhelming sadness that made my knees weak. If their perfect family could fracture, what hope did it give the rest of us? I couldn't imagine what it must feel like for Grace, especially when her mom was her best friend and biggest cheerleader.

I always felt bad for Grace because of her metabolic disorder. Even though she never talked about it, being overweight really bothered her. And she might have laughed when people teased her and poked fun at herself, but I recognized the unfazed face she put on. The same one I had when people picked on me and said I smelled. You pretended it didn't bother you, even though you wanted to die on the inside. Her parents, but especially her mom, had always been so amazing and supportive of her through all of it. I'd tried to talk to Grace about what happened once, shortly after I found out.

"Your mom called my mom and said she really wants you to call her or write her back. She's really worried about you and just wants to know if you're okay." I treaded water next to her while we waited for Blakely and Thera to make it back out to us with the raft they'd gone to shore to get.

Grace narrowed her eyes to slits. "Did she tell you what she did?"

I nodded. "I'm so sorry, Grace." I would've given her a hug if we hadn't been in the water.

"Then you understand why I'm not talking to her." She dove underneath the water before I could respond. She swam almost to shore without coming up for breath. I never tried bringing it up again. I hadn't known what to say anyway, so if she didn't want to talk about it, I was more than happy to ignore it too.

When the person you trusted and relied on the most in the world turned out to be someone else, you never looked at the world in the same way again. Of course Grace trusted nobody, especially Blakely, but she was right—we weren't teenagers anymore, and we had to think for ourselves, especially about something this important. I couldn't let Grace or Thera influence what I thought about Blakely. We didn't have to make decisions as a group. That's what Grace had said, too, and she was right. We were independent women who could make decisions for ourselves, and I needed to decide what I wanted to do. How I felt about all this.

# REGINA

I lost my husband in the most brutal way, and it's nobody's fault but my own. I utterly annihilated my life. That makes it harder some days. And then there are my children. I lost Jared just once, but I lose them over and over again. That's much worse. Each time I try to reach out, they reject me. They're grown men with lives of their own, and neither of them want me in them. I've never stopped trying, though, and I never will.

I wrote letters to them every week from prison for over a decade. My sister-in-law was their legal guardian, and she sent them back unopened every time. But I never quit sending them, even if it wasn't as often as the years passed into their adulthood. They're stored in boxes in my mom's basement over on Seventh Street. Maybe someday they'll read them. They also get Christmas and birthday cards from me, and those aren't returned, so there's still hope. I know there is.

It's one thing for them not to know me, but I want them to know their father. Not that Jared's family doesn't love them to pieces and take great care of them. They do. Or talk about Jared with them all the time. They do that too. It's just that there are things I can tell them about their father that nobody else knows. Little things about him. How he was with them. All the things he talked about and wanted them to know. The way his face lit up when he saw them for the first time every morning.

Jaylen and Jordan also need to know they were created in the most glorious of love stories, because that's the part nobody ever talks about with them. People liked believing we were this troubled and disturbed couple, but we weren't. We were always wildly in love with each other and our family. Our love was the type movies are made of and books are written about. But the most important thing I wanted them to know?

They might have the world's worst mother, but they had the world's best father.

They're still so young, so they still have a lot of growing up to do. And maybe someday they'll give me a chance to know them for real. Until then, I just keep sending the letters. I have secret accounts on social media to see what's going on in their lives because they blocked my personal ones.

I get it, and I'm not even mad at them.

I killed their dad.

I wasn't like some other women, who stood by their man after they'd been accused of a terrible crime, or mothers who chose to protect their husband over their children. From the moment the story broke, I believed those girls, because that's what you do with child abuse victims. I believed they were right. That Jared was guilty of everything they accused him of.

And I wanted him dead.

My attorney insisted on using the insanity defense. That I wasn't in my right mind. Didn't know the consequences of my actions because they were all intertwined with what happened to me as a kid. And yes, my memory got all jumbled with then and now, but I always knew what I was doing—exactly what I was doing—and I would've done more if I could've. Jared deserved to suffer. Death was too easy an out, but I had to kill him because it was the only way to stop him from hurting another child. Because people like him? Ones that sexually abuse young girls who look up to them as heroes? They don't ever get better. They don't ever change. So, I wanted to make sure he'd never hurt anyone else. That was the only way, and I wasn't sorry.

Up until the point I started suspecting he might not have done it. Then, everything shifted.

# CHAPTER TWENTY-SEVEN
## *NOW*

### THERA

I knocked on the door, even though Blakely had asked to be left alone when she went upstairs. But I couldn't let her be by herself. Not when she was so upset, and especially not after everything she'd just told us. She sat on the bed, facing the window. Her back toward me. Her shoulders shook, like she was sobbing and trying to be quiet.

Sadness flooded me. Blakely had always been so lost. It wasn't that she'd grown up without a mother, even though she had. She'd grown up without a dad too. That was the worst part. It was the thing that damaged her the most. I'd always thought that, but she never talked about that part, so I didn't force her. I couldn't imagine what it must've been like growing up in that house.

I sat next to her on the bed and put my arm around her. She fell into my arms weeping, and I held her while she cried. I'd been to her house a few times when we were kids. My dad made sure to send me there a couple of times a year after we'd met at camp. The first time we drove up to their home, my dad couldn't hide how impressed he was with their money. Their house was so big it'd been officially labeled an estate. Her backyard was as big as the park I played in as a kid. Part of him just always felt like he wasn't enough, but he'd always been perfect to me. Still was.

Her house had reminded me of Rapunzel because it was so huge and there was a private wing upstairs reserved especially for Blakely. Rapunzel was one of my favorite stories. But all I kept wondering the entire time I was there was why two people needed such a big house. There were enough bathrooms for them each to have at least three. And what did you need seven bedrooms for when you only had two people? Blakely always wanted to play hide-and-seek in that great big ole house, and it would literally take hours, even though it was just us playing. There was just so much space to hide in. Once, it took her so long to find me in one of the bedrooms that I fell asleep in the closet.

I've never forgotten the time she showed me the basement. She took me through the kitchen and showed me the maid's quarters first. Then, she led me through a small door in the back of the pantry to a concrete basement underneath their laundry room. Dark, cold, and dingy. Such a dramatic difference from the bright sparkling white of the rest of the house. Each stair creaked as we walked down.

"This is where I come to play by myself," she said, leading the way in front of me into the pitch black. "I've never brought anyone down here before. You're the first."

I laughed nervously and forced myself to keep moving. She flicked on the light when we got to the bottom of the stairs, and that's when I saw them. Her dolls. Well, not her dolls, exactly. Only the heads. She'd ripped their bodies off, and those lay in a heap over in the corner. Their heads dangled from string tied around their necks, stretched from one end of the basement to the other. All their hair had been cut off too. Some of them were grossly disfigured. Stabbed with scissors or marked with black Sharpie.

"No one can hear us when we play down here," she said with a wicked grin. "That's why I like coming down here."

But I refused to go down there again. It was too creepy for me, and I didn't like to play in the dark. It scared me.

Blakely's sobs brought me back to the present moment. She was still pretty worked up. "Thank you, Thera. Thanks so much for being here for me. You don't know what it's been like," she sniffled, wiping her nose on the back of her long sleeve. "Nobody does . . ."

"How old were you when you married Phillip?" I asked. She'd done her best to fill us in on the story, but it was so traumatic, most of it had come out in fragmented pieces.

"Nineteen. Exactly two years from our last summer together. I was just a baby then." She started crying again. "I didn't have a choice. I don't care what anyone else thinks, but they don't know what it's like growing up in a family like mine. And I was a child, so I had no options. No money. No resources. I was trapped. Sorry, I can't help but defend myself because I know everyone's judging me. I didn't expect those reactions."

"Grace did come at you rather hard."

Blakely snorted. "You think? And from her? I mean, come on. Who is she to judge about anyone else's life? I'm sorry. Maybe if I took my clothes off and flashed my boobs in front of the camera, I'd be a millionaire too." She slapped her hand over her mouth after she'd said it. "I'm sorry. I didn't mean that. I'm just angry."

"Grace does porn?" I had no idea. I guess that explained how she drove a Mercedes. Was I the only one that hadn't looked the girls up on the way here? I just hadn't. I was weird. One of those people that hated social media and didn't use it. Still to this day. No matter how real you pretended to be or said you were, it was all fake. I'd lived through Myspace and Facebook without ever creating a profile, so it seemed pointless to get on Instagram or TikTok now.

Blakely nodded, trying hard not to smile, but I could tell she wanted to. She loved sharing any juicy gossip. Always had. "I was totally shocked too. She's one of the top-earning OnlyFans accounts in the entire country."

"Wow," I said. I couldn't imagine taking my clothes off or showing any part of myself in front of the camera. I didn't even like taking pictures. "I'm sorry she stormed off. I think Meg's talking to her and seeing if she can get her to stay."

Blakely shrugged. "I don't really blame her for being mad or leaving. It was a big risk getting all of you here and telling you the way I did. It seemed like such a good idea at the time. Like I'd finally figured a way out, you know? It all made sense in my head, but then when you were all here . . . I don't know. Suddenly, it made me doubt everything, even myself."

I didn't know what to say to that. Blakely had always said she was a killer. That's how she liked to introduce herself at camp when we were really young. Whenever we got matched with our counselor, the first thing they made us do was go around the room and introduce ourselves. Blakely always said the same thing.

"I'm Blakely, and I'm a killer." She'd giggle as they looked back at her with horrified expressions. None of them ever knew what to say after that. She loved shocking people. Anything to throw them off balance. She'd give them a few more seconds to squirm before saying the next part, "Really, I'm a killer. That's the first thing I did when I was born—killed my mom. Daddy keeps saying it's not my fault, but that makes no sense when she literally died squeezing me out of her vagina. She bled out on the table."

Every year when it came to be her turn, I'd cringe and hope she wouldn't say it. She finally stopped the summer we turned twelve. She was more interested in the attention and responses from the boys than she was in the counselors. Thankfully, the boys were all grossed out by childbirth, and they definitely didn't want to hear anyone say the word *vagina*.

Had she spoken it enough times over her life to make it true? Created a self-fulfilling prophecy? That's what I said to the psychic clients I worked with who considered me their spiritual adviser. I stressed how we had to be so selective with the words we used because our words have power. But I didn't really believe it. I said lots of things to my clients that I didn't believe, though. I'd pretty much say anything to make someone feel better about themselves.

"How'd you do it?" I asked her, even though earlier she'd said she didn't want to tell us specifics. Said the less we knew, the better. But that wasn't going to work with me. She had to tell me.

She leaned in closer. "You really want to know?"

I nodded. Of course I wanted to know. Human behavior fascinated me. She knew that.

"It was so easy." She let out a small giggle, almost like she'd sounded when we were little and she was telling me all her secrets. "I'm sorry, I know I shouldn't laugh. That's so terrible. It's not funny, but I'd just been terrified of Phillip for so long. Like totally out-of-my-mind scared. You have no idea what that's like. Living in constant fear. Every single day. All the time." Her eyes clouded at the mention of it, but she quickly pushed the feelings aside. She was good at that. Almost as good as I was. "And then, when I finally did it?" She smiled. "It was just so easy. I couldn't believe how easy it was to get rid of him. All I kept thinking that night while I hid in the closet was how I should've done it years ago."

"Yeah, but what exactly did you do? I want details."

She punched my arm. "Psycho."

I shook my head. "I just want to know what I'm getting myself into."

"Mm-hmm," she said with a teasing smile. "Well, if you must know, I did him just like he did to my sweet Camille." She grabbed my hand and leaned in closer. She smelled like sweat and expensive wine. "He didn't give me any kind of access to medications either. Nothing. I couldn't even take a Tylenol without him giving it to me like I was a child, but he messed up with the rat poisoning. He just left the rest of it in the garage sitting next to where the gardener keeps the gas for the lawn mower, and I found it when I had to let the gardener in there because he forgot his keys." She giggled again. She couldn't help herself. I didn't miss the irony in it, and part of me wanted to laugh too. "I gave it to him in his favorite meat loaf—his grandmother's recipe. As soon as I saw it on the menu for that week, I knew it was my chance, so I took it. The meat loaf was perfect because I could cook the powder right into it and didn't have to worry about him trying to make me eat it with him, like he did with practically everything else. But he doesn't allow me to eat red meat anymore, so I took that as another sign. Anyway, at first, I thought it hadn't worked. He was acting totally normal after dinner, and then, right before he went to bed, he started feeling sick and said he threw up in the shower. I was so crushed." Her face fell. Probably just like it'd done that night. "I could've cried right on the spot because I just figured he'd gotten all of it out of his system by puking. It'd taken me so long to prepare, and then it was just over. It'd gotten my hopes up for the first time in a long time, and it just came crashing down. But then . . ." Her grin was back. "Then, he started shaking and seizing once we got in the bed. Probably like five minutes after we laid down."

"Oh my God, really? What'd you do?" I scooted closer to her. Grabbed her hand for this part. I'd always wanted to be inside a murderer's brain.

"I jumped out of bed super fast. You would've thought there was a fire, how quick I got out of that bed." Her voice was pressured and hurried, like she was reliving it as she told it. "I didn't even look at him. Didn't dare go near him. I was too afraid he might try to grab me or say something to get me to help him, you know, and I couldn't risk chickening out. So, I just scooped up my babies and ran into the closet. I slammed the door and put on my headphones." She mimicked the action, holding her hands over her ears, much like I was sure she'd done that night. "I turned the volume up as loud as it would go and stayed in there for hours. Just holding my babies and rocking. I don't know how long it took for him to actually die. Maybe it was minutes. It could've been hours, but when I came out of the closet, he was dead." She didn't look sad or remorseful, but I didn't blame her. Not like some other people might, but I've never been like other people. He sounded like a terrible man who'd treated her even worse. Bad people should be punished. We didn't do it often enough.

"What'd you listen to?" I asked. Her face was finally relaxed. She'd stopped crying. My unconditional love had brought her back from the darkness. Allowed her to spill her secrets and get the relief that comes from the truth-telling. Gave me the high from being the one to provide the release.

She was staring back at me with a confused expression. "What do you mean?"

"Like when he was dying and you were in the closet, what'd you listen to?"

She shoved me back on the bed, and I toppled onto my side. "Oh my God, you really are sick, Thera!"

I laughed like it wasn't a big deal, but I really wanted to know.

# CHAPTER TWENTY-EIGHT
## *NOW*

### MEG

I knocked on Blakely's door in the same way I'd knocked on Grace's earlier tonight. I wasn't surprised to find Thera inside with her. They were cuddled up on the bed together. Blakely had clearly been crying. Crumpled-up tissue surrounded her. Thera patted the bed, inviting me to join them.

Blakely turned to me. Eyes swollen and red. Face blotchy. All her makeup washed off. She looked like the Blakely I used to know, and for a second, it took my breath away. Especially with Thera sitting next to her, the way she was. "Did Grace leave?"

I nodded. "I tried getting her to stay, but her mind was made up."

"It's okay," she said. "I don't blame her."

But I knew it hurt. Whatever was going on. Whatever happened, she needed us.

"She's right, you know. I never should've done this. I shouldn't have brought all of you into this." Blakely shook her head. Completely dejected. She wrung her hands together on her lap. "I just didn't know what else to do. I really didn't. I meant what I said earlier, Meg. If I'd reached out and asked all of you to come, it never would've happened.

We would've all agreed to meet. Said how much we missed each other, but you know it wouldn't have happened."

I didn't want her to be right, but she was. If she'd reached out and asked us to get together, I probably would've said no. I definitely wouldn't have cleared everything off my schedule and gotten on the first plane headed to Atlanta. Most likely we would've reconnected and gone back and forth about it a bunch of times but never actually done it.

I put my hand on her back. She was sweating and trembling. I'd never seen her like this. Not once. She prided herself on always being put together. My heart went out to her. I couldn't help it. Her pain was literally oozing from her body.

"Is he here? Like still in the house?" It was a strange question to ask, but I had to know if I was spending the night with a dead body. Everything about this was so unsettling.

She shook her head. "He's in the garage." She said it like she was referring to extra wine.

"No one's noticed that he's missing?" I asked next. Thera nodded her head in agreement, like it was a good question and she wanted to know the answer too.

"Nope." She shook her head again. "Because I've been pretending to be him ever since I did it. For nine days now. God, I can't believe it's been nine days already."

"What have you been doing?" Thera asked. She was staring at Blakely with the same expression she used to get when she was tackling a tough math problem during Olympics week.

"I emailed all his clients and staff from his work account that he was out sick with the flu so he'd be working from home for the next week and doing his best to stay on top of things. I've been texting and calling myself from his phone so it looks like we've been communicating this whole time too. We've even had some FaceTime dates." She giggled at that. She couldn't help herself. "I've answered all his texts from his family and friends. My dad." She rolled her eyes and kept going. "Me and his assistant have been communicating multiple times a day like nothing's wrong, and I can tell you right now, she doesn't suspect a thing. She totally thinks I'm him. I've been doing everything from his phone, obviously. His computer. All his things. You know what else I've even been doing?" She flipped her hair over her shoulders and glanced at each of us. A smile pulling at the corner of her mouth. "Messaging with all his little mistresses on the apps too. I've been staying current with all them. Even sending pics. I'm telling you, nobody has any idea he's missing." She said it like she was proud of herself.

He wasn't missing—he was dead.

And I'd decided just like Grace that I didn't want to know how she'd killed him. I had no idea what kind of help she wanted from us or if I was even going to agree to be a part of it, but no matter what—there would be the risk of Blakely getting caught. If she got busted and they asked me about what happened, then I wouldn't have any information to give them. I wouldn't be pretending to be ignorant—I really would be.

"What are you going to do now?" Thera's voice was hesitant and unsure, but there was no doubt in my mind that she would help Blakely no matter how Blakely answered the question.

"See, that's the thing. It's not like I'm trying to stay in this life. This life isn't even mine, and I'm not sure what my dad is going to do when he finds out Phillip's gone." She was trying to sound brave, but the fear had returned to her face. "It's not just about getting away from Phillip. It's getting away from my dad, too, so that's what I'm trying to do. Disappear . . ."

"And just how do you plan to do that?" I asked.

"It's not just pretending to be Phillip that's important. Everything I do is still being monitored through all of his devices, so I've made sure not to veer a single inch from my normal routine either. I haven't done anything out of the ordinary. I'm assuming once the detectives have all his stuff—which at some point they will, even if it's just through the cloud—then they'll see exactly what I've been doing in the weeks leading up to his disappearance." She put *disappearance* in air quotes.

"They're going to know all of my steps, just like Phillip always did, which is why I have to be so careful and deliberate with them. Also, why I need you . . ."

And then she looked at us. The same look she used to give us at camp when she was coming up with one of her plans. Most of the time I had no idea what she was plotting because my brain just didn't work like hers and she was way too impulsive for me. This time wasn't any different. She kept staring at us like we were automatically supposed to know what she was thinking.

"I don't understand," Thera said, and I quickly nodded my head in agreement.

"Me either," I said.

Blakely laughed, but we weren't kidding. At least I wasn't. Where'd we fit in all this? She'd never actually said what she needed our help with. She got up from the bed and walked to the closet, taking a minute to gather herself. I quickly looked at Thera, and she shrugged. Blakely turned back around.

"Basically, I'm just trying to scatter as many pieces of the puzzle as possible to give myself the best chance of getting free and starting a new life. I'm going to wait for like another week and just keep doing what I've been doing—pretending to be Phillip and sticking to my usual routines. Phillip is supposed to be going on a business trip to Chicago the following weekend. I'm going to drive him to the airport to drop him off like I always do, except this time the only thing I'll be dropping off is his phone. I'm going to leave it in the flowerpot in the lobby. That way when they first start searching for him and retracing his steps, that's where it'll ping." She paused, making sure we were following her before continuing. "I'll wait until Monday to call my dad in a panic that Phillip hasn't returned home from his trip. And see, that's the thing about my dad. He's going to look into things himself first before calling the police. Because the other thing I found when I finally broke into Phillip's computer was that his business was tanking. He's been stealing money from my father." She shook her head with an evil glimmer in her eye. "That's not going to go well with my dad, and I'm willing to bet that my dad will think Phillip is running away from him. He already knows that I don't have access to any of my funds, so he's going to give me money until we figure out what's happening, especially if I get all frantic and sound like I'm going to go to the police. After that—while he's busy distracted with Phillip—I'm going to slowly disappear. I'll do the same thing with my dad that I pretended to do with Phillip. I'll keep communicating with everyone for a while, so they still think I'm here, but I'll already be somewhere else. Hopefully before they have any clue I'm gone. Eventually, I'll just stop communicating entirely."

Thera stood and took Blakely's hand. "You still haven't told us how we can help you."

Glad I wasn't the only one who noticed she'd still bypassed our part.

"I need you to help me get rid of the body," Blakely said, and even though it's what I'd been expecting and waiting for, hearing her say it out loud still felt incredibly strange and unreal.

Thera stiffened. "If the body is in the garage, then why not just leave it there?"

"Because then they'll know Phillip was murdered, and that will change everything. They'll treat the case totally different. They need to think he's missing. They can't think he's dead. The point is to distract them with Phillip to give me long enough time to get away. Far enough where I can start over completely fresh and they can never find me. Not the police or my dad. Not to mention my mother-in-law. My mother-in-law would never stop trying to come after me if she thought I killed her son. I'd be running from her for the rest of my life, and I don't want to do that either. For the first time ever in my life, I just want to be free. Do you know what it's like to be owned by someone else your whole life?" She looked into each of our eyes imploringly, and I'd never felt more privileged than I did in that moment. Because I might not have grown up rich, but I'd always grown up loved.

Blakely continued. "I'm going to leave a note when I go too. Throw them off even more. Basically sounding like a distraught and destroyed housewife who's just found out her husband of twenty years has been cheating on her and also has another sexual harassment suit filed against him from one of his former employees too. By the way—all those things are true. But anyway, I'll talk about not being able to handle any more and feeling like a total failure to my family and the company. I'll make it super sad and sappy. Tug at all the heartstrings and ask them to give me my space while I try to figure things out." She shrugged. "I'm just hoping they never find out what happened to either of us."

I could tell Thera was thinking hard. So was I. It felt just like the moral-dilemma game we used to play when we were kids. Except this time it was real. We used to play the game late at night, long after lights-out—what we'd do in different scenarios, and they inevitably led to murder. Some version of: What would you do if your friend murdered someone and needed your help? It depended on the reason. That'd been my answer when I was twelve, and it was still the same answer.

Blakely walked over to the bed and knelt in front of us. She took each of our hands. "Please. I want you to know that you don't have to decide anything right this minute. I want you to take some time and really think about it. This is a really big decision. A huge ask. I understand that. So, if you can't do it, I'm still going to love you just as much as I always did. Nothing is going to change that. I'm just so happy that you came . . . and that you stayed," she said, giving each of us a huge hug.

There was no missing the fact that Grace hadn't stayed. She was probably halfway back to Miami by now. She'd looked so different from who she used to be. Out of all of us, she's the one that had changed the most. Her transformation might've started that summer.

"How does it feel?" I asked. Being a murderer. That's what I was asking. What I wanted to know. The question I'd been holding back.

"I know I'm supposed to feel bad, and part of me still can't believe I did it. That I was capable of that . . . but I don't know." She shook her head, looking wasted and depleted, like someone who'd been up for days.

"After what he did to my baby Camille, I just feel vindicated and . . . safe. Finally safe. And I'm not sure I've ever felt safe in my entire life." Her eyes filled with tears, and she looked up at me. "I know you must think I'm a terrible person for what I did to Mr. Crosby when we were kids, but I'm not. I swear I'm not. I know I did all kinds of messed-up things for attention back then." She took my hand again, squeezing it tight while she went on. Thera put her hand on her back. "I hurt people all the time without even thinking, but it's just because I was in so much pain myself, and I was so young, Meg. I didn't even know how to give words to what I was feeling. So, I just acted out. And that last summer? What we did to Jared?" She shook her head at herself. "I mean, what *I* did to Jared. All of you were just following my lead. I know that." Her eyes hadn't left mine. "And I know it was wrong, Meg. It was wrong, and I'm so sorry I put you through that." She glanced at Thera. "You too. I mean it. I really am sorry for what I did to that poor man and his family."

The immediate rush of relief throughout my entire body felt better than any drug I'd ever done.

There.

The secret was out. In the air, where it could breathe. Where it could finally have a life of its own instead of eating away at my insides and destroying my chances of ever being truly free. Finally. After all this time. She'd taken responsibility. This was why I'd come. This was what I'd needed to hear for twenty-six years. I hadn't realized how badly I still needed to. It was like this part of my soul had been twisted up inside me and it had finally uncoiled and released. I let out a deep sigh and put my hand on Blakely's back.

I'd come here to tell her no. That I was incredibly sorry for what happened to her and how she'd been treated, but I couldn't help her with whatever she'd done to her husband. It was too much to ask, and I had too much to lose. But she had nobody. She was truly alone in the world, and I couldn't imagine what that was like for her. How could she not be damaged?

Grace would think I was a fool. Claire would probably agree with her. But I promised to be there for Blakely—for all of them, when they needed me—and I always kept my promises, especially when someone was hurting and in trouble. Now that she'd admitted her mistake, I felt like I could trust her again. Not completely and not like I had before, but it was enough.

I squeezed her hand. "Tell me everything you need, hon. I'm here for you."

# CHAPTER TWENTY-NINE

## *THEN*

## BLAKELY

I frantically scrubbed the blood off my hands, desperately trying to clean it, but it wasn't coming off. Why wasn't it coming off? I smacked the soap dispenser, trying to get more. Barely anything came out.

"Dammit!" I shoved my hands underneath the faucet again. Water sprayed everywhere. Red covered the sink. Swirled down the drain.

"Hurry up, Blakely. Hurry up!" Meg yelled, jumping up and down beside me, slapping my back like I was a horse and it'd make me go faster. The other sink was stopped up, and she couldn't use it. She was covered in blood too. It was all over her shirt.

Grace was holding on tight to Thera. She had it on her face. Blood-splattered freckles.

"We have to go back there! We have to save him!" Thera screamed like she'd been doing ever since we left the athletic building. We had to drag her with us, pulling her along and forcing her to run, as we plowed through the trees, blindly racing back here. Thera kept tripping and falling, skinning her elbows, her knees. They were bleeding too. There was so much blood. How was there so much blood?

"He's gone. You can't save him," Grace shouted at her, trying to get her to calm down like she'd been doing for the last ten minutes, but it wasn't working. She was hysterical. Words didn't reach her.

"Thera, shut up!" I called without looking around, scrubbing my skin as hard and as fast as I could. "We can't go back there. What if they think we did it? That we had something to do with it? Absolutely not. No." I shook my head. My skin was raw and burning now.

"But we did. This is all our fault. What if she killed him because of us? Because of what we said? We have to tell them. We have to help her. What about the babies? He has two babies. Oh my God, we killed a man with two babies." She covered her hand over her mouth while she wailed. "He was a dad, you guys. A father."

I whipped around and pushed Grace off her. I grabbed Thera's shirt and pulled her close to me, just like she'd done to Clint when he stole the picture a few days ago. Tears streamed down her face. Snot bubbled from her nose. "We didn't kill anyone, Thera. You understand me? That crazy woman killed Jared, not us. We had nothing to do with that."

"Yes, we did. How can you say that?" she cried. "We had everything to do with that. Everything."

I shook my head ferociously at her. "That woman is a crazy psycho."

Meg grabbed the paper towels, running them under the water, and started frantically wiping at her face in the mirror. But it only made the splatters worse. Grace took her shirt off and tried using it to help her while Thera kept screaming in my face. Her breath thick with fear.

"We have to tell them what happened. They have to know what we did."

"We didn't do anything!"

"Are you kidding me? We destroyed a man's life! We did this!" She frantically pointed behind us, where the sound of sirens wailed in our ears, growing louder by the second. She pulled herself away from me. "Ohmigod, Blakely, we killed someone."

"We didn't kill anyone! Stop saying that! *Stop saying that!*" She was screaming so loud someone was going to hear her. Nobody knew we were in here. They still didn't know we were the ones to call 911.

"Shut up, Thera! Just shut up!" Meg hissed from beside me. We locked eyes. She was thinking the same thing. She wasn't stupid. She knew exactly what we had to lose. Same as me. Something like this might ruin us, and we were too young to have our lives ruined.

Thera wouldn't stop screaming. She pushed me aside and grabbed the door like she was going to leave, and I grabbed her again, snapping her back. "What are you doing?"

She whipped around. Her eyes were lit. "I'm going down there. We have to help. We have to do something."

I shook my head. Cupped her face in my hands. "It's over. He's gone. There's nothing to do, Thera. We can't save him."

"But we have to tell them. We have to tell them what we did," she cried. She wouldn't stop saying it. Screaming it louder and louder every time.

Suddenly, there was the sound of people outside the bathroom. Someone was coming. They were going to know we were in here. Thera needed to be quiet. She needed to shut up.

"Be quiet. Stop screaming." I dropped my voice low.

"We—"

I didn't know Meg was behind me until her hand connected with Thera's face. A sharp smack right across her cheek. It stunned Thera into silence immediately. She raised her hand to her face.

"They're coming inside! They're coming inside. We have to hide," Grace whisper yelled and motioned for us to hurry into the back stall around the corner.

I held on to Thera and dragged her into the stall, just like we'd dragged her through the woods. We crammed ourselves in with Meg and Grace as the bathroom door opened. Thera and I were on top of the toilet. Meg and Grace plastered against the back wall, trying to hide their feet. I clamped my hand over Thera's mouth in case she started screaming again. Nobody breathed. Nobody moved. Grace's heart thumped against my back.

The footsteps made their way into the bathroom. I eyed Meg again. Her eyes were wide with the same fear in them as mine. There was blood all over the sink. Everywhere. What were they going to think? I waited for the scream to follow at the sight of it, but there was nothing. Just the sound of the running water followed by the sound of them pulling out a paper towel from the holder. They didn't use the restroom. It was another few seconds, and then they were gone. As quick as they'd come.

We all released our breath at once. Collapsing and melting with relief in the stall. Everyone breathing hard, trying not to panic.

"I don't understand. How'd we pull that off?" Grace shook her head, looking stunned. "Like were they wasted or something? Because who sees that bloodbath in the sink and doesn't totally freak out?"

"Maybe they thought someone had a bloody nose," Thera said softly, finally sounding like herself for the first time since she'd run into Jared's office and witnessed the brutal scene.

"I can't imagine not freaking out over it, either, but we got so lucky," I said, with the adrenaline still pouring through me.

"We didn't get lucky." Meg turned to me with a smile. She gave a long dramatic pause. "I wiped the sink."

"Ohmigod, are you kidding me?!" I threw my arms around her and lifted her off the floor as we squealed. I'd never loved her more than I did at that moment.

# REGINA

Prison gave me lots of time to think. To process what had happened and analyze things. But the one thing it gave me that I'd never had before? Being around criminals.

Real hard criminals like the ones I used to watch on *Dateline* and *48 Hours*. I thought I knew things about life and people before I got locked up, but I'd been naive. Completely misinformed and prejudiced about a lot of things, people, and systems, starting with the other prisoners themselves.

They were the ones that saved me from myself. It all happened by accident.

I started acting "better" so I could get off suicide watch. Lots of women killed themselves in prison. It happened all the time. People always think the leading cause of death in prisons is inmates killing each other. That's not it. It's suicide. Death by suicide is the number one way people die in prison, and I wanted to add my name to that statistic. I had nothing to live for. Nothing. I was fully aware that I'd destroyed everything and everyone in my life.

Fake it until you make it.

That's what I started doing and figured I had to do it long enough to be left alone. Because the ones that die by suicide aren't the ones on suicide watch. That's why I started talking to other inmates. Actually leaving my cell and mingling with the others. The old me would've been terrified. But new me didn't care about dying, so I wasn't scared at all.

Surprisingly, most of them were good people, especially my cell-mate, Yolanda. She was one of the smartest people I'd ever met. Just as smart as those girls at Pendleton, and if she'd ever been given the opportunities they'd had, she probably could've become the first female president or built the world's next computer. But she'd been born to drug-addicted parents that sold her and her siblings to support their habit. Keeping them locked in the kitchen cabinets and fed dog food when they weren't forcing them to turn tricks for their customers. Drugging them into submission with Benadryl. She'd run away when she was thirteen, but there was nowhere to go when you were that young. So that was how she'd ended up on the streets. Also why she was so smart. She'd gotten her first prostitution charge at fourteen, and the charges had been piling on ever since. She'd never actually committed a violent crime. Lots of the women in here hadn't, though. But that's what happened when your skin wasn't white and you lived in oppressive systems conditioned to fail you.

"He didn't do it." That was the first thing Yolanda said after I finally told her my entire story from start to finish. Beginning to end, leaving nothing hidden. Her proclamation had throttled me and planted the first seeds of doubt in my mind.

It felt wrong at first. Incredibly wrong. You always believe the victims. The biggest reason I'd never told anyone that my coach was abusing me was because I was afraid no one would believe me. So, there was no way I was going to do something like that to those girls.

But Yolanda had opened a door that I couldn't close, and once she did, there was no going back. I just had to go through it.

During one of our middle-of-the-night-and-can't-sleep conversations years earlier, I'd told her all about the feeding issues my boys had been born with. Neither of them would eat, and they'd almost been diagnosed with failure to thrive, which was a terrifying diagnosis. Our days were filled with doctors' appointments and specialists to get them to gain weight. They had to be fed every two hours, no matter what. That's why I was so sleep deprived. It didn't matter if Jared took care of the feeding for me. I still woke up automatically, like my body was on its own internal clock attached to theirs. Once I was awake, even if it wasn't my turn, I couldn't relax or fall back to sleep until I knew they had been fed.

I'd told Yolanda how they'd used that in their narrative about me in court. Trying to say that postpartum depression and sleep deprivation were part of the reason I did what I did. But I told Yolanda the truth, just like I'd told my lawyers, even though they'd never wanted to hear it—Jared and I were getting along just fine. We really were, despite what everyone said about us. But that was just because they didn't want to believe something so terrible could happen to people that were happy. Except it was the truth.

The twins' issues were the first real, significant challenges we'd faced as a couple. Up until then, things had gone pretty smoothly, and even though not sleeping was brutal, it brought us together as a team. Made us love each other even more, in a way we'd never had to before.

But that wasn't the important thing Yolanda remembered from the conversation.

"We've got to go over your records," she announced just as we were falling off to sleep.

"What do you mean? I've already showed you everything." One of the first things she'd done after she'd heard my story was help me get all my records from trial. My lawyer hadn't wanted to hand them over, but she made him, spouting off some statute I'd never heard of before. She'd brought them to Bev in Unit A to go over because Bev was almost finished with her law degree at Middleton. She made lots of money consulting on people's cases, but she hadn't given me much hope with mine. "Bev said the prosecution did everything by the book, remember?"

"That's not what I'm talking about." Yolanda shook her head. Jumped down from her bunk to sit next to me on mine. "You know how you told me your babies were so sick when they were born?" I nodded. "And remember how you said you had a huge calendar in the kitchen to keep track of everything? Did you have a smaller version somewhere? Like a planner or something? An app on your phone?" She quickly burst out laughing when she realized what she'd said. There were no apps in 1998. But she'd hit a gold mine.

I'd been one of those people that couldn't live without a day planner before we all had phones. The only way I'd kept anything straight during those days was to keep really detailed notes. I kept diligent records about all the boys' appointments and everything happening with them. I'd never have thought to ask my mom to bring it to me if it hadn't been for Yolanda. My mom brought all of them with on her next visit, and we dove into them as soon as she left.

The one thing immediately clear was how many dates didn't add up. Jared was with me during many of the dates that he was supposed to have been at camp giving private lessons to the girls and abusing them. Jared was as involved a father as he was a husband, so he insisted on going to almost all their appointments with me. He was constantly moving his schedule around to accommodate them. It was all there. Everything in black and white of where he'd been. And most of the time, he'd been with me.

That was the turning point. When I started considering that the victims might be lying.

I'd never believed Jared's stories. I'd never even given him long enough to get them out of his mouth. Every abuser said they didn't do it. And the things they were accusing him of? Nobody ever admitted it. Every single man that's accused of abusing little girls denies it.

But what if he'd been the one telling the truth?

That was the last thing he'd said before he died.

It wasn't *I'm sorry* or even *I love you*. I guess it's hard to tell someone you love them after they've just stabbed you one hundred and seventeen times. Sometimes I still couldn't believe I stabbed him that many times.

When the prosecutors reenacted it during trial, I started flinching on twenty-three. After fifty-one, the judge made her stop. Point taken.

But all the way to the end, that's what Jared said, his last words before he took his final breath, while blood gurgled up from his throat and spilled out of the corners of his mouth—*I didn't do it.*

# CHAPTER THIRTY

## *NOW*

## THERA

I rolled over and looked at my phone to see the time: 3:12. I still hadn't slept. I'd been staring at the ceiling all night. Blakely had laid out the plan. She'd put careful thought into how we could help her get rid of the body. After that, she'd spent the rest of the night crying on and off as she shared stories about what it'd been like growing up with her father and the years she'd spent with Phillip.

I'd already decided I was going to help her before she'd shared more details of her life, but afterward, I was more convinced than ever. It also felt like, for the first time in our entire friendship, I knew who she was. Really knew who she was. Even though I'd been her best friend, there was always this part of herself that she'd kept secret.

"I'm going to help you with whatever you need. I'm here for you," I said when I tucked her into bed the night before, like she was a small child, just like my mom used to do. It dawned on me while I was doing it that she'd lived her entire life without anyone ever tucking her in, and something about that broke my heart for her all over again. It wasn't right. Only reinforced my decision.

"Are you sure, Thera?" She'd looked deep in my eyes. Hers filled with tears.

I nodded at her. "I'm positive. Blood sisters for life, remember?"

That'd made her smile. The kind that went all the way through her eyes and into her soul.

"Okay, but I still want you to think about it tonight, and we can talk about it again in the morning. You can totally change your mind if you want to. There's no pressure." She leaned up and gave me a quick kiss. "I love you, Thera. Thank you for everything you did for me today. I don't know how I ever got so lucky to be friends with someone so good inside."

I'd smiled back at that. The same way I always did when someone said it.

People always thought that I had this strict moral code because it was connected to some kind of God, but that wasn't it at all. Rules created order, and I needed order; otherwise the world didn't make sense to me. Rules made sense. They defined what was right and wrong. That's why I followed them, because if I didn't, I felt like I would fall off the earth. They told me how to behave. Gave me order and structure. It'd been that way since I lost my mom. It was my way of existing and coping in the world—follow the rules. It had nothing to do with God or any sort of spiritual conviction about the morality of right and wrong. Or even being a good person.

We all had our secrets. That's one thing I knew for sure about life. What we looked like and how we represented ourselves on the outside were often two entirely different things. I fully understood how Blakely could function in the world like nothing was wrong while she was being tortured in her own home. There are parts of yourself that you hide from others, especially the ones that are dark. Meg might not know that, but Blakely and I did.

I'd worn my own public face since I was seven years old. My dad? The one who was supposed to know and love me more than anyone else on the planet actually had no idea who I really was. How I really felt or existed in the world. He saw me as this bright, optimistic overcomer and achiever. Everyone did. The incredible girl with the golden heart that had tragically lost her mom to cancer when she was so young.

The mom-dying part was true. So was the tragedy.

When she died, I didn't think I'd ever stop crying, even though I knew it was coming. Even though I'd said all my goodbyes and everything else I wanted to say. It still hurt as much as if it'd come out of nowhere, because I'd believed with my whole heart, all the way up until her last breath, that she was going to be saved. That's what we'd prayed for. That's what we'd believed.

*God's got your back.* That was what Dad would say all the time after Mom passed away in our living room, and I would nod. Smile. Give him a big hug. Because that's what he needed to hear from me, and I wanted him to be okay. He couldn't be okay if I wasn't. On some level I knew if I wasn't, it'd break him in a way he'd never recover from. I was his reason to live, so I had to be okay. Always good. Always hopeful. Saying the right thing at the right time. And I always knew what the right thing to do was.

"God's got me," I'd say, settling into his arms and listening for the sound of his sigh. The deep release of his muscles untensing because I was okay and that's all that mattered to him. I was his purpose. The reason he got up in the morning. And all I wanted to do was make him happy.

But that was the thing. God didn't have my back. He didn't even have a single vertebra.

We'd never been Christian people before Mom got cancer. My parents had never taken me to church. Not once. Not even on Christmas or Easter, which was super strange in the small religious town I'd grown up in. But they hadn't.

They were wrecked when they told me about Mom being sick. You should've seen their faces. I'll never forget that moment. There was nothing I could grab onto. No solid ground underneath my feet. And I needed something. I needed a miracle.

So, I found Jesus. Quick.

I'd turned into a Jesus freak because, ask anyone who knew me, once I got something in my head, that was it. I devoured the scripture in the Bible. Listened to it constantly. I only had worship music playing in my Walkman twenty-four seven. Over and over again. The same uplifting songs. I made note cards and covered all the mirrors with healing scripture. Stuck notes on the doors. The refrigerator. Kept a folded-up piece of paper with all of them in my pocket, too, so I could yank it out whenever I needed to. Anytime I had an anxious or fearful thought about my mom dying or her cancer not going away, I took it out and quoted health and healing in Jesus's name over every part of her body. All her body cells. Just like I'd seen the preachers do. Raising my arms up high to the Lord:

"First Peter, two twenty-four," I'd declare as loud as I could and with as much authority that I could put into my voice. *"He himself bore our sins' in his body on the cross, so that we might die to sins and live for righteousness; 'by his wounds you have been healed.'"*

That one was always quickly followed by my other favorite healing promise in the Bible, James 5:14–15:

*"Is anyone among you sick? Let them call the elders of the church to pray over them and anoint them with oil in the name of the Lord. And the prayer offered in faith will make the sick person well; the Lord will raise them up. If they have sinned, they will be forgiven."*

And the things I did never bothered my parents. They loved it. This religion—this God—I'd found to cling to in this dark hour. The one giving me hope. Filling me with love and light.

I never expected them to come to church with me, but that's what happened, and it wasn't long before we were the center of Riverdale Community Church. They had bake sales and garage sales to raise money for us so my dad could take time off work to be with Mom. They came to the hospital and prayed with us. And not just praying. They anointed her head with oil. One of the ladies swore she was speaking in tongues. It sounded like gibberish to me, but who was I to say what the Holy Spirit sounded like? I was just a baby Christian.

We kept going with our faith despite what the doctors told us. We ignored their death sentences. They had no place in our house of healing. Mom must've read Dodie Osteen's recovery-from-cancer booklet hundreds of times. She'd highlighted all the same verses from the Bible that had healed Dodie from her cancer, and she walked around our house shouting them at the top of her lungs, just like Dodie. Mom did it every morning until she was exhausted and we made her stop to rest. She did all the right things. And despite what was happening, she continued getting sick instead of better, but we refused to give her cancer any power. After all, faith was believing in things you hadn't seen. You had to believe it before you could see it, and on and on the promises went. There wasn't supposed to be any firmer foundation than standing on the word of God, so that's where we kept our feet solidly planted.

Mom was in the middle of her fourth round of chemotherapy when she caught pneumonia. It weakened her immune system and gave the cancer an open door to ravage her cells, which is exactly what it did, like a monster. Mom was too weak to pray. She could barely open her eyes, but Dad and I became prayer warriors. We never stopped. Round the clock, we took turns by her bedside. The people from church came in shifts too.

The pastor came on Tuesday. He prayed over Mom first, and then he turned to us. "There's a story in the Bible where Jesus tells his disciples that if they have the faith of a mustard seed, they can move mountains." He opened his hand, revealing tiny seeds resting in his palm. "You see these? How small they are? That's the only amount of faith you need for Jesus to step into your life and move mountains. Give you your miracle." He pointed to Mom, then back to his hand again. "This is all the faith you need. Just that much, and anything is possible in Jesus's name. Do you hear me?"

I eagerly nodded. Things didn't look good at all for Mom, but I could do that. I could have the faith of a mustard seed, if that's all it took for Jesus to save her. I really could. So could Dad. We'd do it together. Anything for Mom.

The pastor gave us the seeds before he left. Dad and I raced out to the backyard as soon as he was gone. We dug up a plot of dirt by the fence and planted the seeds. We repeated the mustard seed scripture while we worked. The pastor had given that to us too. He said we needed to have faith followed by action and to remind God what his word said, so that's exactly what we did.

We held hands so tightly after we were finished, praying it over our newly planted mustard seed garden a final time. *"Truly I tell you, if you have faith as small as a mustard seed, you can say to this mountain, 'Move from here to there,' and it will move. Nothing will be impossible for you."* So that's what we declared as loudly as we could into the night air—we told my mom's cancer to move out of her body. To heal her immediately. We ended it in Jesus's name with the final declaration: *"'If you believe, you will receive whatever you ask for in prayer.'"*

Dad and I stood in the backyard, holding hands and feeling like superheroes. Real-life superheroes. We believed it. We did. I'd never been so filled with the spirit. I'd barely slept that night, but I hadn't needed to. I was on fire.

And then Mom died.

Within ten days of planting our seeds.

It all happened so quick. I held tight to a very thin thread of faith all the way to the end. Even after she passed, I diligently watered and cared for those seeds. Checking on them every single day. Multiple times. I covered them in the fall and all through the winter, because I wasn't taking any chances of them freezing. Part of me thought God was growing my mom in those seeds, as if they had the power to bring her back to life. I trusted that if he'd taken her from me, then he was going to give her back to me. Because that's what his word said. And he'd brought plenty of people back from the dead before. He'd done it with Lazarus, and he wasn't even his son, so I wouldn't waver in my faith.

*This is only a test, Thera. And you're good at tests.* That's what I told myself over and over again, because it had been true. I always got As.

The morning I raced outside and saw those tiny green sprouts peeking their way out from underneath the dirt, I threw myself on the ground and sobbed like I'd never cried before. My dad found me like that and snapped a picture. He still keeps it on his nightstand in a beautiful frame. I spent the entire day out there in the sun with her—chatting, laughing, crying, reading her our favorite books. I would've slept on the grass underneath the stars all night if Dad would've let me, but he hadn't.

"Come on, bug," he said, winking at me. "She'll still be here in the morning."

I'd skipped inside the house and was so excited that I woke up with the sun and long before Dad did. For the first time in forever, my heart didn't ache quite so heavy. It still hurt, but it had lost some of its weight overnight. I wore a huge smile on my face as I ran outside to say good morning to my mom. I froze when I saw it—the spots in the ground where the new mustard plants used to be. Gone. Empty dirt holes instead. The squirrels had dug up every single one of them and eaten them for breakfast.

That was the day I stopped believing in God. In meaning. In life.

I'd walked back into the house like I was in a trance. My dad still wasn't up yet, and I watched from my window as he discovered the same horror for himself an hour later. He still thought I was asleep, though. He sprinted into the house, and I heard him scrambling around downstairs before he raced back out of the house and into the car. He'd never left me alone before, and I couldn't imagine where he was going or what he was doing, but I didn't move from my spot in the window. He didn't come back in the house when he got home. Just went straight out to the garden and planted new plants in the exact same place the others had been.

I never told him I knew the truth. That I'd gotten up first. That I'd seen it. To this day, we still talked to Mom in that garden.

I lived life for my dad. He needed me to be okay, and I loved him more than anything or anyone else. I was the only thing he had left, so I made myself be okay for him, no matter what. Do you know how much work it takes to pretend like you're fine every day? To be the sunshine when you're really the darkness?

I realized tonight that I might not be as different from Blakely as I'd always thought. I didn't know what Meg's answer would be or if she would even be here in the morning, but I knew what mine would be—I was going to help her.

# CHAPTER THIRTY-ONE
## *NOW*

### GRACE

I pressed my lips together and puckered them in front of the mirror. Still too dark. I grabbed a Kleenex to blot them just as my assistant knocked at my door.

"I'm literally getting up at this second." I jumped up and turned around.

But it wasn't just Tessa in the doorway of my dressing room. Two men were with her. Serious-looking men. Ones wearing suits, and nobody came to visit me at work dressed like that.

Tessa eyed me cautiously, her eyes just as skeptical as mine. "Grace, this is Detective Wallace and his partner, Greg. They let themselves in downstairs," she said, giving me a knowing look.

The one with the crew cut stepped forward. He stuck out his hand. "Yes, I'm Detective Wallace, and we're here on behalf of the Houston Police Department. We had a few questions for you this morning."

"Okay," I said, shaking his hand and trying to think fast. What was this about? I didn't know anyone from Houston, did I? "Questions about what?"

"Mind if I sit?" Detective Wallace asked, pointing to one of the chairs in front of my mirror. The one Tessa usually sat in.

I shook my head. "I'm sorry. I don't have much time. I'm about to do a photo shoot."

He gave me a clipped nod. "This shouldn't take too long. We just had a few questions to ask you about Regina Crosby, and then we'll be out of your way."

The room spun. Fell open underneath me. I put my hand on the table to steady myself. Tessa raced over to me. She put her arm around me.

"Are you okay?" Her face was lined with concern.

I brushed her hand off me. "I'm fine. I just stood up too fast, and I've had too much coffee this morning," I said, trying to recover as quickly as possible. I motioned for the door. "Really, I'm good. Why don't you give us a minute?"

She cocked her head to the side, like she was really questioning whether or not I was okay now, because I never took any important meetings without her. She was my organizing brain. The one that kept track of all the important details. Her brain worked so differently from mine, and she always picked up on things that I didn't. Always.

I nodded at her. "Yes, yes, I'm fine."

She gave me one last look over her shoulder to see if I'd changed my mind before she shut the door behind her. The two officers stood menacingly in front of me.

"When was the last time you saw Regina Crosby?" Detective Wallace asked.

Hearing him say it the second time was still just as jarring. I rubbed my face. "Regina Crosby?" He nodded at me. His face impassive. I shrugged. "I haven't seen Regina Crosby since I was a kid at camp."

What did he know? Why was he here? Had something happened? I hadn't talked to any of the girls since I left Atlanta a little over a week ago. I figured I never would again. I'd made it clear I wanted no part of whatever they were doing. But that had to do with Blakely's husband. Why was he asking me about Regina?

"Did you know she got released from prison?" Detective Wallace asked the next question too. Was that their approach? He did all the questioning while his partner just sat back and studied whoever they were interrogating? Because his partner's eyes hadn't left mine. The way they both just stared at me without showing any emotion was unnerving.

"I didn't," I lied.

"Have you seen her since she was released?" Another question from him.

"I just told you that I haven't seen her since Camp Pendleton." I wanted to tell him *Nice try*, but I held back. Where was this going? Did I need an attorney? Was it too soon to ask for one? What would it look like if I did? Was his partner reading my mind? It felt like he was trying to read my thoughts.

Detective Wallace's eyes never left my face. Neither did his partner's. "Have you seen or been in contact with anyone from Camp Pendleton lately?"

I shook my head.

He raised his eyebrows. The first sign of emotional life. "Really? How about any of your old cabinmates? Thera? Blakely?"

"Meg." His partner finally spoke. His voice a deep baritone.

My mouth went dry. I couldn't swallow. What did I say? What had they done? Where was this going? *Look calm. Keep it together.* I silently instructed myself while I asked, "I'm sorry. Can you tell me what this is about? Am I in some kind of trouble here, Officers?"

I was glad my makeup and hair were done. I hadn't been lying when I told Tessa I was coming out of my dressing room and ready to film. My boobs were practically spilling out of my bra. I hoped it made them uncomfortable. My lashes and wig made me feel like I was wearing a costume. It made it easy to pretend I wasn't terrified of whatever was happening. What my friends might've done. Because my old friends were vicious creatures.

"Have you done something wrong?" Detective Wallace was back to asking the questions. I shook my head. "Then, no. You're not in trouble. We're just trying to locate Regina Crosby."

I waited for him to continue. To explain more. But he just stopped. Like I was supposed to know what that meant. Or he was waiting for me to say something, but I didn't have anything to say. I was totally lost.

His partner reached into his back pocket and pulled out an envelope. He handed it to Detective Wallace. "See, here's the thing, Ms. Howard. Regina Crosby was released from prison about seven weeks ago. She's been staying with her mother right outside of Houston ever since she got out. Three weeks ago, Regina left for her job at the grocery store and never came home. Turns out, she never made it to work either. Her mother didn't tell anyone right away. She figured her daughter skipped town, and she was going to let her be. But Regina didn't check in with her parole officer, and that's when he called the house. Her mother told him she was missing. They put an APB out on her, but you can imagine that our detectives haven't worked too hard on trying to locate a paroled prisoner. Lots of them disappear onto the streets after they've been released, and we never hear from them again. Then, last week, her mama was going through her things, and she found this letter." He paused, holding it up. "You know anything about this?"

Another white envelope. Almost exactly like the ones we'd all been sent. But Blakely was the one who sent ours. That's what she'd said. Had she been lying? What was going on?

"I told you. I don't know anything about Regina Crosby." My heart thudded in my chest. Pulse pounded in my ears. It was all supposed to be made up. The story about Regina coming after us. Blakely said it was her. She said she sent the notes. What was happening? This was supposed to be over. I'd walked away so my hands didn't get dirty in another one of their messes.

"You look pale," Greg interjected, feigning concern. "Do you feel okay?"

"Oh, I'm fine. It's just like I was saying to my assistant. I got up too fast. And at this point, I drink so much caffeine, it's probably safer just to use crack." I laughed, then quickly realized who I was talking to and stopped short. Neither of them was smiling.

"Regina's mother found this letter, and that's when she called the police." He stuck his hand out to me. "Here. It's probably just easier if you read it yourself."

I took it from him slowly because, at the same time that I wanted to know what it said, I also didn't, and I definitely didn't want both of them watching my reactions while I read it.

"I'm going to sit," I said, turning around and quickly trying to rearrange my face and pull myself together. My thoughts were scattered. My emotions jumping all over the place. I sat down at the seat in front of my dressing table. They could sit wherever they wanted. I didn't care. I moved the chair slightly to the side. I felt their eyes on me while I started to read.

"Take your time," Greg instructed. "It's a lot to digest."

"Thanks," I said, feigning politeness and a smile. Easy to do behind my lipsticked lips and fake lashes. I let out a slow deep breath, then started reading.

Dear Mom—
If you're reading this letter, then it means I've gone missing. Or maybe you've already found my body and this is the last part of you going through my things. Either way, something terrible has happened to me, and I'm gone. I'm so sorry, Mom. I wish I didn't have to hurt you again, but there wasn't any other way. I had to try to get you the money for your surgery. I couldn't let you suffer. You don't deserve to live in pain

every day. I couldn't stand by and watch that happen. Not after the way you've always stood by me.

None of this would've happened to our family if it hadn't been for those girls at Camp Pendleton. Those spoiled entitled girls lied about Jared, Mom. One of them grew a conscience a year ago and she sent me a letter explaining everything. Said they all lied. Jared never touched any of them. He was a great coach. Those girls toyed with my family and ruined our lives just for fun. Just because they could.

After everything you've done for me and my sons, I had to at least try to get the money from your surgery from them. All of them have money. Every single one of them, especially Blakely Reynolds. Remember that name. She'll be easy to find. She was the girl in the picture. The one that started it all. Her father is worth millions. I'm headed straight to her to get your money.

If something happens and I don't make it back, give the police this letter. Also give them the letter from Meg Watson. It's in the box with my diplomas in the basement. I love you so much!

Always and forever,
Regina

# CHAPTER THIRTY-TWO

## *NOW*

### GRACE

I slowly looked up from Regina's letter to her mother from before she went missing. I had no idea what to say to the officers. There must've been shock stamped all over my face. There was no way I could hide it. Meg had written Regina a letter. She'd lied to me. She'd lied that night when we got together. She never told us about the letter. Granted, we didn't talk much about Regina after Blakely told us the real reason she'd brought us there, but what if there was something else going on too?

"Pretty intense stuff, right?" Detective Wallace interrupted my thoughts.

"Yes . . . I . . . just . . . wow . . . that's a lot." I couldn't formulate thoughts. Nothing made sense.

"Imagine how her mother feels."

Everything inside me frozen. Emotions. Thoughts. Words.

"It's really sad about her mom," Greg said.

This time I managed a nod. Meg had written Regina? What had she told her? I wanted to see that letter. Had they seen that letter? Of course they had. Did Meg blame us? I'd been so angry at Blakely, I hadn't looked at or questioned anything else about the others. Was it possible the two things were related? Were Meg and Blakely somehow working together? Or were they working with Regina?

"What's wrong with Regina's mom?" I asked when I finally found my voice.

"Such a tragic story. You'd think after a family goes through one tragedy, they'd be exempt from having to go through another, but that hasn't been the case. Usually isn't, unfortunately. Three years ago, her mother got into a freak diving accident at the local pool. Did some nasty damage to her third vertebrae. She's been wheelchair bound ever since and has lots of complications. One of them being she's in pretty excruciating pain most of the time. She was contacted last month about a medical trial with a new experimental procedure that stimulates the spinal cord for regrowth. Problem is their insurance won't cover it because it's still in the beginning phases and doesn't have FDA approval. The procedure alone is over two hundred thousand dollars. That doesn't cover the cost of whatever new hardware they put in there. Amazing what modern medicine can do these days, you know? But the Maustons couldn't afford something like that. Do you know they took out another mortgage on their house to help fund her trial?"

I just stood there, shaking my head, dumbfounded. My brain still whirling and spinning.

"Why don't we go into the other room?" I suggested, even though I didn't want them in my recording studio. I needed a second to gather myself. A moment for them to stop looking at me and analyzing all my reactions. "I'm going to run to the restroom real quick. Why don't you have a seat in there?"

I didn't wait for them to respond. I just turned around and bolted to the bathroom. I locked the door and leaned against it, trying to calm my breathing and relax. Where was everyone else? Had the police visited all of them, too, or just me? What was going on? Nothing made sense.

God, I should've looked at their social media or something. I should've kept track of them when I came home. You couldn't just have your best friends from childhood pop up with some fake notes about a murder and then just return back to your regular life like nothing had happened. What was I thinking? How had I just gone back to my life like that? Where were they? What if they'd somehow set me up for something and I didn't even know it?

This was what I'd been afraid of all along. Just being at Blakely's house that night connected us to her and whatever she was doing. It was the same thing parents told their kids when they went to parties. *It doesn't matter if you didn't do it, you were there.* But yes, it did. There was a difference between being there and doing it.

There had to be. Even if we'd pushed Regina over the edge to the point where she killed her husband, it's not like we'd actually killed him. She stabbed him. She'd had to put the knife in her hand and push it through his flesh. That's what I told myself when I woke up in the night, sweating in terror and guilt. The weight of what we'd done pressing down on me. That's what I told myself now as I headed back into my studio.

The two officers were standing up next to each other, deep in conversation, but they stopped as soon as they spotted me. Greg gave me a clipped nod.

"Can't really say that I blame Regina for getting smart and deciding to frame the girls responsible for killing her husband," Detective Wallace said. This time there was no mistaking I was some kind of a suspect. Or that I needed my lawyer, but I didn't have one. Who has a lawyer other than people who get in trouble? That wasn't me.

I couldn't shake what Meg had done. That meant the entire time we were at Blakely's—and she'd been the first person to arrive, which also made me question everything—she had sat there and said absolutely nothing about sending Regina a letter. The fact that she'd told Regina what we'd done—confessed our sins—was huge, and she knew it. That should've been the first thing out of her mouth, no matter what Blakely had going on. Were Regina going missing and Blakely sending the letters actually connected? Were Meg and Blakely working together?

Had they been working together this entire time? Since the summer? But what for?

The detectives were waiting for me to speak, so I had to say something.

"I'm sorry I can't be more helpful, but I have no idea what's going on." Everything else might've been a lie, but that was the most truthful statement I could've given them. I cleared my throat. Anxious to ask. Worried about what they'd think of me asking and equally worried that they'd think something bad about it if I didn't ask about it. "Can I read Meg's letter too?"

Detective Wallace didn't take a second to think about it. He just shook his head immediately. "That letter's been sealed for evidence and taken down to the district."

I tried not to show my annoyance, but wasn't Regina's letter evidence too? And they'd let me see that. Why weren't they showing me Meg's? There had to be a reason. I didn't know anything about these guys, and I'd never been in any kind of trouble with the law—I didn't even have a speeding ticket—but that didn't matter. All you had to do was look at them and know they didn't do anything without a reason. Their steps were deliberate and ordered, so if they hadn't shown me Meg's letter, then it meant there was something in there that they didn't want me to see. What was it?

# REGINA

I killed the love of my life, and he was innocent. Totally innocent. That had been a whole different kind of shock. When I first got Meg's letter, it sent me hurtling back to my early days in prison. To the dark days.

I'd been stunned when the guard slid the letter underneath my cell door. I rarely ever got mail anymore. At the beginning of my incarceration, my mom sent me lots of letters, but once we got computers in the library, we'd started doing most of our communication through email. When she sent me anything now, it was usually care packages filled with all my favorite toiletries and treats. At first, I'd thought it was a mistake. It wouldn't be the first time they'd accidently given me someone else's mail. But no, there it was. My eight-digit inmate number written on the front and stamped on the back.

I'd just stared at the letter, already opened by prison security, like they did every other piece of mail that came through the system. But even though they'd opened it, the return address was still clear:

Meg Watson
11714 Kline Street
Seattle, WA 91675

I hadn't been able to read it for three days. I'd just carried it around with me everywhere I went, like I was a kid and it was my favorite blanket.

"Girl, what are you waiting on?" Yolanda asked when I showed it to her. I didn't even have to unseal it. All I had to do was pull the letter out, but I still couldn't.

"I just . . . I don't know. I can't imagine what she has to say to me, and I'm not sure I want to know." It'd taken me so long to put myself back together; what would I do if this shattered me again? I didn't have another rebuild in me. You can only come back from that kind of bottom once.

Yolanda had been the one to finally open it.

"Here," I said, shoving it to her shortly before lights-out on the unit. Tomorrow would mark day four since I'd received it. "You open it for me and see what it says."

She raised her eyebrows at me. "You sure, girl?"

I nodded. "Just read it and see what it says. Then you can decide if you think I should read it or not. But I don't want to read anything that's going to flip me out."

She snatched the envelope and pulled out the letter immediately, since she'd been dying to read it since it'd come. The letter was hand-written on lined notebook paper. Old-school style. Her eyes grew big as she read. "Jesus. Jesus." She just kept saying it as she shook her head. Once she was finished, she looked up with an expression I'd never seen on her face before. One I couldn't read. "You definitely have to read this yourself." She handed it back to me.

I slowly took it from her. "You sure?"

She vigorously nodded her head. "Positive. Girl, read it."

I took a deep breath, bracing myself for whatever it said, and then, finally, looked down. My eyes took a moment to register the words and even longer for the words to catch up with my brain.

Dear Regina—

I've thought about writing this letter so many times over the years. I can't tell you how many times I've stopped and started it. To be honest, I'm not sure this one won't end up just like the others.

You don't know me, but my name is Meg Watson. I was one of the girls that attended Camp Pendleton while your husband worked there. I was one of his students. He gave me private lessons and I was part of his tennis team. Before I get into anything else, I want you to know that your husband loved you. More than anything else. You and your boys. You're all he ever talked about when we were together. I think he'd understand why you did what you did, and I'm pretty sure he'd forgive you too because your husband was an incredible man despite what people said about him and all the rumors they spread.

The most important thing I want you to know is that the things they said about him were wrong. Totally false. Mr. Crosby never hurt me or my friends. It started as a stupid prank that grew into something we never imagined would happen. I'll never fully understand exactly what happened. How things spiraled and snowballed. How I even let myself be involved in something so awful.

I'm sure you know Blakely. The girl in the picture. The one they showed at your trial. She was one of my closest friends and I was the one who took the picture that started everything, all the rumors. I've never told anyone that before. You're the first. I took the picture and even though it looks like something happened between them, I can assure you that it didn't. Blakely tried to sit on your husband's lap and he shoved her off immediately. He wanted nothing to do with her or cheating on you. He wasn't the monster they made him out to be.

But I want you to know that I did tell the dean nothing happened, but he didn't believe me. Neither did anyone else. They just kept telling me it did and acting like I was lying to cover up for him or that I was a confused abuse victim. It really started messing with my head. It made me question my reality and what I'd seen. I was barely seventeen. So young and so confused. That doesn't make it better or give any kind of excuse for my behavior, but it's the truth. We'd never interview young girls now in a situation like the way they did to us, but that's how it was. And then when all the other girls started coming forward, it got even more confusing. I started thinking maybe they were right. Maybe it did happen.

I don't know what made those other girls come forward and say he'd hurt them too. We weren't even friends with them. We barely talked. It's haunted me since it happened no matter how hard I tried to push it down. So, finally last year, I started reaching out to those girls. I had to know for myself. I knew we'd lied, but what about them? I was still 99.9% sure that your husband was a good guy. If we'd made it up, chances are they'd done the same.

Regina—I've talked to every single one of those girls in the last year, and they all made it up too. The things they accused him of never happened. Most of them are just like me. Adult women now, looking backward and trying to understand what they did. Why they were ever part of such a huge lie. No one ever really believed there would be any kind of consequences like what happened.

I don't know why or how we were all a part of something so horrendous. It was like we all adopted a shared delusion and it just spread like a contagious disease throughout camp and while it was going on, everyone believed they were telling the truth. That actually happens with groups of teenage girls, you know. I've looked it up. Social contagion is a real thing.

Or maybe I'm just grasping at straws because I so desperately want an explanation for our incomprehensible behavior. Not that this makes it better or is any excuse for what we did to you and your family. I know that. I realize that. We did a terrible thing and nothing will ever change that.

I'm so sorry for what we did to you. What we did to your husband. Your children. Your lives. I know that doesn't mean much or give him his life back or yours, but I had to apologize. Nothing will ever make what we did better, but I'm hoping that finding out the truth might at least give you some peace. Or help you out of prison. Maybe if you show your lawyers or the parole board this letter, they'll let you out early. I don't know how things work in the justice system. I just know you were wronged and if I can do anything to make it right, I'm available to help.

I have no idea how to end this letter. I've never gotten this far. I'm crossing my fingers that I have enough courage to send it. You deserve to know the truth. Words can't express how sorry I am. Please forgive me. Forgive all of us.

Sincerely,

Meg Watson

# CHAPTER THIRTY-THREE
## *NOW*

## MEG

I tried to pay attention to what my wife, Claire, was saying, but it was like she'd been muted. I watched her lips but couldn't hear the sound. I might've physically been in the living room watching TV with her, but my mind was everywhere. My phone buzzed against my thigh, over and over again. Grace had been blowing up my phone all night. I knew she would. From the moment that detective from Houston left a voice message to tell me Regina was missing and asked me to call him back so he could ask me a few questions. She'd probably called all of us. I wanted to talk to Blakely before I talked to her, but I didn't think Grace was going to leave me alone. I'd already texted Blakely three times, and she hadn't texted me back.

What was I going to tell Grace? Did the officer say something about the letter to her? It was the first thing the officer mentioned in his message. I meant to say something about the letter to everyone that weekend. I fully intended to confess what I'd done, but when things took a turn and Blakely told me what we were really there for, I reconsidered. Did it do any good to let them know I'd sent it? None of them had any interest in reparations. But I did.

I couldn't live my life knowing what we'd done to that woman. And not just her. We'd taken two parents away from innocent children, and the moment I became a mother myself, I had to do something to make it right. If I was her, I would hate us and want to punish us too. That's why I wasn't surprised when we got the letters. Not like the others. Part of me had always hoped she'd contact me after I sent the letter. I just hadn't expected it to be that way and in such a cryptic manner.

But then Blakely told us she'd done it and what was really happening, and I don't know . . . everything just shifted to helping Blakely. I forgot about it almost that quickly. I hadn't thought about it since.

It was much easier for Thera and Grace to move on after the murder because they hadn't been in the room when it happened. They didn't witness the brutality. The mutilation. Maybe that was why I'd felt so compelled to write the letter and they hadn't. They'd only seen the aftermath for a few brief seconds. Grace might not have even looked. But not me. I saw all of it, and I was completely traumatized. Wrecked. For weeks after we got home, all I kept seeing every time I closed my eyes was Mr. Crosby's slashed-up face. Regina had made Xs over his eyes with the knife. Sliced his mouth ear to ear. It'd looked like he was continuously throwing up blood.

That's what I saw in those first few weeks back home. I went twenty-three days without a good night's sleep. The worst insomnia of my life because, on one hand, I wanted to sleep, but on the other hand, I was terrified of the nightmares. I didn't know which parts were real and which ones I was imagining.

We did a lot of terrible things that summer. And maybe we were responsible for triggering a rage bomb that exploded inside a fragile individual. But someone with that much anger? That much pent-up rage and trauma? Who's to say something else might not have triggered her in the same way? How did we know she wouldn't have walked into the grocery store and lost it over food? Or that she wasn't one road rage incident away from exploding on some innocent bystander?

At least that's what I told myself. I said anything I needed to say to keep the memories at bay. To fight off the images that were constantly threatening to burst their way into my consciousness. It was the only way I'd been able to go on with my life. Complete denial and repression.

But the door to my unconscious had been unlocked, and the memory from that night pummeled me. Hit me full throttle.

I'd heard the screams and run into Mr. Crosby's office. Regina was screaming, writhing her head back and forth. As possessed by the devil as anyone I'd ever seen. I wanted to hold up a cross and scream Bible verses at her. I was frozen, but Blakely immediately sprang into action. She grabbed her wrists and wrestled for the knife, pulling Regina off him. Blakely finally got it from her, and she flung Regina backward, sending her flying into me. I wrapped both arms tight around Regina and screamed at Thera and Grace to go get help. I could hear them outside the office door. Thera was crying. Grace was yelling at her.

And then Blakely turned around.

She had the strangest look in her eye. One I'd never seen before or since. As if the demon that had been in Regina had left her body and traveled into Blakely's. Everything happened in slow motion. I don't know if she moved that slowly or if it just felt like time was moving that slowly. Blakely took another two steps over to Mr. Crosby and stood in front of him, just like she'd done when I'd taken the original picture.

Mr. Crosby's body was jerking, spurting with blood. A violent, bloody seizure.

Blakely pulled down his pants, exposing him. I'd never forget that moment of horror. I thought she just wanted to see his privates. Know what it looked like. Or expose him so he'd be humiliated. I never could've predicted what she did next.

"Blakely . . . ," I'd started to say, but my words sputtered out.

She turned her head and smiled at me. Then turned back to him, and she sliced his member straight off. In one quick movement. Lopped it like she was chopping down a tree. And then she just flung it across the room, like she'd surprised herself or come back into herself. Right as Thera and Grace thundered through the door. Back from running to the pay phone and calling 911. The bloody handprint on the phone was Thera's. The police always glossed over that part, and I'd never understood why. They didn't seem concerned with finding out who'd made the call.

It was funny the way your mind played tricks on you. How you could tell yourself something enough times that eventually you believed yourself. Maybe that's what made a good liar. You're your biggest con.

I blocked that memory out from the moment it happened. Faded it out to the edges of my memory and pushed it away whenever it tried to get back inside the inner circle. The part of how she mutilated him. We all talked about Blakely like she had more responsibility for what had happened, but that wasn't all she had more of. Was she full of psychopathy too? Was it possible she'd done something to Regina?

# REGINA

Lots of the other women paid careful attention to their time served, but I never did. Because what for? I had nothing to look forward to. Not in prison or when I got out. But from the moment of my mom's diving accident, I counted down the days until my release. My dad had been gone for years. Taken by the widower's heart attack, but the two of them had drifted apart long before that. She said it wasn't over me, but it was, even though she'd never admit it. He wanted her to leave me. To have nothing to do with me, the same way he'd done after the trial. My dad was one of those who believed killing Jared was one thing—horrible but forgivable. Trying to drown my babies in the lake was another.

But my mom refused to cut me off. Her love was eternal, no matter what I'd done, and I'd never felt so powerless as I did after her accident. She'd been showing one of her students a dive, and she'd slipped on the board. She'd smacked her head on it and then again at the bottom of the pool, severing the eighth nerve root at C7. It was a miracle she'd survived, and I'd begged to visit her in the hospital, but they only let you visit your parents when they were dead.

They put her back together, but they didn't fix her. There was permanent damage to her spinal cord. The fact that there was a way for her to not be in excruciating pain every day and the only thing holding us back from the cure was money infuriated me. It just wasn't fair that the people who got the best treatment were the ones who could pay for it. While the rest of us were at the mercy of our meager bank accounts, even though we worked just as hard.

"Get it from those rich bitches," Yolanda said one night after I'd spent the last hour ranting and carrying on over the unfairness of it all.

At first, I'd laughed. I thought she was joking, but then I started really thinking about it. What if I did? How would that work? I'd be out in less than two years. Nineteen months and eleven days, to be exact. That was plenty of time to prepare. Plot.

That's when I'd asked Yolanda for her help figuring it out. She was more than happy to help. She loved my mom, and my mom returned the feelings. She appreciated the way Yolanda had always taken care of and looked after me. She made sure to wave at her in the visiting room, and she always threw in a few extra things for her in my care packages, like her favorite toothpaste and the next book in whatever urban fantasy series they were currently binging together.

Yolanda and I went back to my court documents and easily found Blakely's name. She was the girl in the picture. The one everyone knew. Once I found her, we started watching everything she did. Social media made it so easy. People were so stupid with the details they posted about their lives. I'd never understand it. What happened to keeping your private lives private?

Yolanda wanted to gather as much information as possible on all of them, but I disagreed. I was only interested in one person—Blakely Reynolds. If I could get to her, then I wouldn't have to bother with the others. She was old money rich. The kind that never runs out. And besides, I remembered her. Very distinctly remembered her. She'd wrestled me. Grabbed the knife. Sliced off Jared's most intimate part.

Out of all the fragmented parts, that was the one I remembered crystal clear, even though I'd never shared it with anyone else. Not that I was keeping it a secret. At the time it was just more proof of Jared's guilt. Another reason that I'd never considered he didn't do it. During the trial, I learned Blakely was one of his victims.

Not just any one. The first. The girl featured in the picture that they must've flashed on the screen at least ten times. They'd put it up there next to his mutilated body.

"Ladies and gentleman of the jury, do we really think this?" He dramatically pointed at the screen during closing arguments, and all their heads turned to look. "Deserved this?" Flash to his mutilated corpse that somehow had stayed upright in his padded office chair. Some of the jury members closed their eyes. A few gagged.

They assumed I'd been the one to mutilate his privates, but it'd been her. Except I didn't bother telling them the truth. Wouldn't have made any difference anyway. I didn't care about my trial. While my lawyer was trying to get me a lesser sentence because of mental impairment, I was praying for the death penalty. I never set them straight.

Because that's what you wanted to do when vile creatures abused you with their member. Chop it off so they couldn't use it, which was exactly what Blakely had done. It was exactly what I'd wanted to do to the coach that abused me. I'd had similar fantasies about him. Slicing it off and leaving him to bleed out. So, the fact that she'd done it never surprised me. It only reinforced his guilt.

But now that I knew Jared hadn't done it? That he'd never touched her? Or any of those other girls? It made me furious. She'd mutilated his body for no reason after she'd set the entire thing up. There was something wrong with her. Seriously wrong with her.

That's why I didn't care how I hurt her or what I did to her. She deserved every ounce of it. Part of me wanted to hurt her. Maybe even kill her. It was weird what happened inside of you once you knew you were capable of murder. It changed you forever in a way that you could never come back from. It was just like anything else: after you'd crossed over a line once, it was easier to cross over a second time. I didn't want to go back to prison, though. I had to take care of my mom. She needed me.

So, I'd done what I needed to do. And I wasn't sorry. She'd taken everything from me in the most brutal way possible, and she needed to pay. Literally pay.

"And if she doesn't?" That was what Yolanda had asked me a few weeks before I got out, after we'd just finished going over the plan for the thousandth time. I was going to miss her so much after I was gone. She helped me figure out where Blakely was. Where she lived. Her husband. House. Job. Life. All of it. Even hacked into the security system Blakely had on her house.

I'd shook my head. "I'll do whatever it takes to make sure she gives me the money."

216

# CHAPTER THIRTY-FOUR
## *NOW*

## MEG

Grace's face filled my phone screen. "What the fuck is going on?" she asked as soon as I got on the FaceTime call. "I called Blakely, and the number is out of service."

I hurried around to the side of my house, scurrying behind the back shed. I didn't want Claire to overhear. I was terrified that she would. My heart had been pounding ever since I remembered what Blakely had done to Mr. Crosby. I almost passed out right on my kitchen floor. I'd never passed out in my entire life, but in that moment all the blood left my body. I'd gripped the counter while my head spun. Claire had come in while I was still spinning.

"Are you okay? You look really pale," she said, immediately noticing something was wrong. I turned around so she couldn't peer at me with her dagger-truth-seeking eyes.

"I'm just a little dizzy. I think my blood sugar dropped. I just realized I haven't eaten since lunch," I said, thinking quickly as I opened the refrigerator and grabbed an apple.

I leaned my arm against the shed, breathing heavy even though I hadn't exerted myself. "Jesus Christ. Jesus Christ. Jesus Christ." I'd given up waiting for Blakely to text and tried to call her too. I'd gotten the same message.

"Meg, I don't understand. Make me understand what's happening, and make me understand fast, because I'm about to lose it. Detectives showed up at my studio today, talking about how Regina Crosby is a missing person. She's been missing for days. Her mom is the one that filed the report, and she's convinced somebody hurt Regina." She spoke fast. It was hard to keep up. "Not only that. Oh no, it gets so much better. He's got a letter from Regina that she left with her mother basically calling us spoiled, entitled brats and that if she ever went missing, we killed her." She snorted. "And all this happens one week after we all got those fucked-up letters that were really Blakely? Except when we show up at her house, she decides to tell us she murdered her husband. That she needs help? What the hell is happening? You better start talking, and I want the truth."

"I know. I know. Ohmigod. Ohmigod." This was what I got. This was what happened when you did bad things. Bad things always got punished. It didn't matter, even if you tried to set them right. "I don't know what's happening. I really don't. I'm just as confused as you are."

"Bullshit. You know exactly what's happening. You probably helped plan this entire thing."

"Grace, I swear, I didn't. You have to believe me. I had no idea. When we got those letters, I hadn't heard from Blakely or anyone else since we left camp. Really, I hadn't. I don't know why you don't believe me. I'm freaking out just as badly as you are." More. I was freaking out more because I knew Blakely was evil.

"Oh, I don't know why I don't believe you, Meg. Maybe it's because you sent a fuckin' letter to Regina and never told us about it. Maybe that's why."

My throat squeezed. All the blood left my body, just like it'd done in the kitchen. What else did the police say? I hadn't talked to them yet. They'd just left a message. I was too scared. What would I say?

Were what happened at Blakely's and Regina related? It was too big of a coincidence on timing for them not to be.

"Didn't think I knew about that, did you?" Her voice was cold. "Now you see where I'm coming from, huh? Makes things a bit clearer. So, yeah, I don't trust you as far as I can throw you, but you're going to tell me what's going on because you got me into this mess."

I shook my head. "I didn't. I mean, I did send the letter to Regina. That part I did. Last year. But that was different. That has absolutely nothing to do with this." Except maybe it did. But if it did, I didn't know how, and I hadn't been a part of it. "Look, why do you think I was so eager to get to Blakely's? Why do you think I took it so seriously? Because I knew that I'd sent the letter to Regina and told her what we'd done. I'd basically given her the ammunition to hurt us, and I swear, Grace, I know you have no reason to believe me, but I swear, I truly believed that's what she was doing. I thought she was going to destroy all of us. That's why I was so nervous. The entire reason I went. Did you see how much I was drinking that night?"

She searched my face through the screen, trying to see if she should believe me. If I was telling the truth. I looked back at her imploringly, trying to get her to see that I was.

"You had no idea Regina was missing?" she asked, still not entirely convinced.

I adamantly shook my head and tried to look as transparent as possible. "None, Grace. I swear, absolutely none."

"Do you think Blakely did?"

I paused for a few seconds. "I'm not sure . . . we never talked about Regina again after Blakely told us she was the one who sent the letters. Not once. You were there for that entire conversation. We waited for you to have it. I said like two things about the trial before you got there, and that's it. Everything shifted into talking about her husband and her situation. That was the rest of the night."

"I told you so, Meg. What did I say that night when I was leaving? What exactly did I say that night? I told you not to trust her. I told you that you didn't know her. And clearly, I was right. All of this is connected, somehow. I just don't know how. I've never been so pissed about being right in my life, and now you've got me into this mess."

"But you didn't do anything."

"Didn't do anything? I was there with all of you. Because I left a few hours early? Like they're going to believe that. What did you do?" Her voice dripped with vitriol. She didn't want to even look at me.

"I haven't let myself even think about it." And I hadn't. That's the only reason I'd agreed to do it in the first place. Blakely had needed our help, and she deserved a chance to be free from abuse. So when I got up that morning, I decided to help her and pretend like it never happened. I'd bury the memories the same way I'd buried them before. That was my coping strategy. It wasn't a good one, but it was all I had, and I'd needed a plan. Now it just made me sick.

"Tell me what you did, Meg."

I kept furtively glancing over my shoulder. Back at the house. Straining for sounds. Claire would never understand. Or maybe she would. Clearly, I was the friend you could count on when there was a dead body in your living room. But was she? Maybe I should just tell her. I didn't know what to do. How to make this right.

"Tell me what you did," Grace repeated. Her voice rising. Even angrier this time.

"You heard what she said. He was hurting her. Making her sleep in the garage. Tying her up like a dog. Controlling all of her finances. Every part of her life. She was a prisoner in her own home. And I believed her. Every part. I met her dad at camp. So did you, and he was one of those men that curled my stomach. And that feeling only grew the older we got, and I knew what those eyes meant. We all did. You did, too, I'm sure. So, her story that he'd given her into the hands of another awful man? That was believable too."

"Yeah, I was there for all that. How awful her dad and husband were to her. Blah. Blah. Blah." She was as unmoved by Blakely's story now as she had been that night.

"You must just think I'm an idiot." How could I have been so dumb? So easily fooled? I'd believed all her stories. Part of me still did. We didn't know for sure if this was connected.

"I don't think you're an idiot. I think you have a big heart and Blakely can be very convincing of just about anything. It's not your fault for believing her."

I couldn't tell if she actually believed that or if she was just saying it to make me feel better so that I'd hurry up and tell her the rest of the story. Either way, I needed her help out of this. I talked fast. A few more minutes, and Claire was definitely going to come looking for me. I didn't just disappear into the dark backyard in the middle of the evening for fun. I glanced around me again before speaking.

"After you left, it was weird for a while, obviously, but then we started talking again. All of us in her room—me, Thera, and Blakely. She seemed so wrecked. I mean, she was wrecked. I don't think she was faking that . . . Maybe she was? God, what if she was?" I shook my head, dislodging all the questions that wanted to intrude. I had to stay focused. "I felt really bad for her. I know it's so stupid, but I've always felt so responsible for what happened, you know? Like if Mr. Crosby had never taken an interest in me, then none of this would've happened. And I guess my adult self knows that's not true, but it just feels like I have this huge karmic debt hanging over my head. It keeps me from ever truly being happy, because deep down I know I was part of a terrible thing. So, in some messed-up way, helping Blakely felt like maybe it was making things right with the universe? I couldn't help Regina, but I could help Blakely . . ." It had made sense at the time, but saying it out loud made it sound ridiculous and made me doubt my decision.

Grace was silent on the other end. Finally, after a few more beats passed, she asked in a quieter voice, "So, what'd you do to help her?"

I dropped my voice even lower than hers. "We got rid of the body." A sentence I never thought I'd utter in a million years. It didn't sound right coming out of my mouth. It didn't feel right either. "She wanted to put different parts of him in different places. She told us—"

She interrupted me, covering her ears and shaking her head. "Never mind. Never mind. Forget I asked. I don't want to know. Just the fact that I was there makes me look guilty, and I don't want to know anything else, especially if they're going to come back and ask me more questions."

"Do you think they will?"

She shrugged. "I'm not sure. It was pretty impossible to read either of them."

"I don't know why I'm still so twisted up in all this. But it felt like a way to make it right, and I can't explain it, other than it did. I feel guilty, Grace. So guilty I wrote a letter to Regina a year ago and tracked down all the girls. Do you know everybody made it up? Did you read my letter?"

Her face softened at the mention of the other girls. In the end, there'd been six girls to come forward. Seven, if you counted Blakely. "What do you mean?"

"I contacted all of them. Well, not Robbie Keho. She died of a drug overdose at twenty-four, but everyone else? The others? I had a conversation with every single one."

"And they all lied?"

I nodded. "All of them."

"I'll never understand that summer. What happened to us. To me. How did I do any of that?" Her face twisted in confusion and pain. "That's not who I am. I'm not that person."

"Whatever happened, it just happened to me again." She'd been strong enough to resist it this time, but not me. I'd fallen under the spell of that summer all over again. Or was it the spell of Blakely?

# CHAPTER THIRTY-FIVE

## *NOW*

## THERA

"Bug, honey? Did your friends leave?" Dad called out to me from the living room. From his spot in the beat-up orange recliner where he spent most of his days.

"They did, Dad," I yelled back, shutting the front door behind the police officer.

"That gentleman sure was a nice man, sweetie. You should have him come over more often. It's about time you started moving on past Steve." He broke into a coughing fit at the end of his sentence.

Steve was my college boyfriend. He'd been married for thirteen years, had two kids and a receding hairline, and was living in West Virginia. I hadn't seen him since graduation.

"Maybe I will. I'm going to run into the kitchen and get your medicine. I'll be right back, and we can watch another episode of *Judge Judy*, okay?" I hurried into the kitchen and grabbed a glass of water. I gulped it down. Filled it again, then drank halfway. I couldn't believe that just happened, and I couldn't believe I'd handled it so calmly. How'd I do that?

When the police officer first knocked on the door, I assumed something had finally happened to my next-door neighbor, Hilda. I'd heard her and her husband fighting again last night, and I swear it's only a matter of time before one of them kills the other. But it wasn't about Hilda.

"Ma'am, I'm Officer Dale Corrigan, and I'm here on behalf of the Houston Police Department. Mind if I come inside?" He asked like it was a question, but you couldn't say no to the police.

I opened the screen door wide and motioned him inside. "Sure, come on in." Houston? I didn't know anyone in Houston. I hadn't been to Texas in years. And even then, it was only to drive through it on the way to Phoenix to visit my grandmother.

I'd let him in, and when he'd told me he was there about Regina, I made an audible gasp, even though I hadn't meant to. And then he'd showed me a copy of the letter she'd written her mother before she went missing, and I had to sit down. That's how we ended up in the living room, because the dining room and table were a mess. Otherwise, we would've sat there, but that's where I worked and saw all my clients. There was confidential information about them splayed out everywhere, and I didn't want him to see it. I take my clients' privacy very seriously.

I'd never been so grateful for Dad's cognitive impairments as I had been while he'd asked the police officer the same questions over and over again. Or that he'd thought it was 1994 and the officer was coming to take me out on a date. Dad kept embarrassing the officer and making him uncomfortable. Normally, I would've jumped in to stop it, but I liked that it was making the officer as off kilter as me. I just sat for a few minutes, watching it play itself out.

"Like I was saying," the officer said to me as soon as Dad gave him a break in the conversation, "we'd really like to know if you've seen or heard from Regina Crosby or anyone from Camp Pendleton in the last two weeks."

I'd looked him straight in the eye and lied. My insides were trembling. I was sweating down both legs and in my armpits. I felt like I couldn't breathe. But I smiled politely and denied having seen them. I promised to call him if I heard anything.

He'd left it alone. Hadn't pressed me further. Being in the living room with Dad made him uncomfortable, and he just wanted to get out of here as quick as he could. Would he be back? Would he bring someone with him? What would I say if he did?

The last time I saw Blakely, I'd carried pieces of her husband's dead body out of the house in a big Samsonite suitcase.

"Thank you, sweetie. Thank you so much," she'd said after I got back, with tears glistening in her blue eyes and emotions thick in her throat. "I'll never be able to repay you."

"You're welcome," I'd said, squeezing her back just as tight. Feeling so incredibly proud of the job I'd done.

Meg had a suitcase too. She went forty miles north to Lake Lanier, but I went south to Okefenokee Swamp where the Chattahoochee River drained into the basin, creating the perfect home for alligators. Blakely drew us maps on paper with detailed driving instructions and exactly where to go and what to do once we were there.

"The police can track all that stuff in your phone, and you don't want them to find anything if it ever comes up," she'd explained when she made us leave our phones at the house with her and handed us the maps. Handwritten ones on paper, like the old days.

It was smart. I never would've thought of that, but she'd thought about so many of the details. Like Meg's suitcase had a set of ten-pound dumbbells inside it, along with Phillip's body. Since she was dumping her suitcase in Lake Lanier, she wanted it to sink fast and stay down there. The longer it was immersed, the longer it had to decompose, giving Blakely more time to get away. Once it did, if it did, she hoped it'd come up in pieces, and it'd take them a long time to identify Phillip. But she'd gone the extra mile and done another really smart thing that I wouldn't have thought of either. She'd kept his teeth. She'd yanked them out with pliers.

"Besides his DNA, and unless he's in their database, he's pretty much a blank slate. They'll probably just chalk him up to one of the homeless bodies that gets dumped in there every year. Or"—she gave a wicked grin—"maybe he'll just disappear."

That's what she was really hoping for. Bodies went missing in the lake all the time. Just vanished. Never found again. Twenty-seven just in the last ten years. It was the most haunted spot in Georgia, and it'd taken over seven hundred victims in its water. That's why she picked it.

The other half of Phillip went into my suitcase. My suitcase didn't have any weights because we didn't want mine to sink down to the bottom of the lake, like Meg's. We wanted it to pop open, and she worked the latch so that it could easily undo once it hit the water or something bumped against it. Then, the alligators would feast like they feasted on any other red meat that came near them.

"Whatever you do, don't touch that." She pointed to the golden clasp. "It's super loose, so it'll fall open in the water, but you definitely don't want it falling open beforehand. Can you imagine?"

She'd been so thoughtful. She knew exactly where I should park so that if someone spotted me, I wouldn't look suspicious lugging a suitcase. She'd drawn me a map of that, too, just in case. She really didn't want us to get caught doing anything wrong. Or maybe she was just protecting herself.

We never asked how she'd gotten Phillip into pieces. How did she cut through his bones? That's all I kept wondering. You couldn't cut through bone with a kitchen knife. Did she use a chain saw? And where'd she do it in her crystalline house? I kept picturing her in the garage with a chain saw, splattering blood all over the gleaming white walls. I watched Meg while she was going over the instructions with us a final time, and her eyes held the same questions. And the same strange excitement too. She couldn't believe she was doing it either. That's what her eyes said every time she looked at me. *Are we really doing this?*

And we were. We did.

I woke up that morning feeling really important. Like what I did during the day was going to matter, and nothing I'd done in a really long time had mattered. I'd been starving and had a huge breakfast. French toast slathered in syrup and extra butter, with a tall glass of orange juice to wash it all down. It was delicious. All of it. Then, I'd set out for my drive with a suitcase in the trunk of my car. I had my own car, since I'd driven from Greensboro, but she rented one for Meg. We'd said goodbye in the driveway, like we were heading off to work. Blakely even packed us lunches so we wouldn't have to stop anywhere, and she'd remembered I hated mustard, leaving it off my turkey sandwich.

It was a beautiful drive. All the alligators lived below the fall line, so that's where I was headed. To one of the most popular spots to be, if you were interested in seeing them. They crawled out of the swamps and roamed people's yards, eating their pets if they weren't careful. They'd also been known to show up on the Oxbow Meadows golf course and send all the golfers scurrying to their carts in a mad panic. Meg fed Phillip's body to ghosts, and I fed him to alligators.

I was terrified of getting pulled over on the way there, so I went exactly the speed limit. Not too high. Not too low. Just right. I was obsessed with which parts of him I was carrying. It was all I could think about on the drive. How'd Blakely split him up? Did I have his arms? His legs? What had she done with his big head? It was huge. She never would've been able to fit it in the suitcase without smashing it first. How did you flatten a skull? Did she use a hammer?

I really wanted to pull over and stop. Open the suitcase just to see what was inside. But I didn't. That wasn't a part of the plan, and we needed to stick to the plan. Anything else was too risky.

The drop went perfectly. Absolutely flawless. Nobody else in sight.

My last thought when I finally dropped the suitcase into the water and watched the murky bubbles rise was completely unexpected: What if I was the one carrying his penis? One of us had to be, and there was a 50 percent chance it was me. Something about the possibility of it being me just gave me the biggest case of the giggles. I'd laughed all the way back to the car.

I wasn't laughing now. I had no idea what was going on.

I gathered all Dad's medicines on a tray, along with the applesauce he'd need to eat first. His nighttime meds always made him sick, so he couldn't take them on an empty stomach.

The truth was exactly as I told the detective—I hadn't heard from Blakely. Not since I told her goodbye in Atlanta. She'd wrapped her arms around me on her porch and squeezed me so hard I could barely breathe. The kind of hugs my grandmother used to give. I'd inhaled her scent the same way so that I could hold her with me for as long as possible.

I couldn't help but realize how alive I felt. Really, truly alive, after all these years. Like how you do when you're a kid and each day is a brand-new and exciting adventure. Where you wake up sprinting out of bed rather than wanting to immediately lie back down and pull the covers over your head. I spent most of my days sleepwalking through my life, with all the days blending together as one. Unattached and adrift. Not that I didn't love my dad. I loved my dad. Always would. He was the only thing tethering me to the planet, except he spent more and more of his time not even knowing he was here. Yesterday he thought I was his great-aunt Betty.

I'd felt more alive in the last two weeks than I'd felt in fifteen years. From the moment I'd gotten the letter from Regina. It made me remember what it was like to actually experience things. It wasn't like I hadn't tried to revive my life when I noticed it sputtering out. I had. Going on fancy vacations. Treating myself to new clothes. A fresh haircut. Long walks. Getting laid. Spa treatments. I'd done everything you're supposed to do when you're trying to breathe life back into your being. None of it worked.

Then I got the letter, and it pumped life straight into my veins. All my emotions on high alert. And I remembered what it felt like to feel. *Really* feel. To be scared. Terrified. Happy. Excited. Nervous.

Brave. I'd ricocheted through all of them since it happened. It totally rejuvenated me.

"Here you go, Dad," I said, setting the tray down next to his recliner. The one he spent his days in now. Even sleeping there at night because he no longer liked his bed. Said it was too uncomfortable. I handed him the small bowl of applesauce. "Let's have you eat this first."

I watched him as he carefully spooned it into his mouth and took small cautious bites. I wiped the drool from the corners of his mouth as he ate, and I tried not to smile.

I didn't know if the police officer would come back. I had no idea if I'd hear from Blakely again either. But if I did? If she called again? Well, I hated to admit it, but the first question out of my mouth would be "What are we doing next?"

# CHAPTER THIRTY-SIX
## *NOW*

### GRACE

The last ten miles to go, and this time I didn't get a flat tire. I'd also shaved an hour off my time. Last trip, I'd gone slow. Using the hours on the road to unwind my mind. This time I'd seen how fast my Mercedes could go and how well it really handled turns. I hadn't been to Atlanta in ten years, and now I was about to be there twice in just over a week.

I'd tried going to bed last night after my conversation with Meg, hoping I could shut my brain off. I even took a sleeping pill, but it had absolutely no effect, other than to give me a terrible headache. I'd lain there for two hours, with my brain replaying different scenarios over and over again. Meg said she was telling the truth, and her story sounded plausible, but I didn't know if I believed her. Not fully. She'd hidden crucial information. Would she have told us about her letter to Regina once we were outside if Blakely hadn't dropped the bomb about her husband?

I'd gone back and forth what felt like a million times, and I just couldn't say for sure. If she'd purposefully kept it a secret, then what else was she hiding? How did I know she wasn't working with Blakely? That's when I decided to pay Little Miss Blakely a surprise visit, since her phone still said it was disconnected. I'd tapped out a short email to Tessa to tell her to post some of my prerecorded stuff in the morning and to let her know that my mom was sick so I was going home to pay her a quick visit. Which was a total lie. I barely spoke to my mom anymore. Mostly just saw her on the holidays, if then. Our relationship had never recovered after her affair, especially not after she went on to marry the man. Not that I hadn't forgiven her. I just couldn't stomach being around her. The moment I'd caught her kissing another man besides my dad, she'd stopped being who she'd been to me, and I'd never gotten that person back. Sometimes there were wounds you just couldn't heal from, even after they became scars.

Blakely lived at the end of a long cul-de-sac. The last house at the end of the street, right smack in the middle. I didn't want her to know I was coming, so I parked over on the next block and walked the rest of the way. I spotted the For Sale sign posted up in their front yard as soon as I made the corner.

Blakely clearly hadn't wasted any time on her promises of getting out and starting over. I couldn't help but be curious how much she was listing her house for, so I pulled it up on Zillow. It wasn't the amount she was asking for that stole the air from my lungs—it was how long the house had been listed on the market. Twenty-one days. Over a week before she'd sent us the letters and we'd met at her house. She'd already been planning on moving.

Why?

I stared at the house. A huge traditional white colonial built in the 1950s and recently remodeled, like all the other houses on the block. Flanked with huge windows framed in black. A perfectly manicured front yard leading up to the porch. They'd been planning to move before we got there? That didn't make sense. Phillip was still alive then. I walked slowly toward the house. Each step deliberate and slow, trying to fit this new information into the already complicated puzzle.

I got to the house and walked up to the front door. But I knew before I got there that it was pointless to be here. The glass door let

me know she was already gone. The house was barren. Sparkling wood
floors and shiny white walls flanked in windows, but empty. They hadn't
even staged the house, or maybe they already had multiple offers. Either
way, she was gone and she wasn't coming back. That was clear.

I walked back out to the yard sign and found the agent's phone
number. I quickly tapped out a text letting her know I was interested
in the house and asked her to call me when she had a chance. I'd barely
made it to the sidewalk when my phone buzzed with her call. Real
estate agents were the fanciest of used-car salesmen, even the best ones.

"Hi, Grace. This is Jackie. I just got your text about the house
on Myers Street. Such a great property, isn't it? Four bedrooms. Six
bathrooms. The kitchen is absolutely incredible. Done with imported
porcelain tiles. Concrete countertops. And it flows so seamlessly into
the entertainer's backyard. Stunning. If I didn't love my house, I'd think
about buying it." She laughed. "Anyway, I just want to be completely
transparent and let you know we've got an offer accepted on the house.
But . . . no money has actually been exchanged. Still seventy-two hours
for the deposit to go through. So, what I'm saying is that if there was
an offer that blew them out of the water, I'm not saying my clients
wouldn't take a look."

"Oh bummer." I feigned disappointment. "It's such an incredible
place. I stopped by twice for the open house last weekend and absolutely
fell in love with it."

"Open house?" The friendly salesperson instantly left her voice.
"My clients only allow private showings."

I thought fast. "Really? Hmm . . . Maybe I'm confusing it with
the house on Williams behind it?" I noticed all the other listings when
I pulled up theirs, and my brain had instantly memorized the address
because my brain had a mind of its own. Always has. This time it saved
me, because she was immediately back to being a saleswoman.

"Yes, that's a gorgeous property too. Unfortunately, it's not one of
Keller Williams's. Are you already working with an agent?"

"Yes, and he's fantastic," I said, not wanting to raise any of her suspicions after I'd just lowered them. "Richard Mandaue from Sotheby's, and he should be landing any minute. He's just getting back from New York or I would've just had him call you. I'm sure you'll hear from him within the hour, as soon as I tell him about the house. He's old school and insists on writing the sellers a letter. If we're in a time crunch, I really want to get an offer in, though. I've never done anything like this before, but I actually really love the property, and if I can talk my husband into it, we might just have to go in cash, if that will sway the seller in our direction. Who should we address the letter to?"

I could feel her practically buzzing with energy at the mention of a cash offer. "Phillip and Blakely Reynolds. They are wonderful people. Absolutely wonderful. Phillip especially. I was just telling him yesterday how easy he is to work with and how much I appreciate it. You know, sometimes sellers can get so stressed out because there are so many moving parts involved. And I won't lie, there's plenty of times that the sellers take it out on their agents. I can't say I blame them. But Phillip? He's a great guy. Never bats an eye, no matter what comes his way."

"Did you say yesterday?"

"Yes."

"You spoke with him yesterday?"

The hesitation was back in her voice. She drew out her yes. Instantly curious as to why I would care. This time I had nothing to give her.

"Great. Great," I said quickly. "That makes me happy. Well, look, I'm going to jump off and give my husband a call. We're going to start putting our offer together, and you'll be hearing from my agent soon. So nice to meet you. Thank you for all your help." I hit end before she'd finished saying goodbye.

I practically ran back to the car. My heart thudded. My head pounded. She'd talked to Phillip yesterday. She was one person that had no reason to lie. But how did she talk to Phillip if he was supposed to be dead? I slid into the passenger seat and pulled my phone back out. I quickly pulled up Instagram.

I hadn't gone to Blakely's Instagram last night, no matter how badly I wanted to, because I was afraid the police would be able to tell I'd been there, and I wanted to stay as far away from her as possible. I had no idea what they were capable of or if they even had to ask my permission to snoop on my online behavior, so I hadn't been willing to risk it then. But I was now.

She hadn't posted anything since the dinner she'd had at El Floridita's two months ago. But the red circle around her profile pic was there, letting me know she'd posted something in her stories. I clicked on it.

And there it was.

Her and Phillip on a sailboat in the middle of an ocean somewhere. They were at the helm, and he had his hand around her waist, almost like they were trying to mimic the scene from *Titanic*. The pose was so Blakely. And then the caption:

On our way to the Cayman Islands for our second honeymoon followed by a string of various heart emoji and exclamation points.

I couldn't believe it. She might as well be giving us the finger. Of course she'd set us up. Probably from the very beginning. What had we been a part of? Was it too late to stop it? I immediately called Meg. She answered on the third ring, like she'd been waiting for my call.

I skipped the hello and went straight to the problem. "Phillip is alive, and Blakely's the biggest liar on the planet. She played you again. She played all of us."

"What are you talking about?"

"I'm in Atlanta, and I just left her house. Her house that's for sale and already wiped spotless. Not just that, though. This is where it gets good. The house has been on the market for twenty-one days. Whatever's happening, whatever she did, she's been planning it all along. I talked to the real estate agent. She said she talked to Phillip yesterday. Yesterday, Meg. How the hell do you talk to a dead man?"

"I mean, I mean . . . maybe she had another man pretend to be him? She told us she was making everyone think he was still alive and she was going to keep doing it until she had a good chance to get away. That she didn't want anyone to think he'd gone missing. She'd been answering all his emails and his texts."

"No. No. That's not it. The agent said she spoke to him multiple times."

"But that still doesn't mean anything. Blakely probably has someone take his phone calls too. How would the agent know if she was talking to the real Phillip or someone else that Blakely had pretending to be him?" She said it with way more confidence than I felt.

"Exactly how would that work? Another man in her life? She doesn't have any brothers besides Jonathon, and we know he's not helping her out with anything. And if Phillip's so controlling and doesn't allow her to have any friends, then how'd she meet someone to help her? And even if, by some chance, she did, no guy in their right mind is going to just meet someone and pretend to be their husband."

"You said it yourself, she can be really convincing."

"None of that matters," I said, shaking my head. We didn't need to get hung up on that part anyway. "He's alive. It's not just that the real estate agent said she talked to him. I just checked Blakely's Instagram, and she posted a story with the two of them. Her and Phillip. They're in the middle of the Caribbean right now."

"No way. Not possible." She shook her head like she refused to let the information inside. "She said she's monitoring his social media too. Doing all that too. She probably just posted an old photo of them. People do it all the time. You know that."

"I checked the time stamp. It was taken this morning." Any picture or video taken on an iPhone had a time stamp you could look up even if you hadn't been the one to take it.

That's when the air finally went still. Only Meg's breathing. The space stretched on between us as she finally let all the information sink in, shattering the last pieces of her denial. Her voice was hesitant and scared when she finally spoke. "Then whose body did I carry out of Blakely's house in a suitcase?"

# CHAPTER THIRTY-SEVEN
## *NOW*

### MEG

I spotted the squad car the moment I turned down our block, and my heart sank in my chest. Apparently, if you avoided the police long enough, they showed up at your house. It'd only been two days since the detective left the voicemail, but the detectives must not have time to wait for people to talk to their missing friends before talking to their suspects. Both Thera and Grace were convinced we'd never see or hear from Blakely again, but part of me was still holding on to hope that she'd at least contact one of us.

Claire's car was in the driveway, which was strange since she was supposed to be working late tonight. Hopefully nothing was wrong with the kids. She would've called me if something was wrong with the kids, though. I grabbed my bag and the files I'd brought home from the office and hurried to get inside. Now that the officer was here, I just wanted to get this over with as fast as I could.

I opened the door to find Claire sitting in the living room with two officers dressed in regular clothes. Everyone froze when they saw me. Claire's face was stricken. Maybe I was wrong. Maybe this had nothing to do with Blakely and Regina. What if this was about the kids?

"Oh my God, did something happen to Molly or Shad?" I ignored the officers and directed my question at Claire.

She shook her head in quick jerks and cleared her throat. Then opened her mouth and tried to speak, but nothing came out.

"Are you okay? What's happening?" I rushed toward her, and she jumped up before I got close, knocking the coffee table with her knee and spilling some of the coffee onto the floor and all over everything. But she didn't even care. Not like she usually would.

"Get away from me. Don't come near me." Her voice trembled with fear. She clutched the arm of the officer standing next to her.

I froze. "What's going on?" This time I turned my attention to the police officers. What had they told her? Why was she terrified?

The other officer stepped forward and stuck out his hand. "I'm Officer Jameson, and this is my partner, Erik." He motioned to the man standing next to Claire. She was still clinging to his arm. Her eyes wide. Body rigid and stiff. I'd never seen her like this. "We just had a couple questions about your whereabouts a few weeks ago." He reached into his pocket and pulled out a small notebook. He flipped it open like he was going to take notes old-school-style, even though he looked way younger than me. "Can you tell me where you were the weekend of September twentieth?" He glanced at his notebook. "Let's see. September twentieth through September twenty-second. Do you remember where you were that weekend?"

I was at Blakely's. That was the weekend. My throat tightened. Mouth went completely dry. I couldn't swallow. Claire's eyes drilled into me.

"Yeah, Meg, why don't you tell the officers where you were that weekend?" Her voice was still trembling, but this time it wasn't fear. She was angry and looking for blood.

I tried to smile, but still couldn't. My lips were stuck to my gums. A piece of skin tore when I tried to talk. "I was in Atlanta. Downtown at Woodruff for a conference." My voice didn't sound like mine.

"Really? There for work?" He scribbled on his pad without looking up. I kept my eyes on him. I couldn't look at Claire and lie at the same time.

I nodded. Gulping, desperately trying to swallow. The lack of oxygen made me feel dizzy. What if I just passed out right in front of them? Would they still be there to question me when I woke up?

"Did you go anywhere else besides downtown? Go to a fancy dinner somewhere? Take in any movies?" He looked up at me from under his long lashes. "See any old friends?"

I shook my head.

"You didn't see anyone else? Didn't go anywhere else? Just stayed down there the whole time, did you?" He raised his eyebrows at me. Not even trying to hide his disbelief.

"Yes," I lied, because I didn't know what else to say. What did they know? Why were they here? What had they told my wife?

"Stop lying!" Claire's scream cut through the air. "They have you on video. All the traffic-cam videos."

A pit opened in my stomach. Bile rose in my throat. What had they seen me do? How'd I end up on camera? We'd been so careful.

"Would you like to sit down?" Erik asked, pointing to the couch.

I couldn't do anything but stand there while the world spun around me. The air warbled like it did when I ate shrooms. All the blood rushed to the back of my head. My pulse pounded.

He waited for me to respond, and when I didn't, he walked over to the coffee table and grabbed the manila folder sitting on top of it. I hadn't noticed it when I walked in. He opened the folder and pulled out a stack of glossy photos. Then, walked slowly back to me, drawing out the moment. He handed me the photo on top.

"This you?" he asked, pointing at it.

I didn't want to take the picture but I had no other choice. I reluctantly grabbed it from him and stared in horror at an enlarged photo of me driving the rental car up I-85 on my way to the swamp. There was no denying I was the woman in the picture. I nodded slowly. He handed me another one.

"How about this?" The camera had captured a perfect side profile of me this time. My forehead was lined with concentration as I crossed over McEver Bridge. It was so obviously me there was no reason to respond.

"What were you doing out by Lake Lanier? Awfully far from the High Museum of Art, don't you think?" the other officer asked.

What were their names? Had they given them to me? Officer Jameson. That's who he was. My thoughts were so scattered. Why weren't they wearing badges? All of this was so disorienting. I felt my insides shrinking. The same way they'd done that day in the dean's office. I turned around, automatically searching for Claire, because she was my rock. But when my eyes landed on hers, they met those of a stranger. She'd unplugged herself completely from me.

"What were you doing there, Meg?" Her voice was ice cold. Eyes impenetrable.

My head spun. I didn't know what to say. What to tell her. I could handle almost anything besides losing her. I raced over to her and crouched at her feet, grabbing both her hands, but she jerked away.

"Don't touch me!" she shrieked.

"Please, Claire. Just let me explain. It'll all make sense if you just let me tell you what happened. I can explain everything. Please, Claire. I love you. I'd never hurt you on purpose. Just let me explain myself." But I just sounded like every other person who'd been caught lying. "You have to—"

Officer Jameson cut in. "We'd really like to hear that explanation, ma'am, if you don't mind telling us too. Maybe you could start with why you were driving Thomas Reynolds's car."

I whipped around. "Thomas Reynolds's car?" That was Blakely's dad. Blakely's dad was Thomas Reynolds. But Blakely told me it was a rental car. She said she'd gotten it from Enterprise. Had it delivered that morning.

He nodded like he was irritated with me, as if I was purposefully playing dumb and he'd reached his limit. "Yes, that's what we're here about today. We've spoken with Blakely Reynolds, and she let us know that she'd introduced the two of you years ago. Apparently, you'd reached out again to her and asked to speak with her dad? What was it that you wanted to chat with him about?"

"Thomas Reynolds?"

"Yes, Thomas Reynolds."

"The last time I saw that man was at camp when I was a child."

He shook his head. "Mind explaining how you got his car, then? And what you're doing driving it without him in it? Or was he in it? Just in the back seat or the trunk, where the cameras couldn't see him. Because here's the thing—Thomas has been missing since that weekend." He pointed to the pictures I was still holding. "And you're the last one to be seen with him. Well, not exactly with him. Driving his car."

"I don't know what you're talking about." I turned to Claire. "Really, I have no idea what they're talking about. I swear. I thought I was helping Blakely. I was just trying to help Blakely. I don't know what happened to her dad."

Officer Erik stepped forward. "See that's the thing, Meg. We think something pretty bad happened to Mr. Reynolds. Because do you want to know what else we found in his car?" He paused. Staring pointedly at me like it'd make me confess, but I had nothing to give him. "Blood. His blood everywhere in the back seat and in the trunk of that car. Along with lots of other fingerprints and hair matching another person. I'm willing to bet that if we take you down to the station, like we're about to do, and take a sample of your DNA, we're going to discover that it matches all the material left in that car. Up until this point, my partner's been nice to you, but I'm not like him. I have no time for people that don't know how to tell the truth."

All I could do was shake my head.

"Just tell them the truth, Meg. Please do the right thing. He's been missing for weeks. You can't let that poor family suffer. Think about your friend Blakely," Claire cried.

Blakely had drawn me the map. Precisely drawn it out with a black marker. Thera and I thought she was being so kind and thoughtful that day. My hands stuck to the pictures. Sticky with sweat. She'd given me the car. Said she'd rented it herself. I thought a Lexus was a bit extravagant for a rental, but I figured she'd gone for the luxury since over-the-top was her style.

"I *am* telling the truth, Claire. I have no idea what happened to that man."

Erik snorted. "I'm done with this." He motioned to Officer Jameson. "Let's just take her down to the station."

Officer Jameson stepped toward me. "I don't want to go down to the station." I frantically shook my head. "I already told you everything that I know. I have nothing to do with whatever happened to Thomas Reynolds. Nothing. I haven't seen him since I was a teenager."

But he wasn't listening to me. He was reaching for his waist and pulling out the handcuffs. "Mrs. Watson, I'm going to ask you to turn around."

"I'm being arrested? You can't arrest me for pictures of me driving a car. I haven't done anything wrong. You can't arrest me." I said it again.

But that's exactly what they were doing. Officer Jameson gripped my arm in a way that meant business. "Mrs. Wilson, you're under arrest for the murder of Thomas Reynolds. You have the right—"

"What?" I shrieked. "What are you talking about?" This wasn't happening. It couldn't be happening. I hadn't murdered anyone. I'd barely even met Blakely's father. Just a few times in passing, a long time ago. What had she done?

Officer Jameson just kept reading me my rights while Erik talked on top of him. "It's only a matter of time before we find his body, Meg, so you might as well tell us what you did with it. We've already found his teeth. Those were in the back seat too. The back seat of the car you were driving."

# CHAPTER THIRTY-EIGHT

## *NOW*

## BLAKELY

The sun beamed down on my forehead, bouncing off my hat. The wind coming from the east caressed my cheeks. The bluest skies reflecting off even bluer water, making it hard to tell where the sky ended and the water began. Nothing but endless blue beyond the horizon. Nobody else in sight. God, I loved the Caribbean.

I always thought it would be hard to kill someone. I'd considered it before, especially when I was a teenager. I'd thought about killing my stepmom all the time. Like all the time. I'd always imagined it'd be so tough to step over that line and actually do it. But it wasn't. It was way easier than I'd thought. Maybe that's because I've been a murderer since birth, so it's partly in my DNA.

Phillip's arms wrapped around my waist. He nuzzled his face against the back of my neck.

"You smell delicious," he said. He was still in a towel from the shower. We'd slept until noon again. Been up half the night making love in a way that we hadn't since we were first together, when we couldn't keep our hands off each other. That was the thing about living on a boat in the middle of the Caribbean. You lost all sense of time. "God, I love you."

"I love you too," I said, laying my hands on top of his. Killing Regina had brought us together as a couple in a way that no amount of marriage therapy had ever done.

I thought everything was ruined the night Grace left my house in Atlanta. I still couldn't believe she'd left, but then I couldn't believe anything about Grace. I was sure Thera would be the one I'd have to talk into the plan. I'd practiced all the conversations that I might have with her because I was sure she'd be the one that needed convincing. I had the pictures to show her of what Phillip had supposedly done to my face a few weeks ago when he was angry, but I hadn't wanted to pull those out unless I'd absolutely had to. That picture was really hard to look at, and I didn't want to traumatize her any more than absolutely necessary. It'd been an even harder picture to make since Phillip refused to hit me. Finally, we'd put a ball in a sock, and he'd helped me hit myself with it. That got the job done just as well. My left cheek was covered in a nasty bruise, and both eyes were black. The way my lip had split was the worst. It looked hideous and still did underneath all the makeup I wore to cover it up. Painful just to look at. But I would've showed the picture to her if it would've helped her understand why I'd done what I'd done.

Grace was the last person I expected to give me pushback about it. But everything about Grace had been surprising from the moment she walked in the door. I told the others I hadn't followed them, but that was only partially true. I hadn't followed them when there wasn't any way to follow them, but the moment social media was born, I'd been studying all of them like I was earning a master's degree in women's studies. And I wasn't going to lie. I watched all of Grace's stuff. I was obsessed with her.

We all knew how hard she struggled with her weight, but we never talked about it. Just like we never talked about mine or what I did in the bathroom. Don't think there wasn't a reason for that. I made sure those kinds of conversations never happened, carefully steered conversations in the opposite direction. I was great at creating distractions. But all that stuff no longer mattered.

I hadn't binged in three weeks. Not since I killed Regina. Who knew that would finally satisfy my hunger?

I hadn't been all that surprised when I started receiving letters from her. They started arriving in the weeks leading up to her release and continued after she got out. Her letters weren't like the cryptic ones I'd sent to my friends. Hers were much more direct and straightforward.

> You are responsible for killing my husband. I know
> what you did. I was there. If you don't pay me 300,000
> dollars, I'm going to the authorities.

Of course I ignored them. What was she going to say? Tell them she was blackmailing the girl in the famous picture? Like anyone was going to believe that story. And even if they did, what were they going to do to me?

Nothing.

It'd been over twenty-six years. Plus, I'd been a kid in their eyes. Innocent and sweet. A victim of a controlling and abusive predator who'd taken advantage of my innocence. It would be my word against hers, and we all knew who they'd believe. So, the first time she called, I laughed in her face. The second time, I hung up on her. I thought that would be the end of it.

But then she showed up at my front door. Buzzing to be let in at the security gate. When I saw her on camera, that first time, I got a tiny bit scared that I couldn't just continue ignoring her. That I might have to actually deal with her.

"Blakely, you little bitch. Let me in," she'd hissed into the intercom.

I'd pretended like I wasn't home, but she'd come back the next day and the next day and the one after that. "You can ignore me all you want, but I'm not going away. I'm going to show up here every day until you talk to me. You're going to help my mom. Period. This isn't a negotiation. You think I'm playing with you? I'm not playing with you."

It was what she said on day seven that made me take her threats seriously. Also made me the most nervous.

"You understand I've been to prison, right? Do you know everything I've seen? What I've experienced? And I want you to know something else. I'm not scared to go back. I'll do whatever it takes to get help for my mom. And just in case you're wondering, I have absolutely nothing to lose. Why do you think that is? Oh yeah, that's why. Because some spoiled-ass rich girl decided to play with my family just for fun. Well, guess what? I'm going to play with yours."

Regina had been serious. She wasn't playing around. She was the one that killed Camille. Not Phillip, like I'd told the girls that night. But the best lies are the ones partially based in truth.

Our privacy fence enclosed our entire property, so I left the sliding glass doors open in the back. My babies went in and out of the house all day long. They had complete control over the yard in the same way they had complete control over us. They were our babies. We were intentionally childless, and not in the way that I'd told the girls. We didn't want kids, so we'd gotten Phillip fixed, and I took birth control just to be safe. But our babies? They had their own Instagram page. Sometimes there was crossover with my personal one, so I'm assuming that's how Regina found them. And that's how she knew how to kill them.

She was right. Prison had made her smart. She'd checked out the property long before she'd done it, because there was only one blind spot on the entire space where you couldn't see the person if they were standing behind the trees, and that's where she'd stood. The security cameras could still catch what happened on the other side of the fence, though, so they picked up the raw meat being tossed over. She meant to kill all of them. I know she did. It just so happened that Camille got to the fence first. She bit and snapped at the others when they tried to come close.

The raw meat brought out her animal instinct. She'd gobbled it up so fast, she'd barely swallowed. Licking her lips at the end. I hadn't found her lying on the pillows like I'd told the girls. That was another lie. I'd found her foaming at the mouth and twitching on the welcome mat at the back patio door.

I took her to the vet for them to run bloodwork, but I already knew Regina had killed her. Zinc phosphide. That's what the vet said after he got the results. I'd cocked my head to the side in confusion.

"Rat poison," he said with tears in his eyes. He'd treated my babies since they were puppies, and he loved animals as much as I did. "Somehow, she must've gotten into it while you were on a walk. Maybe there was a trap you didn't see. Or some leftover residue on the sidewalk."

But there wasn't. Regina had done it. There was no doubt in my mind. A few days later, she was back at my intercom.

"Blakely, you're going to let me in, and you're going to talk to me. Otherwise? I'm coming after your other babies. One by one. And if that doesn't do it?" She laughed. The cackle exaggerated through the speakers. "Then I'm coming after your husband. Only seems fair, doesn't it?"

That time I'd let her in.

She took one look at me and remembered. She remembered it well. But I hadn't forgotten. Not the way her face looked that day when she burst through Jared's door or the way her entire body trembled with rage. Every part of those moments was alive in me.

She'd crashed into the office just as Jared screamed at me.

"Get away from me, Blakely! Don't come anywhere near me!" He wouldn't stop screaming it. That's all he'd been doing since I'd burst through the door moments before. He'd scooted his chair all the way back against the wall, plastered himself against it, trying to get as far away from me as possible.

Regina stood in the doorway, staring at us and breathing hard. Her bald head gleamed with sweat. Her nostrils flared. Chest heaved. She took a slow step toward us. That's when I spotted the knife clenched in her right hand. The same time as Jared.

He raised his hands into the air. "R-Regina, Regina," he stuttered, talking fast. "Settle down, okay. I want you to just settle down. Take it easy. Nothing is happening. Nothing happened. I didn't do anything wrong. I never touched this girl. I never touched any of them."

Her head was cocked to the side. Stiff. Everything about her was rigid. And her eyes. I'd never seen anyone's eyes look like that before.

She looked back and forth between us. Her movements were so slow. Robotic. Jared was frozen to his chair. His eyes flicking back and forth between us.

"How could you?" she asked through clenched teeth, like it physically hurt her to speak.

Jared kept his hands raised. "Regina, look at me. Look in my eyes. You know me. I would never do anything like that. Never. This girl?" He pointed at me. His face filled with disgust and utter disdain. The same way he'd looked the first time I broke into his office. I wanted to slap the look off his face. "There's something wrong with her. Seriously wrong with her, and she needs help. I've never touched her. It makes me sick to even look at her."

Regina turned to me. Slow. Steady. She locked eyes with me. Her eyes searching, begging for the truth.

I shook my head, then quickly burst into tears. I pointed at Jared, still backed up against the wall with his arms raised in defense. "He just tried to rape me. I just came in here to tell him I was sorry for getting him in trouble, and he tried to rape me."

That was all it took. Sometimes people just needed a little help unleashing what was already inside them. Something in her snapped. I watched it happen.

She lunged for him, and I stepped out of the way. The first stab sounded just like a hard slap. Straight in his chest. All the way through. Smack down to the handle. Then she just started screaming and unleashed. Stabbing him the same way I used to stab my dolls. Except blood poured out of him, instead of puffy white stuffing.

I let her have at him right until Meg ran into the room. That's when I grabbed the knife and started trying to wrestle it away from her, but she was stronger than she looked. I finally worked the knife away from her, and something about the way it felt in my hand made me feel things I'd never experienced before. I hated that he'd rejected me. That he thought he was better. How dare he. But mostly—I just wanted to know what it felt like. I didn't feel things like regular people. So, that's when I'd done it. Grabbed the knife and sliced. It was such a smooth, easy cut. Nothing to it.

The memory of the moment hit me as hard as it hit Regina.

That was when she'd bolted straight for the stairs behind me.

I hadn't meant to kill her. I really didn't. It was an accident.

Isn't that what everyone says, though?

That's no kind of excuse. None that they'd believe. Except it was the truth.

James Bond was at the top of the stairs, and that's who she was going for next. I raced after her and grabbed her by the ponytail, the same way Shamu grabbed his trainer in the story I always told at camp. I just wanted to stop her from hurting another one of my babies. I didn't think she'd fall down the stairs. I definitely didn't expect the crack her head made on the marble or the way the blood spread instantly after it did.

I sat at the end of the stairs, just staring at her body as she lay there crumpled up at the bottom. Blood pooled around her head like a puddle while I tried to figure out what to do. I kept waiting for her to pass out from the pain, but she just wouldn't. At first, she was just groaning and moaning, but then she started screaming for help. I had to put duct tape over her mouth because I was afraid the neighbors would hear her and call the police. That's when I texted Phillip to come home, because I didn't know what else to do.

He found me sobbing at the edge of our tub in the master bedroom, desperately trying to wash the blood off Winston's paws. Winston had run through the huge puddle underneath Regina's body, and I'd chased him all through the house, trying to catch him. There were red footprints everywhere. James Bond was still downstairs, licking it up.

"Get James Bond!" I cried. Something about them being covered in Regina's blood totally freaked me out.

Phillip raced downstairs, and I could hear him cussing as he went. It was only a matter of seconds before he thundered back upstairs.

"She's dead! Blakely, she's dead." His eyes were huge as he scanned the bathroom, trying to figure out what was going on.

"She's probably just finally knocked out. She hit her head really hard." I kept my voice calm, focused on cleaning Winston.

"The tape was over her nose and her mouth. She couldn't breathe."

"What do you mean, she couldn't breathe? I was just trying to get her to be quiet." I did my best to look innocent but still scared.

He frantically shook his head. Beads of sweat were on his forehead like he'd just worked out, even though he'd come from his office. "This is how you had her taped up." He demonstrated while he talked like he was covering his mouth in invisible tape. "You suffocated her."

I sank back on my heels. Holding Winston against my chest. I loved the smell of his new shampoo. Eucalyptus and oatmeal. "I suffocated her?"

I feigned innocence, but I'd watched the way she looked at me while she was lying at the bottom of the stairs. I liked the quiet, but I didn't like her eyes. They were full of hate. So judgmental. But she didn't know me. She didn't know what my life was like. And she was never going to go away. She was never going to leave us alone. So, I'd moved the tape up over her nose and watched in amazement as she struggled to breathe and her eyes bulged. I didn't know a person's eyes could pop out of their head like hers did. I texted Phillip while it was happening. I dashed upstairs as soon as I heard his car in the driveway. That was when the dogs got in all the blood and made such a mess.

"I suffocated her?" I asked again for good measure, making my voice tremble at the end.

"You did." He nodded. He ran his hands through his dark hair as he paced circles in the bathroom. "Who is she?"

I told him everything then. I didn't leave anything out. Well, except for the fact that I put the tape over her mouth on purpose. None of it had been part of my plan, but sometimes that's how the best plans were created. Out of nowhere. I just started talking and filling him in on that summer, concluding with how Meg had written Regina a letter, pointing her finger directly at me for being responsible for killing Regina's husband and putting a target on my back. I still couldn't believe Meg had done that. What did she think would happen when Regina got out? Of course she came after me. I wasn't surprised she came after me once she told me about the letter. I was only surprised that I'd been able to kill her so easily.

That was what had been so amazing about the entire experience with Phillip that afternoon. Just when you think you know a person, they turn around and do something that totally surprises you, and Phillip was full of surprises. He'd switched into action mode almost immediately.

"First thing we have to do is get her out of here and get this place cleaned up," he said after I finished explaining everything, and my heart swelled with love. "We'll decide what to do next after that."

We'd talked while we worked, wrapping her body in cling wrap and dragging it into the guest bathroom. She was way heavier than she looked, and I practically threw my back out heaving her into the bathtub. We filled the tub with ice that Phillip had delivered from 7-Eleven. That was the easy part. Scrubbing the blood and wiping everything down was the hard part. He was the one that had come up with the plan while we stood wringing out the towels in the sink.

"What if, instead of this being something terrible, we turned it into something positive?" he asked as he squirted soap into the bucket and started filling it another time.

"What do you mean?"

"What if we just left and started totally over?"

Turned out Phillip had secrets of his own to tell. Funny how when you bare your darkness to others, they feel free to share theirs with you. His business was in trouble. Big trouble. The going-bankrupt kind. He'd been secretly stealing money from my father's accounts, and my dad was furious with him. And you didn't want my dad mad at you. I knew that better than Phillip did. Daddy had been souring the pot against Phillip already, and he couldn't find any new investors to save his business. Daddy's influence was far reaching.

I liked the idea of wiping the slate clean. Starting over. I liked it even better when he suggested we get rid of my father right along with Regina. We were already covering up one murder. Why not make it two?

Plotting everything out had brought us back together in a way that no amount of marriage therapy ever had. It completely rejuvenated us as a couple. Turned everything around for us, and I'm not going to lie, there was a good chance we'd been headed for divorce. That'll happen when you've been together for over twenty years. I'd suspected him of cheating on me for quite a while, but I didn't actually have any real proof. Not like I'd told the girls. He wasn't stupid. Our prenuptial agreement that my father insisted on didn't leave him anything if there was any kind of infidelity. So, he hid his tracks well. Besides, it wasn't like I hadn't had my own fun. My personal trainer gave me the best head I'd ever had.

But things were like they were with us in the beginning while we worked out all the details. Having a common project and focus really made me feel like we were on a team for the first time in a long time, and everything between us was so easy. It felt good when it'd been hard for so many years. He quickly agreed to frame everything around Meg. She deserved it for writing the letter to Regina. It was too bad Thera had to be collateral damage, but Thera would forgive me. She loved me. I was the me she'd never allow herself to be.

I still couldn't believe we'd pulled it off so well. Effortlessly and flawlessly, like the universe supported our plan. Here we finally were, on our fresh start.

As I looked out over the ocean, I knew we'd been successful. His arm was around my waist. His heart beating against mine in a similar rhythm. Winston and James Bond lay curled up asleep together on the bench. The waves lulled them to sleep most days.

Phillip and I were so connected again. Like one soul sharing two bodies. The perfect family. I'd never be alone as long as I had him by my side. There was so much beauty and exploration waiting for us. Days at sea. Dips in the ocean. Sunsets with the ocean as the backdrop, more beautiful than any on land. There was something exquisitely breathtaking about sunsets at sea. So far, we'd seen eight. Each one more stunning than the next. Maybe this was where we'd always stay. Or maybe we'd land. Settle somewhere off the Greek islands. But no matter where we settled?

It'd be us. My true love. A beautiful new beginning. The world was ours, and I couldn't wait.

# Acknowledgments

This marked book number nine with my developmental editor, Charlotte Herscher, and now I'm afraid of ever writing anything without her brain helping me move things around. Seriously, thank you for endless drafts and always being so easy to work with. And I can't thank Charlotte without thanking Megha Parekh, who's been with me for just as long. Of course, many thanks to my entire publishing team at Thomas & Mercer. Thank you to my agent, Christina Hogrebe, who puts up with my chaos, along with the rest of the team at Jane Rotrosen Agency and all their behind-the-scenes support.

I'm forever grateful for all the love and support of my readers. I don't want to start a list because it'd never fit on a few pages, and I don't want to leave anyone off. Interacting with my readers is my favorite part of being an author. I have so much fun on BookTok every day with y'all, and you've been the best surprise of this journey.

To my forever muse, Molly, who never leaves my side.

Gussie Berry, who's finally old enough to read what I write even though he's probably wishing he wasn't now that he has. My favorite days are the ones where we create. The sound of a pencil sharpener forever the soundtrack to your childhood. That's what I'll remember.

And coffee. What would I ever do without you? All my love.

# About the Author

*Photo © 2020 Jocelyn Snowdon*

Dr. Lucinda Berry is a former psychologist and leading researcher in childhood trauma. Now she writes full time, using her clinical experience to blur the line between fiction and nonfiction. She enjoys taking her readers on a journey through the dark recesses of the human psyche. Her work has been optioned for film and translated into multiple languages.

If Dr. Berry isn't chasing after her son, you can find her running through Los Angeles, prepping for her next marathon. To hear about her upcoming releases and other fun news, visit her on TikTok or sign up for her newsletter at https://LucindaBerry.com.